# THE ANUAN LEGACY

TRACI ISON SCHAFER

Stefan,
Great to meet you
at Enid Comic Con 2019!
May peace surround
you!
Traci

THE ANUAN LEGACY
1
SERIES

INKANA PUBLISHING

The Anuan Legacy



Cover Design: Ana Grigoriu, www.books-design.com
Final Edits: Christina Consolino, www.christinaconsolino.com
Back Cover Author Photo: Amy A. Ward

Published by:
Inkana Publishing, LLC
www.InkanaPublishing.com

First Edition
ISBN: 978-0-9993700-0-1

Printed in the United States of America.

**DEDICATED TO MY PLOT SISTERS,**
**without whom this book would not have been possible.**

Christina Consolino
Cindy Cremeans
Jen Messaros
Jude Walsh
Ruthann Kain

**Also**
**DEDICATED TO MY FAMILY.**
**Thank you for your love and support.**

Destany (Schafer), Larry, and Ison Morgan
Liz and Larry Shaw
Jonathan and Angela Sanders
Todd Schafer, Phyllis Schafer, and A.J. Williams
Bennie Wright Ison ("Granny"), in memoriam

**THANK YOU TO THE FOLLOWING:**

My Beta Readers
The Plot Sisters, Alan Struckman, Destany Schafer-Morgan, Liz Shaw, Larry Morgan, Dennis Strobel, Anne-Marie Cors, Gerald E. Greene, and Kasey Binne

My Technical Consultants
Jonathan Sanders, Thom Shaffer, Tim Jones, and Andrew Allen

# PART I

# CHAPTER 1 - GAIGE

"Gaige, you'll be entering Earth's atmosphere in ten seconds," Nav said over the open mission channel.

"Got it, Nav." I scanned the cockpit readouts to verify that all of the diagnostics still checked out. They did.

"Five seconds."

I braced for the change in velocity.

"Prepare for entry in three, two, one . . ."

Just as I hit the thick atmosphere from the vacuum of space, cockpit warnings blared and diagnostic projections flashed by as the auto-systems tried to pinpoint the problem.

"Nav, something's wrong with the shuttle!" I shouted.

"We know. We think an unexpectedly strong solar burst knocked out your Lexon system. We're working it from here."

The diagnostic projections continued to scroll through the air in front of me, still searching for the problem.

"There's no time," I said. "I'll have to land it mentally." Telekinesis was nothing new to an Anuan, but controlling something that large would be more than a challenge. It would be a miracle.

"Our readings show the electromagnetic interference on Earth's atmosphere caused by the burst won't settle down for another few Earth minutes. Be careful what you're opening yourself up to, Gaige."

"I don't have a choice." The shuttle was going down one way or another. I could take control or die. "Override!"

The warnings fell silent and the cockpit diagnostics faded. The remaining displays dimmed. The shuttle was all mine. I reached forward and touched the control panel. My hands trembled with surging adrenaline until I pressed them so firmly against the panel they couldn't budge. I wouldn't be able to land the craft and maintain a cloaking shield at the same time, but I'd have to worry about being detected later.

The shuttle vibrated under the stress of friction with Earth's atmosphere. Opening my mind, I directed my mental willpower into the shuttle. *Slow to entry speed!* Still, the vibrations rocked the shuttle. If I didn't get the shuttle's speed down, it would break apart under the continued force of entry. I focused everything I could pull from within myself at the shuttle. It slowed—not quite to a normal entry speed—but close enough to ease some of the stress on the craft.

Trying to manage the shuttle was depleting me, not just mentally, but physically, too. The unstable electromagnetic energy in Earth's atmosphere from the solar burst wasn't helping. I couldn't maintain control of the shuttle much longer. Dusk had already started to settle over the area, but the night vision filter of the windshield allowed me to easily see Earth's barren winter trees—lots of them. My eyes scanned for a clearing among all the trees. In the far distance, toward the northwest, I found one. *You can make that.*

I leaned my body and my mind toward the clearing and willed the shuttle in that direction. The craft glided above the treetops.

*Slow to hover.* The shuttle paused and hung suspended in the air over the open stretch of land.

*Landing mode and down.* Drained, I struggled to keep control. My energy level wavered. The craft shuddered then crashed to the ground with a hard jolt that slammed me forward in my restraint.

I laid my head back against the seat, exhausted. Stretching each arm and leg, wiggling fingers and toes, I seemed to be in one piece. But every part of me ached—especially my brain. It felt like an icepick had been driven through my temples.

Dusk offered some visual cover, but I could have easily been detected on radars since I hadn't been able to maintain a cloak during the landing. A stream of sweat ran down the side of my face. I didn't have enough energy to wipe it away, let alone hide a shuttle.

"Gaige? Ship to Gaige."

I heard the static-riddled communications coming from my crippled shuttle, *barely,* but couldn't gather enough energy to answer.

"Ship to Gaige. Respond!"

"Yeah." With some effort, I got the sigh of a word out.

"We're evaluating your medical values now—," Nav said.

"Gaige," another voice interrupted. "This is Mission Commander. I'm sending Conner down with a rescue team as soon as the burst energy subsides. Shouldn't be more than another five Earth minutes."

His words sent a small surge of adrenaline through my body, giving me enough energy to protest. “Tas, no! I mean, Commander, permission to—”

“You can’t stay down there like that,” Tas said. “I’m sending a team to get you.”

“Please, Commander . . .” I couldn’t let my situation affect the mission. I drew in a deep breath, trying to hold on to the quickly fading adrenaline. “I request some time to recover the situation on my own.” I took another breath. “One of us in this area is enough, maybe too much already. Remember, we can’t overwhelm her.”

There was silence and then, finally, Tas answered. “Request granted. But I’ll have Conner and the rescue team on standby. If we don’t receive a positive report from you in fifteen Earth minutes, I’m sending them. Understood?”

I couldn’t respond. Our short exchange had taken what little energy I’d regained. I knew I had to fix the shuttle, get it cloaked, and move it somewhere away from the current site. But I could barely stay conscious.

“Gaige? This is Tas. Are you still with us?”

*Yeah, I’m with you.*

“Gaige?”

No energy left . . . to stay . . . awake . . .

# CHAPTER 2 - TORI

"So, Tori, within the range plotted on this graph you can tell . . ."

I tried to pay attention to my mentor's lesson, but a weariness had settled on me, heavy and sudden. With it came a feeling that something was terribly wrong. My eyes darted from one high-tech gadget to another within the disheveled test lab of Wright-Patterson Air Force Base's world of classified research.

The cheap government setting reduced the technologies' awe-factor, burying it amongst furniture and equipment spread across several decades. Like a time machine had crash-landed here and spewed its contents from a long journey across Air Force history. Everything seemed to be in its not-so-orderly place, but I couldn't stop searching out the reason for my unease.

"Tori? You in there?" Brian waved his hand in front of my face.

My attention refocused across the table on my mentor. *Yeah, I'm with you,* I thought, though I truly wasn't. Something else had me and wouldn't let go. Heat flushed through my body and a trickle of sweat ran down the side of my face. I couldn't decide if the reaction had been caused by embarrassment or the lingering worry over whatever *feeling* had grabbed hold of me.

Brian waited patiently, leaning forward just a bit as if he were hopeful and ready to snatch my words and move forward as soon as I'd recovered. His eyes, hazel-brown and murky, peered at me over the reading glasses perched on his nose. Those glasses and the gray beginning to show at his temples gave his otherwise youthful, fit appearance an authoritative edge, reminding me whose time I was wasting—the nation's top civilian stealth scientist. I was living up to the honor of being selected for the U.S. government's most prestigious college internship program by daydreaming. I had to pull it together and grasped for anything to get myself back on track. The colored graph in Brian's hand brought a few words to mind—frequency, signal ranges. *What about them?* "Uh, the frequency range . . . the signal . . . um, is within the infrared—no, the ultraviolet . . ." I couldn't put the bits and pieces together. "I'm sorry, Dr.—" Calling somebody so important by their first name had been hard to get used to, but Brian gave me his familiar "I'm-not-my-father look," so I started over. "I'm sorry, Brian. I guess I didn't hear you." I swallowed and wiped the stream of sweat off the side of my face with my hand.

Brian smiled and tossed his graph on the table. "This is a lot to take in. You've been a sponge, Tori, but even sponges have their saturation points." He looked down at his watch. "It's almost time for you to go anyway. Why don't we call it a day?"

"Really?" I held my breath, wishing I'd just thanked him and gotten out of there.

"Yes, really. These graphs will still be here in the morning." Brian tipped his head toward the door. "Go enjoy your evening."

***

Even though I'd left work a few minutes ahead of time, darkness overtook the days early during the winter months, so it still felt late. I drove slowly through the family neighborhood that led to our brick, cookie-cutter apartment complex. As I scanned from side to side, watching for any shadow of a small form that might dart out in front of me, I thought back to what had happened in the lab. I'd felt certain something was wrong. The feeling still clung to me like plastic wrap.

An emptiness that longed to be filled had so far refused anything I'd offered. I'd thought following in my dead father's footsteps would satisfy the void, but it hadn't. My soul screamed for me to take my life in *some* direction. More and more, I realized, this wasn't it. My current path didn't fill the lost, yearning spot within me. And being closed up in that classified government lab with its windowless concrete walls felt like wearing a coat two sizes too small—suffocating and uncomfortable. It just didn't fit. My soul needed something else, something more. Perhaps sitting in that environment today had finally brought the realization to a head. It was the best explanation I could come up with, anyway, for the feeling I'd had.

***

I swiped my keycard at the main door of our apartment building, climbed the stairs to the second floor, and walked down the hallway, counting apartments as I went. It was easy to lose track of which identical red door belonged to me and my roommate. When I reached the seventh one, I placed my key in the doorknob. That's when I heard them—the moans, the sighs, the heavy breathing. I removed my key and pounded on the door instead. "Kristen, you home? I forgot my key."

After a quick gasp and some shuffling, the door lock clicked and a disheveled Kristen stood in the doorway with Justin right behind her, still pulling on his T-shirt. His matching blond hair, though different in length, lay equally askew.

"Hey, Tor," she said. "We're on our way out to Justin's. We'll catch you later." She grabbed Justin by the hand and pulled him out the door.

Justin threw a quick glance over his shoulder. "Yeah, catch you later, Tori."

"Have fun," I said, though I knew that bit of advice wasn't needed. How the two hadn't become fused together, I didn't know. Their grades had to suck. Still, the idea of having someone I cared enough about to forget everything else, even grades, made me envy what they shared.

Once the residual racket of their quick getaway settled down, the apartment grew quiet and dead still. Perfect for thinking. I dropped my purse on the floor next to the door and absently picked up the open potato chip bag Kristen and Justin had left on the coffee table. After digging around in the kitchen junk drawer for a few seconds, I found a chip clip, snapped it on the bag, and tossed the bag of chips into the cabinet. Not before stuffing a few barbequed morsels into my mouth, though. That was all the appetite I had. Food could wait. Sorting out what bothered me could not.

Cutting back through the living room, I noticed bright red crumbs against the cream upholstery of the couch and paused to brush them into my hand. Though I'd managed to capture a few crumbs, I'd also left a decent smudge, but I'd deal with that later.

I stepped into the bathroom and dusted the crumbs into the shell-shaped monstrosity of a sink. The design blemish stood out in the granite countertop of an otherwise nicely updated bathroom.

I crossed the hall of our square apartment and entered our one and only bedroom. In a haze of thought that I was anxious to sort through, I changed into the warmest flannel pajamas I owned—pink with white snowmen—and lay down on my bed. Bunching the pillow tightly under my head, I faced the opposite side of the room where Kristen's empty bed sat covered with a yellow, lacy bedspread, rumpled but made. The bed probably wouldn't be occupied that night, like most others. Practically living alone was fine sometimes, but other times, the emptiness in the apartment made me miss my family back home in Florida all the more. I even missed my real parents who'd been gone for so long.

My eyes tingled at the thought and I swiped away a tear. Barely four when they were killed, I didn't remember much about my real parents or our home near Las Vegas, but somehow their scents had stayed with me. Mom's soft floral perfume would waft into a room seconds before she did, followed by her bubbly, energetic presence. And Dad—his musky scent emanated a strength that always made me feel safe. Like he could lift me into his arms, wrap me up, and keep all the monsters away. I inhaled a long breath through my nose and could almost smell them right there in the room with me.

Though my aunt and uncle had done a wonderful job as surrogates, the loss of my parents left a hole in me that had never been filled. Why did the hole seem to be more apparent now? Why were new holes opening up? Holes and uncertainties. Lots of uncertainties. Why didn't I know what path I needed to walk?

And why had it all struck me with such a panic at the lab today? *If* that was truly what had overcome me. I was eighteen now, eighteen and one day. Maybe that was what becoming an adult entailed: figuring out all the grown-up things like where you fit into this world and how you want—no, *need*—to live your life.

Perhaps my aunt and uncle coming up for my birthday had made things worse. Stuck here in the cold, gray Ohio winter, did I simply miss my family and the Florida sunshine? Of course, I did.

*Maybe I just need to go back home*, I thought, as I sank deeper into my comforter.

No energy left . . . to stay . . . awake . . .

# CHAPTER 3 - GAIGE

"Gaige!" I heard Tas's voice in my ear.

I jerked awake, confused for a moment, and then remembered where I was. I realized the team had switched to the communication device in my suit, probably after having given up on the shuttle's crippled system. "I'm here. What time is it?"

"You've been out of link for twenty Earth minutes. They're zeroing in on you, Gaige. A rescue team is on the way to Earth, but you've got to get away from that location!"

"Understood." I released my harness, leaned forward, and rested my head in my hands. The pain in my brain had gone from a sharp, stabbing sensation to a dull ache. I felt better than I had when I'd first landed, but my energy was nowhere close to normal. I couldn't wait until it was, though. I pushed myself from the seat. With the shuttle inoperable and with no spare mental energy, I needed to do things manually. I kicked the latch on the floor behind the cockpit seats and pushed the hatch open.

For a brief second, my eyes caught sight of the Earth clothes I'd brought, but there was no time for that now. I dropped from the shuttle. As soon as I landed on firm Earth, I saw the distant headlights shining through the skeletal trees. The shadowy arms cast by the tree branches reached out in my direction and touched me.

"Gaige to Ship."

"We see them," Nav said. "Do you think you have time to self-destruct the shuttle?"

"I don't think so."

"Then just get out of there. Conner and the rescue team will be on Earth soon."

"I can't leave the shuttle. They'd misuse our technology. You know that." I gripped the rungs on the interior of the hatch, determined to make whatever feeble attempt I could manage to get back into the shuttle and initiate a self-destruct command.

Three vehicles ground to a stop only a few feet from the edge of the craft. Dust flew into the air around them and wafted over me and the shuttle.

My chest tightened. Unable to breathe, I released my hold on the ladder and bent over, gasping. *No. She couldn't have. It was too soon.* I apparently hadn't been able to maintain enough of a filter on my presence during the crash to block her awareness of me. She mentally pulled at me now, draining what little energy I'd been able to recover. I collapsed onto the ground, knowing the vehicles were no longer my only problem.

She'd connected.

# CHAPTER 4 - TORI

*A harness held me back as Earth grew closer. Faster and faster Earth approached. Something was wrong. Maintain. Maintain shuttle. Maintain cloak. Bigger and bigger, faster and faster. Maintain! I slammed into Earth with a hard jolt.*

I sat up in bed and clutched my throat, gasping for air. After a few seconds, I was able to pull in a solid breath, but something was . . . *different*. I felt odd. My head ached and a coldness encircled my wrists as if I wore metal bracelets straight from the freezer. I rubbed my wrists but felt nothing. The room seemed to shrink, locking me inside. I threw the covers back and ran to the bedroom door. It stood wide open. So why did I feel trapped?

Dropping to my hands and knees I crawled back to my bed and reached underneath. Swiping my hand along the floor, I made contact with my softball bat. I dragged it out from under the bed and held it close. Hearing nothing, I clutched my bat and tiptoed to the light switch.

The clatter of ice from the ice maker startled me. I jumped and flipped on the light switch. Squinting in the harsh light, I could see the room clearly enough. Kristen's bed sat empty, still made. Mine lay in a crumpled mess. Everything remained exactly how it had been when I went to sleep, including the closed and locked window. I leaned out of the bedroom doorway and looked down the hall to the main door of the apartment. It also remained locked and secure.

Whatever had woken me must have only been a dream. Yes. A crash landing. But not in a plane. With the dream fuzzy and fading fast, I couldn't be certain of anything. I *did* know that no one had broken into the apartment, so I turned off the light and rolled my bat back under the bed. Pounding the edges of my pillow with my fists, I fluffed up the middle and lay down, snuggling my head into the freshly fattened padding. My heart still raced from the dream, but sleep quickly reclaimed me.

# CHAPTER 5 - BRIAN

"We'll let the interrogators see if they can get anything out of him. Sign language, pictures, I have no idea what they'll use in a situation like this. But that's in *their* swim lane, not ours." The general tipped his head to someone standing farther inside the bay and left to go speak with him.

I couldn't believe what the general had just told me. Called back to work after-hours, I stood in the doorway of a small lab off the main bay of the test facility, where earlier I'd been having a perfectly normal day running experiments and mentoring interns and new hires.

I stared into the smaller room at a man with short, dark hair and tanned skin. A man who looked like any other active young male you might see around town any day. But NORAD had tracked his craft entering our atmosphere *from space. Could it really be true?*

The man watched us through the bars of his cage where he sat in a metal folding chair, cuffed hands resting in his lap. The general had at least allowed the man a chair. A humane gesture that went above and beyond, according to the general.

"Brian!" General Ash snapped his fingers at me.

"Yes, sir." I stepped away from the small room that held the man's cage and stood next to the general so he'd know he had my full attention.

"They're bringing it in now," he said.

The back wall of the hangar-like test facility cranked open to reveal a flatbed truck, accompanied by several smaller vehicles. The general moved closer, but I kept my distance. The driver skillfully backed the semi into the hangar and the crane affixed to the ceiling of the facility slid over the top of the truck. It latched down onto the bus-sized wooden crate sitting on its bed and raised it into the air.

"Take it easy with that thing!" the general yelled.

The crate stopped and swayed gently, then proceeded to glide toward the general. The crane eased the box down in front of him. After the semi pulled out of the facility and the door cranked closed, six men from the entourage surrounded the crate and began prying the edges of the box loose.

"Ready?" one of the men asked.

"Yes. Open it up," the general said.

I bounced my leg, nervous as hell to see what, *exactly,* the crate held. I knew what the U.S. had hidden behind its top secret classifications, and we knew something about what other countries possessed. One look and I'd know if this was really from beyond Earth or not.

The crane lifted the lid from the container, allowing the sides to fall away. They landed with a thud that echoed throughout the bay. Inside sat a dark, pewter aircraft about twenty feet long. Four pencil-thin legs supported the craft. They looked as if they could snap like twigs, but held it solid about six feet above the ground. The nose of the craft came to a point with the rest of the vehicle spreading wider toward the rear, like a spearhead. The midline, thick enough to hold passengers—a pilot, at least—narrowed as it reached the sharp outer edges.

"Holy shit!" It *was* true. "Pardon me, sir. I mean, wow! That's incredible." From where I stood, the man in the cage looked indistinguishable from any other, but the craft . . . That craft was *definitely* not of this Earth. It was *extra-terrestrial.* And whoever flew it here couldn't be from Earth either. ET and his spaceship sat right there in our lab. I looked at the man—or whatever he was—who continued to watch us patiently. I couldn't wait to examine his craft. The opportunity to even lay my eyes on such a thing was mind-blowing. But what the hell were they going to do with *him*?

"Well?" the general asked.

Turning back to the craft, I stepped closer and then stopped. "Have the radiation levels been checked?"

"Of course. At the crash site," he said. "It's clean."

I continued my approach, glancing into the smaller room at the man, torn between my excitement for the craft and my concern about his fate. Regardless of how much he looked like us, he was an alien being. What would become of him here, in the hands of General Ash and others like him? A new world had just opened up to us. Were we going to abuse the opportunity we been given, out of fear or greed or lust for power?

"Brian!"

I jumped and realized I was standing dead still, deep in thought. I continued on, with General Ash glaring at me. When I reached the craft, I lifted my arm toward it. "May I?"

"Yes. I want to know what you think," the general said, waving his arms toward the spacecraft.

I ran my hand along the edge of the sleek, smooth craft. “I can’t even imagine the technologies this thing holds.”

“Can you reverse engineer it?” the general asked.

“If I can’t, no one can.”

# CHAPTER 6 - TORI

The slam of the apartment door woke me.

My head throbbed. "Kristen?" I called out, way too softly for her to have heard, even if she'd been standing right next to me.

Kristen scurried into the bedroom, flipping on the light as she entered. "Hey, Tor."

"Hi, Kristen. Do you need the light? My head is pounding." I rolled on to my side and curled into a ball, shielding my eyes from the light with one hand and gripping my covers tightly under my chin with the other.

"You have a headache?" She flung her clothes off, throwing them on her bed.

"Yeah. Maybe it's your Ohio allergens, or the cold, or whatever. Can't wait to get home to Florida." I tucked my hand back under the covers and, through squinted eyes, watched Kristen rifle around in her drawers trying to find an outfit.

"Don't know why I signed up for a class first thing in the morning. It isn't even light out yet this time of year."

She hadn't heard a word I'd said. "Kristen. The light. Do you need it? Maybe the bathroom light would be enough, instead?"

"Oh, sorry, Tor. I'll be outta here in a minute. Just gotta make a quick change. Can't be doing the walk of shame around campus today."

"No, I suppose not. Why do your parents bother to put you up in an apartment? They're wasting their money."

"They pay because they think I'm a good little girl living with my college roommate. Any real knowledge of my college experiences would put them in their graves." Kristen's hand flew to her mouth. "Oh my God, Tori. I'm so sorry."

"It's okay, Kristen. That was a long time ago." I felt a twinge in my heart, like I was betraying my biological parents. I really did miss them, even after so long, but Kristen didn't need to feel bad about reminding me.

"I really *am* sorry, Tori. I wasn't thinking." Kristen's hand still covered her mouth. Her eyes pleaded for forgiveness, though I'd already given it.

"Really, it's okay. Let's talk about something else." There was one topic that would make Kristen forget everything else. "I take it Justin is doing okay?"

Her hand dropped from her face and the panic in her eyes turned into the same spark of light I saw in them any time her boyfriend walked into the room.

"Justin does more than okay, if you know what I mean," Kristen said with a grin.

"Yeah, I know what you mean." I closed my eyes and pulled the covers over my head. "Just kill the light on your way out, will you?"

"Sure, Tor. Today a class day or work day for you?"

Kristen went back to changing, slamming a drawer closed in the process. I winced.

"Work. Remember? First semester was school. Now it's a work semester." She wouldn't remember.

Kristen clattered around in the bedroom, then the bathroom. Finally, I heard the click of her shoes heading toward the door. "See ya, Tor."

"Kristen, the light."

The front door slammed shut. Or maybe it only closed—any noise was an assault on my pounding head. I lowered the covers to the bridge of my nose and opened my eyelids ever so slightly. "Uh, light, will you go away?" The words stabbed the inside of my skull like knife blades.

The light hissed, popped, and went dark.

I sighed and whispered a quiet thank you for the small miracle.

As I lay there trying to decide if I should get ready for work, I remembered waking in the night, gasping for breath, and thinking someone may have broken into the apartment. A faint trace remained that something else had happened, but the details of that *something* hovered just beyond my reach.

I dozed in and out of sleep for a long while. Eventually, the muted winter sunrise began to permeate the room. In it, I searched. For what, I wasn't sure. The thing just beyond my reach, maybe. I lay quiet, contemplating the thought.

Yes, I was sure. That thing, whatever it was, still lingered.

# CHAPTER 7 - BRIAN

I walked around to the nose of the craft and stepped backward so I could study the sharp lines from a distance. My excitement rose over the unimaginable technologies that sat in front of me, and then sank again every time I looked at the man, not knowing his fate.

Making a wide arc, I circled around to the rear of the craft. I eyed it from every angle, squatting then standing. I took a few steps toward the right side of the craft and squatted again. General Ash stood by and watched.

"You can begin the reverse engineering process as soon as we arrive at the new location," he said. "Determine how to best prepare the craft for a long transport and be ready to leave when the transport team arrives."

*Leave?* I froze in the middle of a squat. Springing to a stand, I jogged from the far side of the spacecraft back around to the general. "What new location? What transport team?"

"There's a team on the way to get this. And *that.*" He motioned to the man in the cage. "Wright-Patt has excellent secured facilities. We were lucky the craft went down nearby. But this place is not isolated enough for what we have here. Not anymore. So we're moving it to a better location. The team is set to be here this evening, after night falls."

As anxious as I was to start uncovering all the technologies that the craft held, something made me nervous about the whole situation. "I didn't know we were relocating the craft. Where are we taking it? And how long will I be gone?"

"You'll be filled in on the details later. Consider the time to be an extended period."

"I can't just—"

"Brian, I realize you're a civilian and as such operate under a different type of structure, shall we say. But, if you'll check your job description, as with all civilian positions, it includes *other duties as assigned.* So, consider this to fall under that category." General Ash's eyes dared me to argue.

I wasn't sure what to say. *Other duties as assigned* was tacked onto every job description. But relocating for an indefinite period of time seemed extreme. As much as I wanted to be a part of the project, being forced to participate caused an uneasy feeling to settle in the pit of my stomach. I opened my mouth, ready to respond, but said nothing. I looked from General Ash to the craft to the man, whose brow crinkled into a heavy ridge.

"It's just that I . . . well . . . this was, *obviously*, a bit unexpected . . . and . . ."

"Jesus, Brian." General Ash flung his hands in the air. "It's a damn alien spacecraft. You *really* want to take a pass on that?"

"No. I mean . . . well, *hell* no. It's just . . ."

"Look," General Ash said, his jaw tight. "You're involved now and this is not the kind of thing you get uninvolved with. Do you understand what I'm saying? You are part of the project now. Whether you planned to be or not, you're in this." He leaned in with each word until his face was too close for me to keep in focus. "Do I make myself clear?"

I took a step back. His eyes, solid and unyielding, stayed fixed on mine. Couple that with the tension in the muscles of his face and I couldn't decide if he looked determined or desperate. Neither option was good for me. Or for ET. I'd always known General Ash lacked people skills, but now it was more apparent than ever that he'd reached his current rank with a good measure of intimidation.

The craft *was* incredible, no doubt, and impossible to walk away from. Still, the situation didn't set well for many reasons. How much control was General Ash about to take over my life? And if I refused to go, what was the general capable of? Would he fire someone with my credentials? And what was going to happen to the man who sat passive and defenseless in his cage?

The caged man listened silently to every word we spoke. *Did he understand what he heard?* The general held his stance, but I needed time to think before taking him on full force.

"Yes, you've made yourself clear," I answered.

A victorious smile spread across the general's face. "Good."

Feeling deflated and less than respectful of General Ash at the moment, I reached for a nearby office chair that sat abandoned next to a tool chest. I dragged it toward me on its lopsided casters and plopped down—a rude move in the presence of a general officer. I leaned back in the chair to make eye contact with him. "If the team will be here this evening, then I'll need to go home and pack—"

"No."

"No?"

"We'll give you a clothing allowance. I want you here in this lab. You need to have the craft ready to go."

"If I'm going to be gone for a while, I have a home to take care of, bills that need to be covered, mail and papers to stop—"

"You have no family responsibilities to deal with. All the rest we can have taken care of for you." He leaned over me. "Your priorities are in this room."

My frustration had ramped up and I stood to hold my ground with the general. "Look—"

"No, you look," he interrupted again, pointing his finger in my face. "You have no idea what's involved here. I suggest you follow orders and quit asking questions, so we don't run into any problems with this project." Spittle gathered at the edges of his mouth as he spoke. "Believe me, you don't want that."

I had to be careful how I handled the situation, not only for my sake, but also for the sake of the man who'd flown his bird into our crazy general's grasp.

I held my hands up, as if in surrender. Which it was. "Okay, not a problem. I'll stay here."

"Good. I'll be back later. Get the craft ready. We can't be delayed. Two guards from Security Forces are on the way to watch that *thing* in the cage. Who knows what it's capable of. You are *not* to leave this room until they get here. Understood?"

"Understood. I'll wait here for them. What about outside the lab? Will you be posting guards at the door?"

"Absolutely not. I don't want any attention brought to this lab today. I want no one who's not already a part of the project to be the wiser." He turned and marched toward the door leading into the hallway.

"Several people have access to this lab," I said. "Once they start arriving for the day, they may be in here."

"Change the code!" he shouted back over his shoulder.

"You're sure you don't want guards outside the door?" I asked.

He stopped and pivoted around like he was in the middle of a formal ceremony. "Are you questioning my decision?"

"No sir. Change the code. I can do that."

"Good. Business as usual. Nothing out of the ordinary." He turned back and proceeded to the door again.

*Locking everyone out of the lab* is *out of the ordinary, General Ass.* "Yes, sir," I said, as the door slammed closed behind him.

# CHAPTER 8 - TORI

A dozen or so cars stretched back from the base gate. While I waited in line to show my ID badge and be ushered through, I watched the video cameras on top of the guard shack scan back and forth. One car passed through the gate, then the next. A nervous anticipation grew each time I moved forward. By the time I reached the gate, an excitement stirred deep inside me. Work had never made me feel that way. *So why did it today?*

I rolled down the car window and handed my government ID to the camouflage-clad airman, then tapped my thumb against the steering wheel, anxious to get to work.

The guard examined the front and back of the card, raising his eyes from it to me and back again. Satisfied I was the person on the ID, he allowed me to proceed.

On autopilot, I wound through the familiar roads that led to my building. The cars and trees and people walking along the sidewalks bundled in their winter garb zipped by faster than usual. My eyes locked onto the speedometer, which read twenty miles over the speed limit. I jerked my foot off the accelerator and slammed it down on the brake, throwing myself forward. Thankfully no one was behind me. I returned my foot to the accelerator, wondering why I'd been so zoned out. My headache was nearly gone, so I couldn't blame it on that.

When I pulled into the parking lot, as strangely anxious as I'd been to get there, I could only sit and stare. Weak sunlight struggled to permeate the thick gray clouds that hung low over my building. I stared at the dreary concrete structure and wondered.

Yes. The same *something* that woke me from my sleep and lingered in the morning light—it lingered here, too.

# CHAPTER 9 - BRIAN

I pushed the office chair back against the wall and stepped into the small lab to get a closer look at the man in the cage. With the general gone, I had to process fast.

What *exactly* did General Ash have planned? I was almost afraid to imagine. We'd reverse engineer the craft. No harm there—depending on what we found and what we did with it, I supposed. But the man in the cage—what were they planning for him? The question gnawed at me.

He sat with his arms resting on his knees just like any human might sit. I took inventory—two eyes, two ears, a nose, a mouth. All in the right places. Even knowing he was an alien, he still looked like any other human male to me.

He didn't move. He only watched me. I wondered if he understood what was going on. I stepped closer to his cage and stopped just out of arm's reach. Up close I saw one difference I hadn't noticed before. His irises were an unusual shade of blue-green—a color I'd never seen on Earth and the one and only physical attribute that might give his alien origin away.

"Do you understand what I'm saying?" I asked.

He tilted his head, maybe trying to figure it out.

"English? Do you understand English?" I asked again.

"I can speak your language," he finally answered.

*Holy shit.* He *could* understand and even communicate with us. He looked and moved and even talked like anybody else you'd meet on Earth. But the craft—no one from Earth flew that craft. As hard as it was to believe, it had to be true. A real extraterrestrial sat only a few feet away from me. I had the opportunity to communicate with ET himself. On any other day—any day an alien wasn't sitting right in front of me—I'd have been able to come up with a thousand questions. But now, with ET staring me in the face, my mind went blank, filled with nothing but shock-induced fuzz.

I closed my eyes for a moment and forced the fog from my brain. Their technologies. Yes, I wanted to know about their technologies. I opened my eyes, ready to speak again, but decided I should ease into the conversation with introductions first, to be polite. *Then* I'd ask about their technologies.

"My name is Brian. Do *you* have a name?"

"My name is Gaige," he answered without pause.

"It's nice to meet you, Gaige." I moved closer, lifted my hand, and then quickly lowered it. As docile as he seemed, I had no idea what he would do if he got hold of me. A handshake might not be the best of ideas.

Before I could ask him any more questions, the door buzzer rang. Most likely, the first of many people wondering why their codes weren't working today.

# CHAPTER 10 - TORI

I pulled my phone out of my purse and tossed it into the car's console—no open signals in a classified building. Thankful for casual Friday, I walked across the parking lot, dodging icy patches and piles of leftover snow as I went. My Nikes managed slick pavement much better than high heels. The air whistled and bit at my neck. I tightened my scarf, pulling it up over my mouth to capture the warmth of my breath.

After scanning through two sets of doors with ID badges and entry codes, I stepped into the warmth of the building, where I tugged away my suffocating scarf and loosened my coat. I had begun to thaw out by the time I reached the lab door, ready to make up for daydreaming the afternoon before. But when I pushed on the door, I almost greeted its thick metal with my head. I gave another shove against it with my hands, just to make sure. It *was* locked. I turned the large combination dial on the door to the right, left, then right again as I entered the code. It didn't release. I tried again. Still nothing happened.

Anxiety gripped my chest like a vice. Why couldn't I get in? I *needed* to get in. Desperately. I didn't know why, but being outside the door instead of inside the lab upset me enough that the hall, the door, everything, became disjointed. A jumble of puzzle pieces that used to be my surroundings spun wildly in my head. I stopped trying the combination, leaned against the wall, and pushed the buzzer instead. Closing my eyes, I tried to wait out both the dizzy spell and whoever was taking their sweet time coming to open the door. I wasn't sure I would outlast either.

Finally, the door cracked open and Brian slid through. "Tori. Hey."

I opened my eyes and managed to stay steady. "What's going on, Dr, I mean, Brian?"

I wasn't sure he'd even registered what I'd said. He repeatedly tapped his hand against his thigh, which created a continuous ripple down the leg of his trousers.

"Brian, are you going to let me in?"

"Um . . ." His tapping hand sped up and so did the ripples. "We have a special project in here today. Just came in."

"Okay. Well, that's what we do here. Are we going in?"

"Actually, no."

"No?"

I looked down at Brian's flapping pant leg, which was almost a blur now. Most of my training took place in the lab. Why wouldn't he let me in and what was he so nervous about?

"Is there a problem with my internship? I'm sorry about yesterday. I . . . I wasn't feeling well—"

"No, no, Tori." He squeezed his hand into a fist, putting a stop to his nervous tapping. "There's no problem with your work performance here. They're just not reading everybody in for this one." Brian's eyes darted this way and that way, not looking at me anymore but searching. "Tell you what. There's a proposal on my desk. Why don't you do a technical evaluation on it for me?"

"Me?"

"Sure." He turned his back to me and hunkered over the combination, dialing in the new code. "Sorry about this project. We'll resume your hands-on training with the next one. The tech eval will be a good learning experience for you. We'll go over it together." He cracked the door enough to slide back through and closed it in my face.

Not sure what to do, but not ready to leave, I touched the dial with my fingertips. Maybe, if I tried it *one more time*, it would open. I dropped my hand to my side. Brian had plainly told me I wasn't read-in, so how would I explain prancing in there, even if by some miracle I could get the door open? I'd have no explanation other than, *I just had to know what was in here.* I could see it now: "*Brian, I'm sorry I broke security protocol. I'll be fired and might even go to jail, but I just had to know.*" Yeah, not a good idea. For now, I'd have to keep wondering what was in the lab that had Brian so frazzled and me so desperate to find out.

# CHAPTER 11 - BRIAN

Tori and the young new hires who had recently started to trickle into our black world were the closest things I had to children of my own, the closest things to a family. I hated having to send them away from the lab that morning with no explanation. But it was for their own good. After finding busywork to keep them occupied, I examined the craft—taking measurements, scanning for emissions and reflective properties, and anything else I had instruments for—while I thought of how to approach our ET, Gaige, about his technologies.

I felt his eyes on me, watching as I worked. I had a million questions about the craft. *The pilot must have* some *answers.* I turned and looked into the room that held his cage. He sat, pensive and calm, not at all like a caged animal. I stared at him. He stared back. I stepped into the room and stopped several feet from his cage. I didn't want to speak to him in the presence of the Security Forces' guards who now stood watch, but it didn't look like I'd have a choice. They probably had no idea they were guarding an alien. In his white, very non-U.S. Government flight suit, he simply looked like a captured pilot from *somewhere* outside the U.S. Somewhere covered a big area and was probably enough to explain his odd aircraft, too. I couldn't contain my curiosity any longer, but I would be careful not to ask Gaige any alien-oriented questions in front of the guards.

"You flew that here?" I pointed over my shoulder to the craft visible through the doorway, not painting a very glowing picture of our species by asking an obvious question.

Gaige glanced at the craft with his blue-green eyes then looked back at me. "I am the pilot."

"It's very impressive," I said.

"Yes, in comparison."

"To ours, you mean?"

"Yes, impressive compared to yours," he said.

"Yep, um. Can you tell me about it?" I waited, holding my breath for the holy grail of space vehicle technology.

"Its operations are based purely on physics, though they're concepts you haven't figured out yet."

"Can you help us figure them out?" I asked, hopeful.

Still seated, he tilted his head, furrowed his brow, and studied me. He looked at the guards who'd been standing silently by—the tall beefy man faced the cage and a slightly smaller version faced the doorway—then back at me. "You *maybe*. But your people—they're not ready. It's best you not know."

He was probably right, but that wouldn't stop us from trying to figure the technology out. My stomach rumbled. I figured Gaige had to be hungry, too. I lowered my voice so the guards wouldn't hear what I was about to say. "Do you eat, like, food?"

He glanced at the guards again and responded just as quietly. "I can eat your foods."

"You're probably hungry," I said, at a normal volume. I wondered if General Ash had any plans to ever feed our ET.

"I am."

"I'll be back. With food."

As I walked toward the guards, I could see the intensity in everything about them. They stood tensely, their heads fixed straight forward. But the eyes—their eyes followed me, waiting for me to make the wrong move. I stopped next to them.

"What are your orders if he should try to escape?"

Both men, standing back to back, moved their heads only slightly in my direction so as not to lose sight of the prisoner or the door. "Shoot to kill," the larger one said.

That's what I was afraid of.

# CHAPTER 12 - GAIGE

With the scientist gone, I stood up from the hard chair. I stretched my cuffed hands over my head and then bent down, placing my palms flat against the floor. The guard facing my direction fixed his eyes on me and held his weapon close, finger on the trigger. He and his comrade both held M-16s in their hands—modified, small caliber, high velocity. My flight suit could handle an impact from that kind of gun. The M-9s holstered at their sides, too.

I walked around the cage a few times, discreetly glancing at the guards. The one watching me soon lost interest in my stretching and relaxed his anxious trigger finger.

Conner and his team should have already arrived on Earth. We needed to plan, but I couldn't take the chance of agitating the guards or letting them overhear. Even if I spoke in my own language, they'd know something was going on. I'd known Conner my whole life. We were as close as brothers. If I projected strongly enough, he'd hear my thoughts. I concentrated while I continued to walk around the cage. *"Conner? Conner, can you hear me?"*

Through the communication device in my suit, Conner's voice vibrated against my eardrums, silent to anyone but me. "I can hear you, Gaige. The rescue team is on the ground and cloaked several miles from where you are. We're trying to maintain some distance and keep ourselves blocked for Victoria's sake."

*"Good. Stay there, for now, and continue to block your energies. Completely. She picked up on me when I barely had any energy left to function, let alone emit much out into the universe."*

"Understood. Do you have a plan yet?"

Even though his trigger finger had eased, the soldier facing me still watched me closely. Not as intently as when I'd first started moving, but I didn't expect he'd *completely* let his guard down. It wouldn't matter, though. Neither would be any match for me.

*"Yes, I have a plan. They're moving me and the shuttle tonight. I have my strength back, and should be able to break free and self-destruct the shuttle on my own. I don't want to bring any attention to myself here, though, so I won't make an attempt to escape until we're away from this area. Once I know where we're going, I'll give you the escape coordinates, so you and your team can move closer to that location in case I need backup."*

"We'll be on standby."

I continued to pace around the cage, trying to acclimate the guards to my movements so I wouldn't catch their attention so readily with them. I gave the guard facing me an Earthly nod as I passed by the front of the cage. He scowled and tightened his grip on the M-16 in his hands. The guard facing the door gave another of his occasional quick glances over his shoulder, then turned his attention immediately back to the door. These two might be difficult to throw off balance, but not impossible.

*"Is the solar activity still high?"* I asked Conner.

"Very. We still wouldn't be able to maintain cloak on the ship, so the shuttles are it. Once we rendezvous, we can take you back to the ship to regroup. Or, if you decide to continue on with the mission, any or all of us can stay and support. The mission commander has left all that up to you as mission lead."

*"Thanks, Conner. I'll forward time and coordinates for escape and rendezvous once I know more."*

# CHAPTER 13 - BRIAN

I hadn't thought to ask Gaige what he wanted to eat, so I piled a sample of everything offered in the cafeteria that day onto my tray. By the time I got back to the lab, my arms burned from carrying the heavy load. I *had* overdone the food, but I wanted to make sure I got something he liked, or at least could eat.

I entered his room and placed the tray on a desk along the wall. The guards stood completely still and silent. I thought Gaige might open up to me, but not with these guards listening. I needed to clear them out. I'd watched the prisoner before they arrived. Maybe they wouldn't consider it a stretch for me to keep an eye on him during their lunch break as well.

"Hey, guys," I said to the guards. "Why don't you go get some lunch?"

Remaining perfectly still, they said nothing. Their eyes, however, revealed I had their attention. They had to eat, but who was I, a civilian, to relieve them from their orders?

"General Ash told me to give you a lunch break," I said. "So go ahead and take that now, while I'm here to watch him. Be back in an hour."

The men made note of the time, and filed out for lunch. If really left to General Ash, they would have probably starved where they stood.

When the guards were gone, I turned to Gaige who'd moved from his chair to the back of the cage. He appeared to be fairly young, early twenties at most. *That* I could tell before. But with him standing for the first time, I could see that he was tall and muscular. And damn intimidating. I'd have hated to be one of the people who had to bring him in.

"I wasn't sure what you liked so I got a few things to choose from," I said. "Pick anything you want."

He walked to the front of the cage and looked down on me. He thanked me and picked out several dishes. I slid the plates he'd chosen through the feeding slot at the bottom of the cage bars, along with a bottle of water, and resecured the small door that covered the opening. He made no attempt to grab me. He just sat back down quietly in his metal folding chair.

We both had to eat. I figured we might as well do it together. I picked out a few items for myself and left the remaining food on the desk. Gaige waited for me to roll the office chair next to the cage and settle in with my tray of food before he took a bite. His movements were well-coordinated, considering he ate with cuffed hands.

"Sorry about the cuffs. If I had the key, I'd take them off."

He looked at me with his unusual colored eyes and then swallowed. "That's okay, I'll manage. That general, he's unstable. You should be careful around him."

*He* was worried about *me*? I found that ironic since he was the one in the cage. "Yes, I know. I also know what you are. Or at least what they think you are."

"They're correct." He picked up the bottle of water and twisted off the lid. "I *am* alien to your world."

I knew it, but hearing him admit that he was truly an alien sent a chill throughout my body. "They're afraid of you. That's why they have you locked up in this cage."

Gaige took a drink of the water and put the lid back on the bottle. "People fear what they don't know."

"That's my point. Well, I suppose I haven't really made a point, but you're right. They don't know. They don't know anything about you or your technology and they'll *want* to know. They'll want the advantages your technology could give us, but they'll also want to know as much as possible about you." I paused, wondering if I should elaborate. "I just don't know what they have planned for you."

He nodded as if he understood, but he didn't seem concerned and even had a slight smile on his face. "You don't have to worry about me." He took the last bite and added the plate in his lap to the others already stacked on the floor of his cage. "Thank you for the food."

I opened the slot and Gaige slid the stack of small plates through, again making no attempt to harm me. I latched the door and placed my tray with all our empty dishes on the desk. Every instinct in my body told me this being was not hostile. I returned to the cage and reached my hand through the bars. "It's an honor to talk with you, Gaige."

Gaige grasped my hand firmly. "And you, Brian."

After spending the remainder of the hour with Gaige, I knew that, alien or not, he was a peaceful being. Whenever the General returned, I had to try and talk to him—as futile as that might be—about Gaige and his fate.

# CHAPTER 14 - TORI

The technical proposal sat on Brian's desk, surrounded by a potpourri of his scientific clutter—text books, reports, and gadgets that had so far kept me occupied while my mind wondered about what was going on in our lab. I put a hand on the cover of the three-inch thick proposal again. Instead of opening it, I reread the awards lining the shelf to my left for about the fourth time, and then pulled back the steel ball at the end of the Newton's cradle that sat on the desk to the right of the proposal.

"Gravitational potential energy," I said, and let the ball go. It slammed into the ball next to it with a loud metal clack that repeated over and over as the energy transferred through all five balls and back again. "Momentum." I watched for a while and then checked the temperature on Brian's Galilean thermometer. Its colorful liquid-filled orbs floated peacefully in the paraffin oil. Seventy degrees. Down a degree since the last time I had checked.

The steel balls slowed their pace. "Sorry guys, you have to give *something* up to heat and friction." I pulled the ball at the end back again, let it drop, and gazed off into space, still wondering what was in the lab and why it had caused Brian's weird behavior.

I came to the conclusion that General Ash must have been hovering over something. I'd heard that whenever Brian had a hot project, the general dropped by from headquarters to put his fingerprints on it. It sounded like he collected credits the way a kid collected lightning bugs on a summer night. That could make anyone nervous. In a building full of civilians, I'd know soon enough. He'd stick out like a sore thumb in his uniform full of stars.

General Ash being around might explain Brian's behavior, but it didn't answer my other questions. What *was* this project? And why was the project all I could think about?

The news played on the TV monitor mounted in the corner of Brian's office—bombings, murders, hostages, more bombings, and more murders. *What were we doing to ourselves? And why were we doing it?* I punched the OFF button on his remote and looked down at the proposal, determined to make a real effort to read it this time.

I turned to the first page, but the ink swirled into black blurs on the white background. I closed my eyes, rubbed them, then opened them and made another attempt. The fuzzy edges of the letters sharpened and went fuzzy again. When they finally cleared into a crisp print, I started to read through the pages, but struggled to make sense of even the simplest sentences. I concentrated on the words so hard I thought my gaze might burn a hole through the paper, but I couldn't get any of the information to stay with me.

Feeling weak, I leaned forward and rested my head on my crossed arms. I'd almost fallen asleep when I thought I sensed someone in the room. I raised my head and looked up, expecting to see Brian or another engineer. Though no one was there, I couldn't shake the feeling that I was not alone. I stood on wobbly legs and turned in a complete circle. I still saw no one and dismissed the feeling to the puny state that had come over me.

I started to sit down, but couldn't. My body, moving almost on its own, one foot in front of the other, guided me from the room. I had a mission, a destination.

When I stopped, I found myself in front of the lab door, staring, still feeling the presence but knowing now I was separated from it by this door. I placed my hands against the cold steel, only to have it warm instantly beneath my palms. I jerked my hands away, frightened at first, and then placed them back against the metal. I stood very still, concentrating, and knew I *had* to get into the lab. I didn't know why, I just knew that I did.

An anxious knot gripped the pit of my stomach. My body swayed and I rested my forehead on the cool metal to steady myself. Again it warmed at my touch. I braced myself, determined to find a way in.

I remembered all the years I'd been the perfect child, the perfect student, never disobedient. I considered going back to Brian's office, but couldn't walk away. I *had* to know what was on the other side of that door.

# CHAPTER 15 - GAIGE

My breath caught and my heart pounded. Victoria drew close. I had to stop her.

As Brian and the general argued nearby, I clutched the bars of my cage and concentrated hard to block whatever energy might have been getting through the wall that I *thought* I held in place between my presence and her. At the same time, I tried to will her away. I sensed a brief hesitation in her, but it passed quickly and she remained determined.

I couldn't let her find me. Not here. Not now. *But how could I stop her?*

# CHAPTER 16 - BRIAN

"Why are you worrying about that *thing* and not out there preparing the craft for the trip?" The general, veins in his temples bulging, nodded his head toward Gaige every time he said the word *thing,* as if he hadn't already clearly established what he thought of Gaige—not as a living, breathing being, but merely an object for us to do with as we would.

"Sir. There's really not a whole lot I can do for the move until the team gets here to crate it."

The general clenched his teeth.

I modified my answer. "But, it's ready from my end. Everything's a go, sir. And I'll advise during the crating process to insure it's properly protected for a long trip."

The general's expression eased. "Good. I don't want any delays." He turned to leave.

"Uh, sir?"

"What?" he said, but continued to walk toward the doorway.

"Sir, please wait." I followed after him. "I still need to speak with you about the plan for Ga—the man. I mean the *thing*."

I gestured toward Gaige, who gazed off in the distance like his mind still resided back in his own world. His hands clutched the bars of his cage so tightly that I almost expected the metal to disintegrate beneath his grip.

"I just think we owe it to another living being to thoroughly examine the best way to treat, um *deal*, with him." I moved closer to Gaige's cage and tipped my head toward the general, encouraging Gaige to say something to defend himself. I hoped at the very least, the shock factor that our alien could communicate with us would get the general to listen.

Gaige's eyes remained fixed far off somewhere, oblivious to my movements.

The general turned back toward me. "That's not my concern. Or yours either. I've been told we're to bring that *thing* and the craft to the remote location. That's exactly what we're going to do. And that's *all* we're going to do."

"Told? Aren't you in charge of this project?" The words slipped out before I could stop them.

The general hung his head and exhaled. I braced myself for the explosion that was sure to come. He raised his head, the fury gone from his eyes now. "No, as a matter of fact, I am not. I have my orders just like you. And I'm telling you to let this go. *Please.* For your sake. For my sake. For the sake of anyone who's ever given a shit about either of us. Drop it. You can't even imagine how badly this could turn out for us. If you could, we wouldn't be having this conversation."

# CHAPTER 17 - TORI

Still leaning my forehead against the door, I turned my head first in one direction and then the other to check for people. The day had slipped by while I tried to evaluate the proposal and not a soul roamed the halls this late in the afternoon. I raised my head from the door and tried the code. As I anticipated, it didn't work. I tried the previous code, then the one before that. I hadn't worked there long enough to know any other codes, so I tried different combinations of the ones I knew. Getting in would take a miracle, but that didn't stop me. The tumblers knocked against each other over and over, but the lock never released.

"Come on lock," I whispered.

*Click.*

I wondered if my ears had deceived me and pushed down on the handle before it could reset. It moved. I *had* unlocked it! I pushed the door open and stepped through into the huge main bay of the test lab.

Tools lay scattered about on the work benches and random items sat here and there around the bay—desks, cabinets, tables full of electronic equipment—but I saw nothing that hadn't been there the day before.

A door near the back of the lab slammed. I heard voices and scrambled to hide behind a nearby electronics cabinet. As the agitated voices grew louder, I recognized one of the voices—Brian's.

It didn't take long to realize the other person was General Ash. I knew I'd be in big trouble if he found me in the lab. I pressed myself as close as I could against the cabinet and waited for them to leave. My heart pounded in my ears so loudly that I was afraid they'd hear it too. But they walked right past me and exited the lab.

After waiting a moment to recover my nerves, I eased my head above the cabinet enough to look around. All was clear. Staying close to objects I could quickly hide behind, I tiptoed in the direction from which Brian and the General had come.

Around a corner, an aircraft like nothing I'd ever seen sat perched on tall, thin legs. I stepped closer to the dull gray, triangular object, but the craft wasn't what called me. My eyes went to a door that led into a smaller laboratory. Something in that room tugged at my soul as strongly as if it had physically grabbed me and pulled me to it. And I couldn't stop myself. I didn't want to stop, consequences or not.

Calm, resolved, and completely unconcerned that Brian and the general could return at any moment, I placed my hand on the doorknob. My head swam and I stumbled back a step, but I didn't let go of the knob. I held to the doorframe with my free hand and steadied myself. Nothing was going to stop me from getting into that room.

# CHAPTER 18 - GAIGE

I squeezed my eyes shut and concentrated as hard as I could to turn her around. Her will was too strong. I opened my eyes, knowing she'd be in the room soon, no matter how hard I tried to stop her. The only thing left for me to do was protect her when she arrived. That meant distracting the guards.

"Guards," I whispered.

The one facing the door turned in my direction and both raised their weapons. With guns aimed and ready to fire, they moved closer to the cage.

"What do you want?" the larger one asked.

"The restroom. I need to use the restroom," I said.

The guards looked at each other. I'd lured them closer to my cage and diverted their attention from the door. That would give me a second or two advantage when she walked into the room.

# CHAPTER 19 - TORI

I turned the knob and opened the door to chaos.

A man—handcuffed and caged like the animals they studied in that very lab decades ago—yanked his handcuffs in two, sending links flying. In the same fluid motion, he reached through the bars and grabbed the two guards standing outside the cage. The guards dropped to the ground and lay motionless. I didn't know what to do. I should have run, but something kept me planted where I stood.

"Get out!" the caged man yelled. "And don't let anyone know you saw me or the craft."

I immediately, and without question, turned and ran from the room. Only partway across the main bay, a hollowness I'd never felt before wrenched my gut, stopping me in my tracks. I bent over, clutching my stomach. I couldn't explain it, but I had to go back—go back or be torn apart running away. I turned and ran toward the small laboratory just as fast as I'd run from it.

When I arrived, I peeked inside before entering. The caged man lowered his head and sighed. He didn't seem surprised to see me—disappointed or worried, maybe, but not surprised. I walked toward him. Stopping at the edge of his cage, I could do nothing, say nothing. I just looked at him. A stranger. Yet I sensed something so familiar about him.

He grasped the bars. "You *have* to go. This place will be flooded with people soon."

I knew I shouldn't have been there, but I couldn't leave. I looked at the men lying on the floor. "Are they . . . dead?"

"Of course not. They're just unconscious."

The caged man had managed to take down two members of the Air Force's well-trained Security Forces team from inside his cage—while handcuffed. At least, he *had* been handcuffed. If he could do that, how had they been able to keep him here? And why? What had he done? "Who are you?" I asked. "Why are you here?"

"It doesn't matter. You *must* go. *Please,* go."

With broken handcuffs and bodies on the floor, I should have been afraid. But nothing about him frightened me, even after what I'd seen him do. Leaving him there, all alone in a cage—I couldn't do it. A tear rolled down my check. "I can't."

Two furrows creased into the man's brow, right between his eyes. He reached one of his now-freed hands through the bars and tore the door's lock from its mounting. The door swung open. I stepped back, not sure what to expect. He walked out and held his hand out to me. "Don't be afraid. I won't hurt you."

I took hold of his outstretched hand. My breath came fast and deep, and my heart rate quickened. But not from fear. No, I wasn't afraid. Captivated, but not afraid. "I know you won't." And I knew he wouldn't. A feeling, so deep within me that I hadn't even known the place existed, told me so.

"We have to go," he said. "But first, I need to take care of something. Kians will not—" He paused. "People of Earth will not respect this technology."

*People of Earth?* Who was this man I couldn't walk away from? His words told me one thing, but logic told me not to listen to the craziness flaring in my thoughts.

He let go of my hand and ran to the craft. He pressed the inner forearm of his left sleeve with the fingertips of his right hand like he was punching an invisible keypad. A hatch on the bottom of the craft swung open. Skipping half the rungs, he ascended the ladder on the inside of the hanging hatch. When he was in the craft I kept watch over my shoulder, worried about what would happen if the flood of people he'd spoken of arrived.

After a moment and without using the ladder, he dropped out of the opening and ran back to the guards on the floor. He pulled something from a side pocket on the leg of his flight suit and touched each guard on the neck with it. "That will keep them out for a while. Just unconscious."

Thin gray smoke billowed out of the craft. Its skin bubbled and began to melt. Drops of viscous liquid metal hit the floor with a plop and the craft started falling in upon itself.

The man grabbed my hand and pulled me toward the door. "We have to hurry. They're coming!"

# CHAPTER 20 - GAIGE

I slowed my initial pace to keep from dragging her across the floor as we made our way through the larger section of the laboratory.

She'd come with me freely—no, not really. She couldn't have made any other choice. She'd already connected and that connection was more powerful than anyone could have anticipated. Too powerful for her to run the other way. I wouldn't take advantage of that, though. Until she gained the knowledge and the strength to make a truly free choice, I'd look after her and keep her safe. Just like her, I had no choice about what I was doing. When she'd walked back into the lab, I'd felt something. Not just feelings *for* her, but something *around* her. Danger. I couldn't leave her there unprotected. That meant taking her with me, out of that place.

We reached the door to the hallway and slowly opened it. Fortunately, the lighting had already been dimmed for the night. Seeing no one, we slipped into the hall, closing the door behind us.

She looked up at me with green eyes that shined like the IC 1295 nebula through her long, dark lashes. Even in the dim light I could see that the excitement had caused the blush of her cheeks to stand out bright pink against her smooth, creamy skin.

"This way," she said, pulling me toward the exit. Her brown hair bounced in wavy whirls against her shoulders as we ran. The eyes, the silky skin, the hair. All perfect. She was more beautiful than any of our display images could have ever captured, and moved like poetry in motion, as the Kians would say. I lost myself watching her until her delicate hand squeezed mine, reminding me this wasn't surveillance. I was right there with her, and I had to control myself. They couldn't see her helping me. I grabbed her and wrapped my arm around her neck. She tensed.

"It's okay," I whispered in her ear.

Her tension eased. She understood. This was only an act. No matter what I said, she didn't have to fear me. And her energy told me that she didn't.

"Don't you try anything sneaky," I said. "You're my ticket out of this place. My little insurance policy!"

"I won't. I promise. I won't try anything," she said.

Thankfully no one had heard us—except their surveillance devices, that is. We made our way through the halls with no interference and broke free into the dark parking lot. But we were far from safe.

"That red car is mine," she whispered. "The one in the back corner."

With my arm still around her neck, we maneuvered together through the icy parking lot to the back door of her car.

"Keys?" I said, holding out my hand.

"They're in my purse, back in the building."

I didn't want to frighten her, but we had to get away from the facility. I placed my palm over the door handle and concentrated.

"I just remembered there's a spare key in a magnetic case under the front bumper."

I pulled my hand away from the door, but not fast enough. The lock released. Before she could ask any questions, I placed her in the back seat, found the spare key, and then sat down behind the wheel.

"Are you okay?" I asked.

"Yes, I'm fine. But how—"

"I have to get you away from here. Maybe for a few days, until I make sure you won't be in any trouble over this. Okay?"

She nodded, though a touch of uncertainty had crept into her eyes.

"Is there anything you need to take with you?"

She clutched at something around her neck, beneath her sweater, and shook her head. "No, I have everything that's important to me."

"Okay, you should lie down in the back seat, just in case."

She did as I said. Of course she did. I started the car and maneuvered us out of the slick parking lot.

"Hurry," she said, quietly, her voice drifting up from the darkness behind me. "As long as there are no issues, we'll be able to leave without being checked. But as soon as the people in my building realize there's been a breach, they'll notify security and every gate on the base will be locked down. We'll be trapped until they resolve the issue—finding us."

*"Conner, change of plans,"* I said, mentally.

"We're following, Gaige. We know she's with you," Conner replied.

*"Have Pags get me out of here."*

"We already have something. Turn left at the next light. That'll be the closest gate out of the base. Then veer right coming out of the gate and get onto the highway going north."

*"Thanks, Conner. I need to get her away from here and see how things go. I have a bad feeling about something, like she's in danger. Have Pags and his surveillance crew find a place where she'll be comfortable until we can figure it out, and let me know the location as soon as possible."*

"Pags is already working on finding a location. We have the same feeling here. The commander wants you to stay with her until we know what's going on. I'll get back to you with a location as soon as Pags has something. Oh, and Gaige—she has a cell phone in the car. It's sending out signals like a Terigon Beacon."

*"Got it, Conner. I'll take care of it. Have Pags find a place in the next few miles, where I can pull off and get rid of the phone—somewhere secluded. I want to talk to her about it first."*

She was quiet now, probably catching up with everything that had happened. I knew when she did, the questions would come.

I could see the gate up ahead. So far, traffic was flowing out easily, with the gate guards either in the guard house or on the other side checking the people entering the base. As we approached—the next to exit—one of the guards stepped out of the building, blocking my lane.

"Why are we stopping?" A shaky voice asked from the back seat.

"I'm not sure. Just stay as low as you can."

While the guard stood in front of us with his hand outstretched in a *hold* position, another guard came out of the building and lifted a metal post from the ground blocking off our lane. I felt no anxiety from these guards so I stayed patient. The second guard returned to the building while the first motioned for our line of traffic to merge with the other. *Evening traffic control.*

"We're moving," she whispered. "Are we out yet?"

"We're exiting now. They were just reducing the traffic flow to one lane for the evening."

"Ahhh. Yes, they do that." She paused for a long while before continuing. "So, the guards, back in my building. What did you do to them?"

The questions had started, like I knew they would, floating up to me from low in the back seat, quiet and hesitant.

"Pressure points the first time," I answered, getting onto the highway. "Before we left, I used a medical device that would keep them unconscious long enough for us to get away. I didn't want them to alert anyone."

"So they'll be all right then?" she asked.

Her soul trusted me, but her Earth upbringing hadn't quite reconciled with it. She'd be conflicted for a while. I had to do what I could to make her feel secure, to point her toward what truly resonated within her versus what she'd been taught in order to survive in this volatile Earth environment.

"Yes, they'll be fine. I wouldn't have hurt them. Not unless it was absolutely necessary to protect myself, or you. We don't like violence."

She was quiet then, but wanted to ask more questions. I could feel it.

"When you say *we*," she finally said, "what do you mean by that?"

# CHAPTER 21 - TORI

I lay in the backseat of my car, waiting, but the man made no quick attempt to answer my question. "*We* don't like violence," I repeated. "As in, your family doesn't like it? Your nation doesn't like it? Who? Who doesn't like it?"

"Search your intuition," he said, "and trust what it tells you. Trust *all* that it tells you."

I sat up and for the first time, took a good, long look at him without the running and hiding to distract me. As much as I could from behind in only dashboard lighting, anyway. Big. His head barely cleared the top of my car. Strong jawline, dark hair, tanned. Like any other nice-looking guy from the U.S. Or Italy, maybe. Spain? But the flight suit. An iridescent white, not the green of our Air Force flight suits. So not U.S., then. The material looked odd, similar to a soft vinyl, but with an unusual sheen. I looked in the rearview mirror to get another glimpse of his face. He glanced back at me in the mirror and an oncoming car's headlights illuminated his eyes like aqua jewels. My heart rhythm stumbled and my mind raced through the bits of information from the past half hour or so: the craft that was like nothing I'd ever seen before, even in the black world; his comment, *People of Earth*; the clothes he wore; those eyes.

What my intuition told me couldn't be true, could it?

But it could. Statistically speaking, it could be true. His craft wasn't from here. His flight suit wasn't from here. And his eyes, those aqua-blue eyes weren't from here.

"Is it true? Are you an alien?"

The rearview mirror framed his alien-blue eyes, which glanced back at me again, kind and patient. "Yes, I am alien to your world."

Even after hearing him admit what I had suspected, I still felt safe with him—this *alien.* But should I? Ted Bundy's victims must have felt safe with him too, until they became part of his serial killer statistics. I reached under the front seat, searching for a screwdriver or anything else I could find to defend myself—just in case I needed to. Finally, my fingers found what I'd been searching for. I gripped the screwdriver in my fist. It felt foreign and wrong.

"I promise you, I won't hurt you. You can put that down."

"How did you . . ." I squeezed the handle. I didn't want to hurt him. I knew I *couldn't* hurt him.

The man pulled the car to the side of the road and turned off the ignition. I held on to the screwdriver, barely feeling it in my hand anymore.

"Search within yourself and you'll know I won't hurt you."

I disconnected from my here and now, and went searching somewhere inside myself. There, I already knew the man's words to be the truth; he wouldn't hurt me.

"We're okay?" he asked.

I dropped the screwdriver. "We're okay." I took a deep breath and prepared to face a new version of reality. "How did you end up in our lab?"

"My shuttle had some issues and your government found me before I could make the necessary repairs." He restarted the car. "I can answer any questions you have, but we need to keep moving. Okay?"

My imagination ran wild with what the government might do to an alien being. Every Hollywood extraterrestrial movie I'd ever seen came rushing back to me. The scenes that flashed across my memory weren't good. But this wasn't a movie. What would they do, in real life, if they caught him? Would they experiment on him? Would they allow him to suffer? Could they hurt another living being? Some could, unquestionably. I knew it firsthand. The person who killed my parents could. But I had the power to stop it this time. And this time I would.

"Yes. We need to go. We can't let them find you."

# CHAPTER 22 - GAIGE

I pulled off the highway into a dark, desolate parking lot far away from any other businesses. "We need to get rid of your phone. Your car is old enough not to have all the traceable electronics. But your phone will lead them right to us."

Still in the backseat, she leaned forward and opened the console, pulling out her cell phone.

I left the car running to keep her warm. "This won't take long," I said, holding out my hand for the phone.

She clutched it to her chest. "What are you going to do?"

"I need to get rid of it."

"But what about my pictures? Pictures of my family? Can't we just turn off the GPS?"

"These things can put out signals that aren't always able to be turned off. Maybe, if I had more time, I could—"

"No," she interrupted. "We don't have time." She laid the phone in the palm of my hand. "*I* might be in legal trouble, but if they catch *you* . . . Go ahead. I have copies of the important ones on my computer back home in Florida."

"Thank you." I got out of the car, hating that I was about to destroy her piece of home, the link to her family when she couldn't be with them. "*Conner, have Pags upload the information from this phone as fast as you can.*" I walked slowly around the car toward the open field behind the building, giving Pags time to make the transfer.

"He's got it, Gaige."

The car door opened and closed. Victoria's footsteps grew louder until she stopped right next to me.

I hesitated.

"Destroy it," she whispered. "They're only pictures."

Her energy said so much. The pictures of her family were important to her, because her family was important to her. She missed them, even the ones who'd been gone for so long.

I closed my hand around the phone, willing energy into it. The electronics hissed and the screen dimmed. It was dead to the world, or anybody trying to track us. I pitched it as far into the field as I could and turned to see the look on Victoria's face.

"How did you do that?" Awe had replaced some of the sadness she'd had in her eyes over the loss of her pictures.

"The mind is a powerful tool." What else could I say? It was as simple and complex as that. "I'm sorry about your pictures."

"I know. But it had to be done." She shivered in the cold.

Without giving it any thought, I put my arms around her. She gripped me tight, pressing her head into my chest. I breathed in the scent of her hair—like freshly bloomed Kinwa flowers from back home—and never wanted to let her go. But I had to. Being that close wasn't good for either of us.

I took a step back. "I need to get you a coat and some supplies."

She laughed. "No, I'm covered there. I have a ridiculous coat perfect for the arctic, bottled water, crackers, protein bars, hand warmers, and a bunch of other stuff. I even have a bag with a few personal things—toothbrush, face wash, stuff like that. It's all in the trunk. My Dad worried about me getting stranded in the snow up here. He watched too many of those *How I Survived* kind of shows."

"I'll get them." I reached in the car and popped the trunk. "Why don't you wait in the car?" I opened the front door for her. "Sit up front with me?"

"Sure." She smiled and got into the car while I pulled a few things from the trunk—the coat, a bottle of water, and two of the bars.

I got in the car and handed the items to her. "I'm Gaige, by the way. Gaige Ardessa."

"Tori Spencer," she said.

"Tori? Is that a nickname?"

"Yes. My real name is Victoria, but I go by Tori."

Her beauty beamed from inside and out. The chopped off nickname didn't capture her whole, true essence. "Why not go by Victoria?" I asked.

She looked puzzled. "I guess Tori is just quicker to say."

"Well, Victoria is a beautiful name and worthy of the time it takes to say it."

She tipped her head down, blushing. "Thank you. I guess Victoria will be fine, if you don't mind taking the time to say it."

"All right then, Victoria it is." I held out my hand to shake hers.

She smiled and took it. "Nice to meet you, Gaige, the Alien."

"Nice to meet *you*, Victoria, the Earthling."

She pulled her hand away and rubbed her palm. I'd felt it too. The warmth. The connection. I looked away, putting distance between us and the moment.

"We need to go," I started the car, but didn't drive away. I had to make sure Victoria was all right with my plan. "I'm taking you someplace where you'll be comfortable. Probably a motel. But I won't leave you there alone. Will that be okay?"

"I'm fine with that."

I felt an excitement in her. Whether it was because of me or the adventure, I didn't know, but I had to be careful not to confuse her.

"Conner to Gaige," Conner's voice rang in my ear. "Be aware the military convoy should reach the lab in about half an Earth hour. It won't be long before they know you're gone."

I thanked Conner mentally. Victoria could probably handle knowing I had others helping me. Maybe it would even make her feel safer. But for now, I had no spare time to explain things. When the convoy discovered I was gone and the shuttle destroyed, measures to reconcile what had happen would ramp up to maximum levels. I had to make sure Victoria was far away from the reach of that chaos by then.

"We need to go," I said to Victoria. "Are you ready?"

She gave a hard, resolute nod. "I'm ready."

# CHAPTER 23 - BRIAN

Even after General Ash's warnings, I continued to plead Gaige's case. "He shouldn't be caged like a criminal. He's done nothing wrong."

When we reached the secondary office the general kept in our building, he slammed his planner down on the desk. "What do you want me to do?" He ran his hands through what little hair he had left. "Let him walk out the front door? Maybe even give him a change of clothes and fifty bucks?"

Before I could respond, General Ash received a call. The convoy was at the back of the building, ready to load the *cargo*. I was out of time. If I couldn't get through to the general, I'd have to try someone above him, whoever that might be.

On the way to the lab, I walked silently alongside General Ash, resigned to the fact that nothing was going to change his mind. I spun the lab's combination dial slowly, stalling for more time to think about how I'd plead my case to whoever else had authority over the situation. Once in the main bay of the lab, I dragged my feet, still trying to buy some time, and was promptly left behind.

The general rounded the corner into the area where the craft sat. "What the hell!" he screamed.

I ran to see what had happened.

General Ash stood, sweaty and red-faced, over an inky black puddle on the floor where the craft had been. "Guards! What the hell is going on?"

I followed him into the side room where they kept Gaige. The door of the empty cage hung open and the guards lay unconscious—or worse—on the floor. While the general raged, I ran over to the men to check for pulses, surprised that Gaige would have hurt anyone. To my relief, both men were alive. The general couldn't have cared less.

"I want to see the footage of this place immediately! Open that back wall up! Get the team in here now! We need to see what we can salvage of this!"

Though I hated the loss of the craft, I was glad Gaige had escaped. But heaven help him if General Ash got hold of him now.

# CHAPTER 24 - VICTORIA

The road stretched out before us like it had no end. The car's headlights illuminated the only remnants of snow left—black sludge along the edges of the highway. I didn't care to see the snow's beauty deteriorate once it became intermingled with dirt and exhaust smoke. It was a harsh contrast to the brilliant, sparkling white of a few days before, when the majesty of it actually made the cold tolerable.

I turned my attention from the road back to Gaige and watched him drive while endless questions ran through my mind. Steering with his left hand, his right elbow rested on the middle console. He didn't fidget or act restless. He seemed comfortable on this planet. *Was that his nature or did he come here often?* He drove a car like he'd done it many times. He could pilot a spacecraft. So maybe a car was no challenge, even for a first-time alien driver.

The flight suit covered most of his body, except the hands, and when his long sleeves pulled up a bit, what I could see of his arms was taut with muscle. So was his neck. By his mature physique and the hint of stubble covering his firm jawline, I thought he might be a little older than me. But not much. He looked fit and strong. So did many men on Earth. I didn't see them ripping open locked cages with their bare hands, though.

"How did you break out of the cage so easily?" I said.

"Our planet's gravity is much stronger. It causes our muscles to develop a more dense structure. I'm sorry if I scared you."

"No. You didn't." He had, actually, scared the hell out of me when I saw him tear metal from metal like tissue paper. But only for that brief second. "If you could break free on your own, why hadn't you?"

"It was a matter of timing."

"So I messed up your plans?"

"No. Things worked out as they should have. When you came into the lab, I knew you weren't safe. It's good you're away from there."

It seemed to me that being inside a secure government building was about the safest place I could be. "Why wouldn't I be safe?"

"My people have a sense about things. I can't really give you any better explanation than that right now. Give me a little time to understand what I'm feeling. Please? I wouldn't have taken you with me if I didn't think it was the best thing for you."

"A sense, huh? All right. You figure it out." He looked so much like us, that I had a hard time remembering he really was an alien. But, he was. I'd seen firsthand proof. How many more ways were we different? How many ways were we alike? I wanted to know more. I wanted to know everything.

"Victoria, I'm going to talk to my team for a minute, okay?"

"Team? There are more of you here?" *How many aliens were running around on our planet? Did I shop at the same stores with them? Work with them?*

"Yes, there's a team here for backup. They're going to help us." He glanced over at me again, never taking his eyes off the road for too long.

"So, you all aren't everywhere, then, mixed in with us?" I asked.

"No, not in years, and never everywhere. We used to have a few here and there. We have a peaceful energy. We thought we could spread that energy around and help the people of Earth. It didn't work out very well. At this moment, only my team is here—four people, plus me."

He'd left the lab with only the clothes on his back, nothing like a phone, walkie-talkie, or any alien version of those things, as far as I could tell. "Okay. How are you going to talk with them?"

"My suit is equipped with a communication device."

"Really?" I remembered him poking at his sleeve before his spaceship's door flew open. "You dial them up on some secret control panel?"

"No, it's done by voice command. Components within the suit respond and connect me to whomever I'm trying to reach."

"Cool!" This I had to hear.

"Go ahead, Conner," he said.

I waited and listened for this Conner person to answer.

"Got it," Gaige said, after a minute or so. "Okay, Victoria. I now have coordinates of a place we can go."

"But, I didn't hear him say anything."

"Oh, no, you wouldn't. Communications from the ship resonate directly to my eardrum through a special device in my flight suit."

I slumped back in my seat, disappointed not to have heard a real-life alien conversation. "Well, I guess if you can zoom in on a spaceship, you would also be a little more advanced than us with your communications." I straightened myself in my seat. "So you have a location, but how will you know if it's okay for me to go back?"

"Our ship is nearby, hidden by Earth's moon. The crew is watching every move at that building."

"Really? You can watch us?" The fact that we could be observed, presumably without our knowledge, was a little disconcerting.

He laughed. "Don't worry. We're not voyeurs. Not in a bad way, anyhow."

"Then in what way?"

"Scientific observations, mostly. Our ship is a science vessel. Your planet is very similar to ours. We can learn a great deal from your planet and people. And the way they all interact." He looked at me then back to the road. "You're uncomfortable with that?"

"Well, it's a little creepy that you can watch us."

"I can understand why you would feel that way. But believe me, we're never intrusive." A mischievous grin exposed dimples I hadn't noticed before. "But I do like that pink nightgown you have."

"What?" My stomach dropped.

"I'm kidding, I'm kidding." He laughed, slapping his free hand against his thigh. "We only observe people in public places. I'm sorry, but I had to break all the seriousness hovering over you."

I sighed. “Good guess. I do like pink, but you must have taken ten years off my life.”

“Nah.” He flipped my visor down. “I put a smile on your face.”

He was right. Staring back at me from the mirror was a smile, and a spark in my eyes I’d never seen before.

“And it’s a beautiful smile,” he added.

# CHAPTER 25 - BRIAN

The team flowed into the lab like an army of ants, surrounding the blob that used to be the spacecraft and attending to the guards, who appeared to be recovering. Meters clicked and people scurried around, scooping samples from the puddle and calling off readings from their instruments like they'd never seen such numbers before. I had to admit, I hadn't either. Who knew what secrets the craft had held or how its destruction may have altered its properties. We could analyze it for years and still not know everything that had just been lost to us.

The general had stormed off with a group of other high-ranking officers to view the security footage. Would that help them catch Gaige? Maybe it didn't matter. Maybe Gaige was in another world by now. I had a bad feeling I'd soon wish I was, too. As worried as the general had been about the transfer going well, I expected him to try and pass the blame to save his own butt. At my count, he had three good candidates—the two guards and me.

Deep in thought, I continued to watch the team fuss over the mess Gaige had left behind. If he wanted to destroy his own craft, that was his prerogative. He didn't trust us with the technology and was probably right not to.

Gaige was free of the general's wrath, but what about me? Would my career be in jeopardy now, even with my credentials? Top scientist in my field—irreplaceable, people said. I suppose if my career with the government was over, I'd find another job. With no wife or family, I could easily relocate if I had to. Plenty of money in the bank meant I didn't have to be in any hurry. But General Ash's words haunted me. *You can't even imagine how badly this could turn out for us. If you could, we wouldn't be having this conversation.*

What did he mean? Was there more on the line than our careers?

# CHAPTER 26 - VICTORIA

Well off the highway now, we'd seen nothing for miles except hills and trees and darkness. Then, a little place appeared somewhere outside of civilization. It seemed the entire world had slipped away, leaving only this patch of existence behind—a grocery store, hardware store, bank, pizza joint, and a few miles beyond that, an old motel. Though it wasn't quite eight o'clock, the early winter sunset and the emotionally draining day made it feel much later.

With only two cars in its parking lot, I wasn't sure how the place stayed in business in such an out-of-the-way location. Gaige and I almost had our own private motel. That could be a good thing if it kept us off the radar of anyone who might be after us. Or a bad thing if I'd been riding for miles and miles in a car with the most patient serial killer in history. I laughed under my breath at the thought.

We pulled into the lot and parked directly in front of the office. A small neon sign in the window announced they were "Open 24 hours."

Gaige shut off the engine. "This is it. Nothing fancy, but secluded."

"*Very* secluded," I said. Beyond the parking lot, only blackness existed. It seemed absurd to me, but what if Gaige *was* the most patient serial killer in history? "Gaige, what if I told you I didn't like being out here in the middle of nowhere?"

"Then I'd take you somewhere else." He shrugged. "But I don't get the sense you mind it here."

"No, maybe not. But what if I told you I wanted to go back?"

"I'd advise against it."

"And if I rejected your advice?"

He twisted in his seat, toward me. "Victoria, I would never force anything on you. Whatever you want to do is your choice. I *would* advise against you going back, though."

I believed wholeheartedly that he'd respect my decision, whatever it might be. "Okay. Your advice is duly noted. We'll wait this out here."

He exhaled and I knew I'd made him a little nervous. "Good. You really don't have to worry."

"Good," I said right back. "Neither do you."

He shook his head and smiled. "I'll try to remember that."

So we would stay in a motel room together, the alien and the criminal who'd broken security protocols. But in that flashy flight suit of his, he looked about as out of place as he could possibly look in the woods. I knew I couldn't let him walk in there. "You're staying put."

"What?"

"You *look* like an alien."

He leaned toward me and whispered. "I *am* an alien."

"Yes, well you look like one in that fancy flight suit. I'm going in. You wait here." I grabbed the door handle then remembered that back at the lab, I'd abandoned my purse and everything in it, including cash and credit cards. I let go of the handle and looked at him, figuring he had no way to pay for the room either.

Gaige leaned back against the seat and crossed his arms, grinning. "Change your mind, bossy?"

"I don't have any money."

"Hmm." Gaige cocked his head and looked me up and down. "How much do you think they'd give you for the parka you have on?"

I grunted. "Not enough. So now what?"

He reached into the sleeve pocket of his flight suit and pulled out several bills. "I guess I'll have to give you some money."

"You have money?"

He held the bills out to me with a handcuff dangling around his wrist. "It's never a bad idea to have some of the local currency." The dimples. "Just in case I want to kidnap an Earthling and take her to a motel."

"Oh, that's always a contingency for you, huh?"

"No, but with you, I made an exception."

I rolled my eyes and took the bills. "You're incorrigible. And you might want to get rid of the bracelets."

I got out of the car and slammed the door behind me. I wasn't mad, but I couldn't let his dimples make me stupid.

Though it was cold, no snow covered the ground and the pathway leading to the motel office was clear of ice. A few little dried up flowers, remnants of summer—so dead and brown it was impossible to know what they used to be—remained along the edges of the concrete walk.

I pulled open the door to the clang of a small cowbell that hung on the inside of the doorknob. Cheap wood paneling covered the walls and the décor hadn't been updated since the

1970s. The mustard-colored laminate countertop curled up at the edges, and the vinyl flooring was so faded and yellowed the original color had been lost to the years. The place desperately needed an update, but it appeared to be clean. I was thankful for that.

Light from a small relic of a TV flickered on the face of the elderly gentleman sitting behind the counter. The table next to him on which the TV sat looked more like a plant stand than a table, but it did a fine job holding the weight of the little TV.

The man turned the volume knob down to silence the black and white horror flick and stood up. “Lookin’ for a room?”

“Yes. Do you have something available in the back?” I asked.

“Sure, we have plenty of vacancies, all with two double beds, satellite TVs, and hair dryers.” He pulled a numbered key off the pegboard behind him. “Can I see some I.D.?”

“I.D.?”

“Yes, you have to be twenty-one to rent a room.”

“I do? I mean, yes, I know I do, but my I.D., I’ve lost it. On vacation. I’m on the way home now. Plan to get a new one first thing Monday.”

We both stood facing each other, him looking at me and me looking at him. Waiting. He held the key in a closed fist like he might not be inclined to let go. I gave him the most tired, pathetic face I could manage, hoping he’d take pity on a young, weary traveler.

*Please, please, rent me a room. Please, please, please.* I wished it, willed it. *Pleeeeease!*

He loosened his grip on the key and handed it to me. “Room eighteen. Circle around to the back and it’ll be toward the center.”

I paid him, thanking him profusely, and turned on my heels to get out of there before he changed his mind. As my hand reached for the door, it occurred to me this man might be my last opportunity to take another course. I pulled the door open, cowbell clanging. I trusted Gaige.

When I got back into the car, the handcuffs were gone from Gaige’s wrists.

“Everything go okay?” he asked.

“Not really. You have to be twenty-one to rent a room.”

“Ah. But you have a key.”

“Yes.” I held the key up and gave it a jiggle. “I used my immense charms on him.”

Gaige raised an eyebrow. “Impressive.”

# CHAPTER 27 - VICTORIA

Just as the clerk said, number eighteen was near the middle of the building. No other cars sat at the back of the motel, so we were able to park directly in front of our room.

With its wood-paneled walls and harvest gold sink, the décor was similar to the office. But also like the office, it was clean. I could stay in any decade as long as it was clean.

"Which bed do you want?" I asked Gaige.

"I'll take the one by the door."

I had the feeling he wanted that bed so he would be the first line of defense should anybody, government or otherwise, break in. A gentlemanly act.

A small breakfast table with two chairs sat in front of the window. I tossed my coat onto the closest chair and climbed on top of my bed. Settling myself in a seated, cross-legged position, facing Gaige's side of the room, I watched him spread out on his back on his own bed. He placed his hands behind his head and closed his eyes. Other than his slow, steady breathing, he remained completely still. I lost myself watching him doing nothing at all. But somehow he fascinated me.

"You should rest, too," he said, eyes still closed.

"Oh. I know. I should. I am. I mean, I will." I fluffed my pillows and stacked them.

He opened his eyes and sat up, swinging his feet over the edge of the bed.

I pounded the top pillow and knocked it aside, giving up on my sham of an activity. I uncrossed my legs and let them hang over the edge of the bed, a mirror image of my roommate, only a much smaller version. "I'm sorry. It's just that you looked so serene, like you didn't have a worry in the world."

"There's no reason to worry. Everything will be fine."

Maybe serene hadn't been the correct interpretation. Sitting face-to-face with him now, I could see his eyes looked tired, a little heavy in the lids. Who knew when he'd last had any decent sleep? Probably not in the cage they'd kept him in.

"I'm sorry," I said. "I didn't mean to interrupt your rest."

"You didn't. I think I need some food first, anyway." He stood and stretched. "You hungry?"

My stomach rumbled as if on cue. "Yes, actually, I am getting hungry."

"Well, coming through town, it looked like we have the choice of pizza or nothing, so I'm going to get us a pizza." He picked up my car key off the table, where he'd tossed it when we arrived. "You can stay here and rest. I know you have to be tired after all that's happened today."

"But—"

"Pick-up window," he interrupted with a grin. "As dark as it is outside, with the dash lights turned down, no Earth clothes will be necessary."

I laughed. "Good. Yes, pizza will be great."

"You'll be fine here. Our ship's surveillance team is watching." He reached for the doorknob, but stopped and turned back to me. "So don't be running around naked." He winked.

"Funny." I tossed one of the pillows at him.

He raised an arm to deflect it, then scooped it off the floor and dropped it on my bed. "Seriously, though. They'll be watching the lab and this area. If anything happens or anybody who shouldn't be comes within miles of this place, they'll let me know and I'll be back here. I will *not* let anything happen to you."

His humor had flipped to dead serious, and I had no doubt he meant what he said. Gaige wouldn't let anything or anyone hurt me.

After he left, a void filled the room. Or me. I wasn't sure which, exactly, but I seemed to *miss* him.

*What was I letting happen?* I paced the room, trying to reason with myself. *Alien. Ridiculously long-distance relationship. Stop being stupid!*

I could talk it through all I wanted. Still, my heart ached for him to return. How would it feel when he was gone from my planet for good? My eyes watered and I didn't want to think about that scenario anymore.

I stopped and pulled out from beneath my sweater the chain that hung around my neck. I gazed at the two gold wedding bands hanging from it and read the inscriptions inside: *May peace and love surround us, always.*

Had my mother not been having their wedding rings inscribed for their anniversary, they'd have been lost the night my parents were robbed and killed. I stared at the rings until they pulled me into their memories and my thoughts drifted back in time. Zoned out on the two thin bands, I saw picnics in a park, kickball in a yard, birthday cake and balloons, and my real parents' faces in every wonderful scene. Then, I saw Gaige's face with his soothing smile, and the same comforting warmth I'd known as a child filled me again. My imagination envisioned us together, happy and in love like my parents had been. I shook my head to scatter the thoughts. What was the point of them? Once this fiasco was all straightened out, he would go back to his planet and I would be stuck here on mine. No good would come from imagining anything different.

I dropped the rings back beneath my sweater and sat on the edge of the bed, waiting for Gaige to return. I fought the urge to lie back and rest, even for a minute, worried that if I drifted off, I'd wake to find everything had been a dream.

# CHAPTER 28 - BRIAN

Summoned by the general, I sat in my office stalling, moving technical reports around on my desk. Whether military or civilian, you never keep a general waiting. But I needed a minute to prepare for the unsurpassed fury I knew General Ash would unleash. His prized spacecraft and ticket to unequalled power lay in a thick black puddle on the floor of our lab and the *thing*, as he called him, had walked out of our building unchallenged. This meeting wasn't going to be pretty. Shit rolled down hill and I figured I was standing in the valley for this one.

I straightened a stack of deliverable sheets, tapping the edges until they lined up perfectly, then I looked at my watch. Fifteen minutes had passed since the general's call. I rose and took a deep breath. I had to face him and the longer I kept him waiting, the worse it would be.

When I reached the general's office, I stopped in front of his door, stalling for one more second, then I entered. The general sat at his desk holding a framed picture of his daughter. He pointed to the chair across from him. "Sit down." His eyes didn't move from the picture. "My daughter, McKenzie." He brushed a finger lightly across the glass that separated him from her photographed face. "She graduates high school this year. I'm looking forward to seeing her in cap and gown. And getting her settled into college. Walking her down the aisle at her wedding. She's very much a daddy's girl." Looking off in the distance now, his eyes had gone glassy. "She'd be lost without me."

A queasiness settled in my stomach. As thrilling as it had been to meet a real live alien, I began to wish Gaige had never crashed his spaceship into my life.

The general clenched his teeth and looked at the blank screen on the opposite wall. "I want you to see something." Still grasping the picture in one hand, he picked up the remote sitting on the desk in front of him with the other. He hit a button and an image appeared on the screen.

I turned my chair to have a better angle. The footage was from the building surveillance cameras. Too nervous to relax, I watched on the edge of my seat as Tori entered the lab and the general and I left. I watched as she found Gaige, ran away from his cage, and then ran back again. I watched as Gaige broke free and, hand-in-hand, the two fled the lab. I watched a weak display of aggression on Gaige's part. And I watched as the two exited the building. I'd watched it with my own eyes, but couldn't believe it. *What had she gotten herself into?*

The general paused the video on a frame of the empty hall. "The girl who left the building with that *thing*—you know her?"

I hesitated, but odds were he already knew the answer, so lying about it probably wouldn't go over well. "Yes, her name is Tori. She's an intern."

He tossed the remote onto his desk where it landed with a hard thud. "And you're friends, yes?"

I looked at the frozen video frame, wondering if he thought I'd had something to do with what I'd just seen. "I'm more of a mentor, really."

"It looks to us like the girl was trying to help that *thing*. She at least didn't try to stop it. We want that *thing* and this friend of yours back. And we want you to help make that happen."

"How can I help? I have no idea where they are." *And wouldn't turn them over to you if I did.*

"We already know where they are," he said, making eye contact for the first time. "We need you to talk her back."

"What makes you think she'll listen to me?"

He leaned forward over his desk. And me. "You'll make her listen."

I knew I had no real choice. And I didn't want anything to happen to Tori, or Gaige either, for that matter. If there was a chance I could be a buffer, I had to at least try.

"All right. I'll do whatever I can."

# CHAPTER 29 - VICTORIA

The door of our motel room opened and realized I'd fallen asleep. Gaige stood in the doorway with a large pizza box and a six pack of root beer, my favorite.

"Did I startle you?" he asked, kicking the door closed.

I pushed myself off the bed, thrilled it hadn't all been a dream. "No, you just woke me. I guess I drifted off."

"Sorry about that." He set the pizza and the drinks on the table.

I flipped the box open and inhaled the aroma of warm yeast and tomato sauce. I hadn't realized how famished I was until I smelled the pizza. We ate until we thought we might burst, then lay on our beds to rest while we waited. But rest escaped me. Instead, I stared at the ceiling with my thoughts spinning, wondering *exactly* whom, or what, I was holed up in a remote motel with.

"Gaige?"

"Yes." He turned his head toward me.

"Can I ask you something?"

"Sure." He rolled onto his side, facing me, and propped himself up on his elbow. "Whatever you'd like."

I got up from my bed and knelt on the floor beside him. Taking hold of his hand, I compared it to my own. It looked the same, except manly, of course. Bigger, stronger. I closed my eyes and felt the warmth of his hand in mine. Kind. Compassionate. A good soul. He was a good soul. My energy-level dropped.

"What are you doing? You shouldn't . . . we probably shouldn't . . ." He pulled his hand back.

I opened my eyes and studied his face. It had all the right parts to be human, but he clearly was not from Earth. "What are you, Gaige?"

He grinned at me. I loved his grin. It wasn't a full-blown smile that included the dimples, but was just as nice. It always seemed to be accompanied by a sparkle in his aqua-blue eyes. "What do I look like?"

I took hold of his hand again and held it next to mine. Sleep that had evaded me earlier pulled at me with unrelenting force. I fought it. Our conversation was too important. "You look like me. Human. I suppose you'd have to, though, since you're here. So you'll blend in. But I want to know, what do you look like, *normally*?" My eyelids fluttered closed, but I opened them wide. I wasn't going to fall asleep until I had my answer.

He laughed. "You watch too much television. I'm not some shape-shifter or something. This *is* what I look like. *Normally.*"

I blinked hard, forcing my eyelids to stay open, and stared at his very non-human eye color. "But your eyes. Humans don't have eyes that color."

"It's a mutation on my planet, just like blue eyes here on Earth."

My head bobbed. I jerked it upright, struggling to stay awake. Gaige stood and lifted me into his arms where my head rested easy on his chest. I felt safe and warm clutched against his body and yearned to stay there. But he laid me on my bed instead.

"I don't know why I'm so freaking tired," I said, without opening my eyes.

"It's because of me," he whispered.

I didn't hear anything he said after that.

# CHAPTER 30 - GAIGE

I sat on the edge of Victoria's bed, watching her. Her chest rose and fell in a choppy pattern—one or two long breaths, then a short, quick gasp—and her eyelids fluttered, but she didn't move a muscle beyond that. Her subconscious was trying hard to connect with me on deeper and deeper levels. That was taking a lot out of her. Attempts to filter my energies hadn't been successful. Not successful *enough*, anyway. She'd read me easily with a touch to my hand. Her abilities were more incredible than I'd expected.

"Conner to Gaige." My communication device resonated in my ear.

*"Go ahead, Conner."*

"I've spoken with Pags. According to the communications his surveillance team is picking up, the Air Force appears to be as interested in finding Victoria as they are you. Another thing. They think they know where you are."

I flinched and started to jump into flight mode. Victoria mumbled something in her sleep. I couldn't understand what, but knew I had to take a moment to clear away my panic. Victoria didn't need to pick up on any negative energy, and from what I'd seen of her abilities, she would.

Gently, I rose from the bed and went to the other side of the room to put some distance between us, hoping the space might help. *"I've got to get her out of here—"*

"Wait, Gaige. You have some time," Conner said. "They're still at the Air Force base pulling a team together. They want to keep any alien connection contained, so they're not reaching out to their counterparts in other communities for help. You still have several hours on them. And their information on your location could be wrong. We don't know yet. It's coming from somewhere outside the building. Surveillance is having an unusually difficult time picking up their communications, but they'll keep trying."

Victoria stirred, still mumbling, and reached her hand to the edge of the bed where I'd been sitting. I thought I could make out my name amongst her mumbles. With a calmer energy now, I moved closer and knelt down next to the bed, so she'd know she wasn't alone. She drew her hand back and curled her arms against her chest. Her mumbling quieted, then stopped. She knew I was close.

*"Okay. In light of the new information, I'd still feel better getting Victoria away from here. No sense taking any chances waiting to find out for sure if they know where we are. Have Pags find another location, somewhere we can have the shuttles cloaked nearby. I want to be able to quickly have Victoria on the other side of the world if we need to."*

"Got it, Gaige."

*"Can you come up with a car, to pick us up? If they're looking for Victoria, they'll be looking for her car, too, so it's best we distance ourselves from it."* I realized I'd been absently running a hand over Victoria's hair as I spoke to Conner and

pulled it back. Her lingering essence continued to tingle my fingertips even after I'd removed my hand. I gripped my fingers into a fist, trying to hold on to the feeling as long as I could.

"Yes, we should be able to obtain a car. Pags already had some backup locations identified. I think one about an hour from you will work well for the shuttles. We'll take the shuttles there now, and then I'll come pick you up."

*"Thank you. And, Conner, don't bring any of the team. For Victoria's sake."*

"I hear you. I'll come alone."

Though Victoria would have some time to rest before being introduced to another of us, I wanted to give her every advantage I could to manage our energies. I leaned over her, placing my hands above her—not touching, but close—and willed calm, restful energy into her body. "Sleep well," I whispered, focusing hard on that thought as I moved my hands above her from the top of her head down to her feet and back. Over and over I willed relaxing energy into her until I had no energy left for myself.

*That should help,* I thought. I lay down on my bed and drifted off.

# CHAPTER 31 - VICTORIA

I opened my eyes to a dim light that shone from the small bedside lamp. It was still dark outside, so I knew I hadn't had a full night's sleep. But I felt well-rested. Energized.

Gaige lay in his bed sound asleep. I barely remembered talking to him, but knew I had. I'd asked what he was. *Had he answered?* Maybe. No shape-shifter. He looked like what he looked like. *Was that an answer?* Not really. I wanted to know more and I knew exactly where to start. I ran to the window and threw open the drapes. "Gaige!"

He bolted from his bed and was at my side quicker than my eyes could follow him. "What's wrong!"

"Damn. You're fast."

"What's wrong?" he said again, scanning me, then the room, then me again.

"Nothing's wrong."

He let out a sigh. "If nothing's wrong, why did you yell my name?"

Looking out the window, I craned my neck this way and that, searching for a good clearing among the mix of thick evergreens and bare maple trees. "Turn off the light and I'll tell you." I waved a hand toward the lamp without taking my eyes off the night sky. "Sorry. I mean, *Please* turn off the light."

"O-kay," he said, flipping the lamp off. "I take it you feel better?"

"Yes, I feel great. Not tired at all now."

"What are we doing in the dark?" His footsteps came back in my direction. "You're not trying to take advantage of me, are you?"

If I couldn't see his alien smile in the dark, I could sure hear it in his tone.

"You wish. Come over here."

He moved up behind me, so close I could feel his breath on my neck. I closed my eyes, pretending for a moment this was what it would be like to live with him, to sleep in the same bed with him, to feel him breathing in the night, so close we'd be breathing the same air. He didn't say anything, just waited on me to speak. But speech wasn't coming easily with him so close.

"Um. Your planet . . ."

"Yes, my planet."

I shook my head, trying to clear out my irrational, hormonal thoughts and focus on our conversation. "Your planet. Where is it?"

"Let me get my bearings." He stayed silent for a moment. "No, we won't be able to see it from the window."

I flipped the lamp back on and grabbed my coat. "Then let's go outside!"

"All right, let's." He laughed. "You must be feeling better. It's cold out there."

I realized then he had on nothing but his flight suit. "Wait. You don't have a coat."

"The suit's temperature-controlled. I'll be fine."

"Are you serious?"

"Yes, I'm serious. I'll be fine. Let's go." He opened the door and stood to the side for me to go through.

Outside, Gaige turned to look back over the top of the motel. He studied the sky for a moment, and then pointed. "There. You can't actually see the planet, but our star, our sun, is right above that thick clump of trees."

I tried to figure out where he was pointing, but wasn't quite sure. "That clump of bare trees or those evergreens?"

He stepped behind me, resting his chin on the top of my head, and pointed over my shoulder so my line of vision could follow his arm. "You see that little cluster of stars right up there?"

*Stay focused on the conversation*, I reminded myself before answering. "Yes, I see them."

"Okay, look to the right. That star all by itself, just to the right of the cluster. That's our star, our sun."

It twinkled yellow, almost winking at me.

Gaige moved his finger in a circle out in front of me. "And in orbit around that star is our planet."

I imagined his planet, circling its life-force sun, full of others like him. "What do they call your planet?"

He let his arm drop, allowing it to drape over my shoulder. "Anu."

"Uh-nu. I like that name."

A howl in the distance suddenly cut through the air.

"WHAT was *that*?" I grabbed Gaige's draped arm and pulled it around me.

"Don't worry. They won't bother us."

Another howl followed, echoing off the hillsides. I turned toward Gaige and locked my arms around his waist. “How do you know that? I think we should go back inside.”

But neither of us moved. Or spoke another word. We just stood, embracing each other. A warmth surged through me. Though I didn’t know much more than his name, beyond logic or explanation, I knew I wanted him.

# CHAPTER 32 - GAIGE

At first I couldn't move, couldn't think. I only wanted to act. Then I did. Losing myself in her, I caressed her back, her neck, and ran my fingers through her hair. She gripped the back of my flight suit, her breath coming fast and heavy. Visions flashed. Me and her—

"No!" I pulled back.

Having been leaning her weight against me, she stumbled forward. I grabbed her by the shoulders to steady her.

She blinked, confused. "No?"

"I overstepped."

"No. You didn't do anything wrong." She reached her hand up and touched my check. "It was . . . that was nice."

I wrapped my hand around hers and pulled it away from my face, reluctant to let go. But I did. "It can't happen."

"It?" She asked, softly.

My mind was going, had gone, places it shouldn't and I was making her all too aware of that. I needed to protect her, not confuse her. "Anything. Nothing. It just can't happen."

"Are you married or something?"

"No. I'm not married or *something*."

She tilted her head like she was studying me, or thinking, or both. "Can't happen or shouldn't happen?"

"Can't. Shouldn't. It doesn't matter."

She held my face in her hands, and then ran them down my neck, then my chest.

It was all I could do not to pull her back against me. "What are you doing?"

"It *does* matter. There's a difference between can't and shouldn't." Her hands stopped on my stomach. "And if you're single, is it that you're . . ."

"That I'm what?"

"Different." She pulled her hands away and looked me in the face. "Are you different?" It was hard to tell in the darkness but I could have sworn a blush covered her cheeks. "You know, not compatible. Physically."

"Oh! We're compatible, all right." I had to laugh, but only for a brief moment. Then, the seriousness of the situation fell back on me. "But you're attracted to me in ways you don't even understand. I'm not going to take advantage of that."

She bowed her head and looked up at me with sheepish eyes. "If I'm willing, it wouldn't be taking advantage."

"Yes, it would." I didn't know what else to say. "We just can't." I shook my head, trying to convince myself more than her. I couldn't let things get out of control. "It's time to get back inside. I don't want you to catch a cold."

I took her by the hand and practically dragged her back into the room. Even holding her hand was difficult now, so I released it as soon as we got inside. She was hurt; I knew that. I'd had no choice, though. I wasn't sure how to make things better, but I had to try.

"Look, Victoria." I guided her by the shoulders into one of the chairs, and knelt down in front of her. "It's not that I don't want to. I mean, I could. So easily. You're . . . you're . . ." I threw my head back, frustrated that logical words escaped me.

"I'm what?" She crossed her arms.

I caressed her cheek. I couldn't help it. "You're beautiful, and you're smart, and you're stubborn—but I like that—and you're important to me. Too important for this." I waved my arm around the crappy little motel room. "And you're . . . you're not ready. There's so much more you should know before making a decision like that. In my world, that act means a lot more than it does here."

She swallowed nervously. "How much more?"

"It's a life commitment for us."

"Life?" Her face paled.

"Yes, life. When we connect with someone and are driven to bond, it's in all ways—physically, emotionally, mentally. That act involves so much more for us. It's like merging two beings into one on every level with every sense we have. Senses you aren't even aware of. And *that* is for life. Our bonds are never broken."

"Never?" She leaned forward in her chair, eyes wide. "But people change over time. How do you know you wouldn't someday grow apart?"

"Remember, we're very intuitive. We listen to something deep within ourselves and when we feel a connection so deep that we're driven to bond, any changes over time are superficial in comparison, and easily managed."

"So it's never just physical?"

"No, it's a package deal for us."

"You're saying that connection drives the desire to bond. But, it seemed like . . . and if that's the case . . .?"

Her words came out jumbled, but I knew what she meant, and she was right. The desire was there, for both of us. But how could I explain the situation without getting into more than she was ready to hear?

"Never mind," she said, saving me from whatever kind of explanation I'd have had to fumble through. "I'm not normally like *that*. Normally. I don't know why . . . like . . . what got into me." She blinked and let out a sigh. "I should go to bed now." She pushed past me, took her coat and shoes off, and got into her bed. "I'm sorry if I did anything to offend you."

"You didn't. And, I'm the one who's sorry. But I'll tell you one thing. If I was a Kian man—Earth man—you wouldn't be sleeping alone tonight." I smiled at her, finally feeling the tension ease. I probably shouldn't have said what I did. Had I confirmed to her that she *was* right? The desire *was* there. But my confession had made the heaviness lift from the room. We needed that.

"Well, you're not, so put the dimples away, Alien." She grinned back at me and I knew the incident was over. For now.

# CHAPTER 33 - GAIGE

Victoria tossed and turned in her bed, while I sat in a chair waiting to hear some word of progress from Conner. I could easily detect that Victoria's subconscious searched for more than she'd ever known was possible to reach. Being in my presence had awakened that in her. I hoped she'd adjust quickly to her new awareness, since I didn't seem to be able to completely block my energies from her. But, like using muscles she'd never used before, eventually she wouldn't even notice. Until then, it would be an exhausting, and maybe even emotional, time for her.

Victoria turned toward me and opened her eyes. "Gaige?"

"Yes."

"Tell me more about your planet." Sleep hadn't completely released its hold on her voice and the words came out slow and husky.

I sat down on the edge of her bed and started telling her everything I could think of. Her eyelids hung heavy, but she fought sleep, and sleep fought her back. I droned on about the commerce, or lack thereof, the landscape, and the architecture.

She laid her hand on my arm to get my attention. "Are there murders?" she asked. "My parents were murdered. During a robbery attempt." Her eyelids still sagged, partially obscuring her green eyes. But now the heaviness looked more like sadness than fatigue. A deep line creased between her brows, adding to the effect.

"I'm sorry."

"Thank you. So, are there? Murders?"

"No, no murders. It's not in our nature. We've evolved into more sensitive, empathetic beings than the ones here on Earth, with abilities beyond the five senses Kians hold to. Kians could be that way too, if they'd work at it."

She raised her head. "We could?"

"Yes, you could." *You* already are, I thought, but didn't dare say it out loud.

She smiled and laid her head back down on the pillow. "I'll work at it then. What about robberies?"

"No robberies either. Even if our nature would allow it, there's no need. Technology provides us with anything we could ever need or want."

With her hand still on my arm, Victoria's eyelids slowly closed and she drifted off easily. I lay down next to her, watching her sleep, so beautiful, so innocent. I felt her connection to me getting stronger. I was drawn to her as much as she was drawn to me, but I couldn't act on it. Getting physical wouldn't be fair to her. She couldn't really understand what she was feeling. Things were too complicated.

I touched a finger to her cheek. She stirred and I froze. Her lips spread into a gentle smile and she rolled against me, still sleeping. *What was she dreaming? Was it of us?*

"Conner to Gaige."

*"I'm here."*

"We have the shuttles in place near the new location and I have a car. I'll be there in about an hour to pick you up."

*"Good. Thank you. We'll be ready. And Conner, Victoria is much more sensitive than we anticipated. Your presence will affect her. So be aware."*

"Got it. See you soon."

I traced a lock of Victoria's hair. I'd let her sleep as long as I could. She'd need every advantage if we had to take drastic measures. "Sleep tight." I kissed her on the forehead and eased off the bed, which responded with a loud creak.

She gasped. "Wait. You haven't finished. Anu. I want to hear more. It sounds wonderful."

"Yes, it is wonderful." I sat back down on the bed.

"And everybody gets along?" A smile hovered at the edges of her mouth and her eyes looked off in the distance like she could see it all for herself already.

"We don't always agree, but we work it out. We're all very close."

"So, you're close to your family, then?" She let out a sigh and twisted her finger in the top edge of the bed sheet. "I miss my family."

"I'm sorry." *It will all be okay*, I thought, sending that positive message silently to her.

"It's okay. That's part of life, right? You grow up, go off to school, run away with an alien." She chuckled and closed her eyes as if the effort of laughing had taken all the energy she had.

"Part of life, yes, I suppose it is. Maybe not always the alien part."

"Maybe not," she agreed, opening her eyes back up. "Your family. You're close to them?" she asked again.

I didn't want to talk about my family when she missed hers so much. She wasn't going to let it go, though, so I hesitantly told her what she wanted to know. "My family is extremely close. Because our senses are so much more astute, families and close friends on Anu become virtually telepathic with each other. That's especially true of what you might call soul mates."

"The bonding thing?" she whispered.

"Yes, the bonding thing."

With the constant seeking her subconscious was doing, she had to be exhausted. I was amazed she'd been able to fight sleep this long. She took my hand and held it up, comparing it again to her own.

"You quack like a duck, Alien."

Though I searched the memories of my language lessons, the meaning of this particular idiom managed to elude me. "A duck?"

"You look human, supposedly function—physically—like a human. But are you? Are you really a human?" Her eyes closed and her hand dropped to the bed.

"Yes, I'm human. Just like you," I whispered.

She pulled her lids open again. "But how?"

"Earth has an atmosphere very similar to our own, so we had an outpost here. That was millennia ago. When our ships became advanced enough to no longer need outposts, the people here wanted to break from us and remain on Earth permanently. They gave up our technologies and any help we could offer. That's how they wanted it. Our culture has a deep regard for individual choices as long as they don't cause harm to others, so we respected their decision. Anu became such a distant memory as the generations passed, that the name began to be known as God of the Sky rather than the planet they used to call home. Their descendants don't know where they came from anymore, or that the planet or the Anuans even exist." I became lost in my thoughts, assuming Victoria had drifted off by now. "They made a lot of mistakes. Without our technologies, living on Earth was not easy—droughts and floods, hard times. They became selfish. And violent. We tried to step back in and help. Even thousands of years later we continued to try, resisting what our intuitions told us. We regretted it. I'm so sorry, Victoria."

I reached a hand toward her to touch her sleeping cheek, but she was wide awake and hanging on every word.

"You're sorry for what?"

"For your loss." I pulled the covers up to her chin and, though she was awake this time, kissed her again on the forehead. "Sleep now."

# CHAPTER 34 - BRIAN

Having been sounds asleep, my nerves jumped when someone pounded on my office door. A sharp pain struck the back of my neck when I tried to straighten it, so I let my head continue to rest against the chair. It wasn't a bad office chair, but it sucked as a bed. "Yes?" I called to whoever was on the other side of my door.

"The general wants you in the test lab in five minutes."

*Of course he does.* "I'll be there." I lolled my neck from side to side before trying to raise my head again. The kinks worked out enough to straighten my neck and stand with only minor discomfort. I looked at my watch. It was after midnight now. Almost twenty-four hours in that place. "Too bad salaried people don't earn overtime." I laughed, definitely punchy from lack of sleep. "Not funny, Brian." If I didn't get myself under control, who would? This was not a situation to enter into slaphappy.

After stretching out and stuffing the snacks from my desk drawer into my coat pockets, I headed to the test lab. Inside sat four black SUVs. A mix of a dozen or so military and civilians stood in groups discussing whatever there was to be discussed. The civilians, dressed in dark suits, looked like they'd just left the presidential motorcade unguarded. For trying to keep the situation quiet, the government sure had enough people there.

I caught one of the civilians in between groups and couldn't resist poking at him. "Hey, why the suits? Shouldn't you guys be doing camo or something?"

For an answer, I received a blank look and a blunt, "We're not special ops. We don't *do* camo."

I wanted to tell him that even in his dreams he wouldn't be able to handle a special ops assignment. I bit my lip instead and swallowed the words.

With a sneer on his face, the suit moved away from me and joined one of the groups.

*Fun bunch.* I was cranky, no doubt, but figured I'd better knock it off, because the general could trump my cranky by a mile.

"Brian!"

I didn't have to turn around to know who screamed my name. "Yes sir, General Ash." I turned to see him blasting toward me.

"We're ready to move out." He flailed his arms toward the SUVs as he moved past me. "Come on everybody! Load up!" He looked back over his shoulder. "Brian. You're with me. Front of the line."

I trudged to the first SUV, hating my life at that moment.

# CHAPTER 35 - VICTORIA

My gloved hands slapped against the concrete floor, searching for something in the darkness. I couldn't recall what I was searching for. Only that I had to find it before . . . *Before what?* Before *something* happened—something bad.

I crawled faster, scanning every inch of the floor with my hands. The sound of my breathing—quick, in and out—bounced around the emptiness before finally fading away, but not before being replaced by a dozen more of my own echoing breaths. I couldn't find whatever lay hidden in the room. But I *had* to keep trying.

Finally locating the target of my search, I picked up the lifeless body off the floor. Out of nowhere, a grunt broke through the empty black void. Until then, I had seen nothing. But, at that moment, I saw the eyes: bright yellow with vertical slits for pupils. Like snake eyes. They pierced me with a look so fierce I could almost feel them burning through my own. I squeezed my eyelids shut.

With a *whish*, the stale air stirred around my neck. I didn't feel the pain. Not at first. A warmth saturated the collar of my shirt. I raised my hand to my neck, inhaling, gasping, drowning, while blood ran through my fingers. *Then* the pain came. A sharp sting deep in my throat. And then nothing. No pain. No sight. No sound. Nothing at all . . .

"Victoria! Are you okay? Wake up. Wake up!"

I opened my eyes. Gaige stood over me, shaking me by the shoulders to wake me. I knew then it had all been a dream, and that they were back. The monsters were back. The same monsters that haunted my dreams around the time of my parents' deaths.

"Are you okay?" Gaige asked again. "You sounded like you were choking."

The monsters' reoccurrence disturbed me. But as scary as they seemed, I knew they lived only in my dreams. Wide awake now, something still frightened me. I sat up, bed covers already kicked aside during my sleep, and pulled my knees against my body, wrapping my arms around my legs to hold them close. "I'm scared."

Gaige sat down on the bed next to me. "Why are you scared? What do you feel exactly?"

"Afraid!" I tucked my head down and held myself in a tight ball.

Gaige laid a gentle hand on my arm. "What are you afraid of? Something in the dream?"

"No, not now. That was only a dream. I don't know why I'm afraid now!"

"Okay. Just concentrate and try to focus."

I felt like the walls were closing in and going to squash us dead any second. "We have to get out of here!" I scurried out of bed to run for the door, but Gaige grabbed me from behind, locking his arms around my chest and pinning my own arms to my sides. I couldn't move.

"I can't believe it," he said. "You know."

"Know what? All I know is that we have to get out of here. Now let me go!" I twisted my body, trying to break free of him, but couldn't overcome his strength.

He leaned over me. "Shhhh," he whispered into my ear. "Shhhhh," he said again, his breath hot against the side of my face. "It's okay. Calm down. Calm down. It's okay. You're safe. You're safe."

His words became reality for me and I felt calmer, definitely safe in his arms. "What Jedi mind tricks are you pulling on me, Alien?"

He turned me around, facing him. He held me with one arm and brushed his hand over my hair. "Just trying to help you control what you're feeling."

I looked deep into his ocean-blue eyes. "And what am I feeling?"

"What *are* you feeling?" he said. "You have to learn to sort that out on your own. Listen to your intuition."

I thought for a moment. The panic was gone, but not the fear. "I'm still afraid. But not as much. Your mind trick helped."

"Good. Now, why do you think you're afraid?" He stopped stroking my hair and rested his hand on my shoulder. The other arm still held me, but not quite as tightly as before.

"I don't know. I . . . I feel trapped in this room, like we need to get out of here or we're going to be suffocated."

"Your feelings are right. You just have to figure out how to better interpret and control them."

"So what's wrong?" I tried hard to hang on to the calmness he'd given me. But with Gaige's confirmation about my feelings, the relatively calm state he'd helped me achieve was beginning to fade.

"Everything will be okay. We're going to alter the situation. You'll have nothing to be afraid of then."

"Go on."

"I've heard from Conner. Conner is the person leading the rescue team. He's getting information from our surveillance team."

"The voyeurs?"

Gaige smiled. "Yes, the voyeurs."

"And?"

"Your government—they know where we are and they're coming for us."

I started to bolt for the door again, but Gaige tightened his hold on me.

"It's okay," he said. "We're leaving. Conner will be here any second with another car—one they won't be looking for—and we'll be long gone by the time they arrive."

Hearing that gave me some relief. The adrenaline that had been driving me dissipated and my legs felt like rubber beneath me.

"Okay?" Without waiting for me to answer, Gaige sat me down on the bed and guided my shoulders back until my head rested comfortably on the pillow.

"Okay. Long gone. Good." I closed my eyes.

"I know this is all new for you and exhausting to try and harness—"

"The intuition thing?" I asked, feeling myself drifting.

"Yes, the intuition thing . . ."

***

I wasn't sure how much time had passed when Gaige touched me lightly on the arm, but I didn't think much.

"I'm sorry to disturb you, Victoria, but he's here now. Conner is here. It's time to go."

I sat up and rubbed my eyes, groggy, but awake enough. Gaige went to the door and opened it. The man who entered wore the same white flight suit as Gaige and stood about the same height, but he had a slimmer build. His auburn eyes matched the color of his hair and glimmered with a wisdom that seemed beyond his years.

"Victoria, this is Conner," Gaige said.

Conner smiled. "Hello, Victoria."

I stood and took several steps toward him, extending my hand. "Hello Con . . ." My head swam and Conner blurred into his surroundings. I dropped down to my hands and knees onto the floor. "I'm sorry. I don't mean to be rude. I . . . I don't know what's . . ."

"Victoria has some things in the trunk. Can you transfer them over? The key is on the table."

"Sure," Conner answered, and slipped out the door without another word.

Gaige bent down and rolled me into his arms, lifting me off the floor. "You're okay. I have you."

I laid my head against his shoulder and kept my eyes closed, hoping it would make the room stop spinning. "What's going on?"

"It's us. You with us," he said, as he walked with me. "To oversimplify, it's the intuition *thing*, as you call it. You're highly intuitive, like us. Well beyond most people of Earth. You've subconsciously recognized the similar, higher-level ability in us and are trying to open up to it, to connect with it in yourself and in us. You're not used to using that part of your being or managing that type of energy and it's draining you. You'll adjust, though . . ." His words garbled and faded. So did I.

# CHAPTER 36 - BRIAN

Sandwiched in between two of the civilians in their dark suits, I sat in the backseat of the first black SUV, its windows so heavily tinted, I could barely see out. Lacking usual general-officer protocol for traveling, the general sat in the front seat, head bobbing as he carried on conversations with the people in the car. I listened carefully to everything they said. Unfortunately, most of their conversations were in code. I had figured out that Tori was *Baby Bird*, who'd apparently fallen from the nest. Flown was more like it. And Gaige was *Tin Man*, who'd come in the *Tin Can.* Not very creative in my opinion. The general also referred to someone with the code name *Reptile*. From the sounds of it, he was the one calling the shots.

"Quiet!" General Ash said. He raised a hand to his ear as if listening to something. "Pull off. They're changing locations. We need to head west now."

The general pointed to an upcoming exit and began conversing with the person feeding him information. "Yes, sir. We're changing course now, sir. We'll get that *thing* and bring it to you as originally instructed. The insignificant pest of a girl will be dealt with back home for you." he jumped. "No, sir. I'm sorry, sir. The girl, yes, we'll bring her to you as well. No, sir. We won't let her escape. If she's that important to you, we'll capture her at all costs." The general paused. "Even at the expense of the *thing*? Uh . . ." His confused voice faded then he jumped again in response to the unintelligible outburst on the other end of whatever communication device he was using. "Yes sir, of course, sir. Even at the expense of the *thing*. Got it. We'll bring her to you, even if we have to sacrifice the *thing* to do it."

A chill ran through my body. *What the hell?* The person on the other end of the conversation wanted Tori so badly they were willing to sacrifice an alien being for her? If they'd sacrifice him, they couldn't want her simply because she'd helped him escape. *But why? Why want Tori over an ET? What the hell had she done?*

# CHAPTER 37 - VICTORIA

Gaige's voice wrapped around me and I floated within it. After a long while, the muffled sound of his words vibrating against my face rattled me awake. Feeling groggy, I lifted my head from his shoulder and tried to get my bearings. We were in the backseat of a car with Conner driving, presumably to our next hideout. Gaige spoke clearly, but I didn't understand the words. I *did* understand that the same fear I'd experienced before was back. It said to run as fast as we could in the opposite direction. I tried to ignore it. I couldn't. I clamped my hands into tight fists and squeezed my eyes shut, willing the fear to leave me alone. It didn't. Nothing I tried eased what I felt. I told myself I was overreacting. I'd been beside myself with fear at the motel and we'd made it out fine. Gaige was much better at interpreting the intuition thing than I was. I had to stay calm and give him the chance to sort out what was wrong and what to do about it.

Conner noticed in the rearview mirror that I had stirred and quietly explained, "He's speaking with the surveillance team from our ship."

Gaige nodded in agreement.

I leaned forward in the seat so I could more easily talk to Conner without disrupting Gaige. My seatbelt strained against my chest. "Is that what your language sounds like?"

"Yes, he's speaking Anuan."

"Is it a difficult language?"

"Not as difficult as English, in my opinion. I didn't think I'd ever get your slang. Still don't sometimes."

I rested my chin on the front seat, finding a conversation with Conner to be a good distraction from the fear that continued to linger. "Are there others on Anu who know my language?"

"Yes, and other Earth languages, too. Since our ship is a science vessel with the specific mission of studying Earth, we have to know at least two Earth languages, along with their dialects and slang, to qualify for our assignments. Nearly everyone on our ship can speak English."

Gaige finished his conversation then placed his hand on my back and began to speak in Anuan. "Sorry," he said, catching himself. "I don't want you to worry, Victoria, but it appears our pursuers have changed course."

"They're coming this way now, aren't they?" I dropped back against the seat, the previously straining seatbelt now relaxed and hanging loose. *Was running to be my life now?* My body began to shake with small quivers that I couldn't control. "What are we going to do?"

"Our backup location is only another minute or two away," Gaige said. "The government officials from Wright-Patterson haven't contacted any local authorities for help and we still have a good lead on them. So, we're going to stop as planned, where you'll be comfortable, then Conner and I will confer with the ship about what to do . . ."

Gaige's lips continued to move but I no longer heard what came out of them. My life had spun out of my control and what happened to it now, I knew, was not up to me anymore. And hadn't been for a while now.

# CHAPTER 38 - BRIAN

We'd pulled into a gas station and parked at the far end of the lot where the lighting was crappy at best. I stood huddled outside the SUVs with the general and a half dozen of the suits, now clad in black trench coats worthy of a Hollywood movie. One of them unzipped my coat and slid a pen into my shirt pocket. A listening device, no doubt. He then held up a set of keys and tipped his head back toward the SUV behind him. I stuck out my hand and he let the keys drop onto my palm.

We were now only twenty minutes away and the general had decided to send me ahead on my own. He was sure I had a better chance by myself of talking out Tori, Gaige, and somebody they called *Hoke*. I might have a better chance than they would, but like hell I'd follow through with it. I'd let them think whatever they wanted, though. I'd been worried about Gaige since the first time I'd seen him in the cage. After hearing the general's side of that weird conversation, my concern for Gaige didn't compare with the concern I now had for Tori. No way were they going to get their hands on her.

"Don't screw this up," the general said.

Not bothering to zip up my coat, I squeezed the keys in my fist and turned without giving General Ass the courtesy of eye contact. Gravel crunched beneath my feet as I walked away from the posse, happy to be free of their company, and anxious to warn Tori.

# CHAPTER 39 - GAIGE

We settled into the backup location—another isolated motel room—with some sandwiches we'd picked up along the way. Victoria chewed slowly, staring at me while she ate.

"Tell me," I said to her.

She swallowed. "Tell you what?"

"What you're feeling. What you're sensing. Interpret it for me."

She laid her sandwich down, leaned back in her chair, and crossed her arms. "There's nothing to interpret. You told me yourself, they've changed course and are coming for us again, even in this new place." She pushed her plate away. "They're going to follow us to the ends of the Earth."

"I didn't say that last part."

"That part was the interpretation. Am I wrong?"

No, she wasn't wrong. My interpretation was the same, and something needed to be done about it. We couldn't keep bouncing from one motel to another.

"Conner," I said. "Can you help me with some things in the car?"

"Sure," he answered.

Conner and I both left our sandwiches half-eaten and stood up from the table.

Victoria went to one of the beds and fluffed some of the pillows into a back rest. She sat down and nestled herself deep into her makeshift chair. "You're not that slick, Alien."

*Slick?* It took me a moment to remember. *Deceptively clever.* I knew Victoria was too smart, and intuitive, to fall for Conner helping me in the car. It had been worth a try, though, to save her from listening to discussions that might continue to keep her upset about our situation. "Not even a little slick?"

She picked up the remote control from the bedside table. "No, not even a little. But you two go ahead and do your conferring in private. I'm going to find a movie to distract myself from this crazy parallel universe I've slipped into."

Her attitude, though not the most pleasant at the moment, showed promise. She seemed to be learning how to process energies she received without letting them overwhelm her. But she was only with two of us. She'd need to improve those skills for things to go smoothly for her, if she ever ended up spending time with more of us.

Victoria turned on the TV and started flipping through channels while Conner and I stepped outside to talk with Pags. This time, the howls echoing in the distance were from the fast moving air and not the animals. The bare trees surrounding the motel didn't help block the winter winds, but the suits would warm to whatever temperature we needed to stay comfortable. They didn't keep the cold wind from cutting at my face. Initiating a plasma shield to protect it wasn't worth the effort for a short conversation, though.

"Gaige and Conner to Pags," I said.

"Go ahead," Pags answered.

"What's the situation now?"

"I was about to contact you. The majority of the group is stationed about fifteen Earth miles from there, but they've sent the scientist from the lab ahead to your location. We don't sense that he's a threat to you. They think he can persuade you back, though. They're not going to let up, Gaige, and for some reason they're even more determined to get Victoria than they are you."

Conner shook his head, and I agreed. *Why Victoria? Could they know?* Things definitely weren't going well. Not at all like they were supposed to have gone with a simple visit to Earth to meet Victoria. It was becoming clear; we needed more than surveillance at this point.

"Thanks, Pags. I need to speak with the commander now." I said.

"I'm monitoring. Go ahead, Gaige." Tas's voice had an anxious edge to it. He'd put his faith in me to accomplish this mission smoothly—a mission he'd probably have preferred to do himself had he not been so vital as commander. I couldn't let him, or Victoria, down.

"Commander, I'm concerned about the way things are going. Even though we have shuttles in the area and navigation standing by to route us away from this location, we need to have a backup plan. Who knows how far they'll chase us. They seem to be able to figure out exactly where we are. We can't keep running from one motel to another."

"We're trying to find out how they're tracking you so easily. But, regardless of how they're doing it, they ARE doing it. So, we need a backup plan in case we can't figure it out in time and block them. I've already set some things in motion in case you have to bring Victoria back here. I know we'd hoped . . . but not this fast. Such a quick transition could be tough on her, so I've contacted Zada. She's assessing any medical risks to Victoria, not only physically, but emotionally, too. Especially considering Victoria seems to have much stronger abilities than anticipated. I've also updated the captain on the situation and notified The Council of the possibility that we may need to bring Victoria on board without having time to complete our full assessments or perhaps even give her a choice about it."

"That's not exactly the way we thought this would go," I said, "but I think we need to be prepared for the possibility."

"Yes, best to be prepared for the worst case. I'll let you know as soon as I hear back from Zada. Command out."

Tas cut communications abruptly. Worst case. Tas was going to make sure worst case didn't happen this time. Not like years ago. I could barely remember that time, but I could hear in his voice that it was revisiting him now.

"Gaige to Pags?"

"I'm still here, Gaige."

"Let me know immediately if the rest of the government entourage moves."

"Will do."

"Thanks. Gaige out."

Conner kicked an errant leaf scuttling by on the ground. "Damn. Why did this have to get complicated?"

"You think your Dad is okay?" I asked.

"He'll be fine. He's focused on his commander duties. That will keep his mind occupied. Enough anyway." Conner followed the dead leaves skipping by, like he was trying to decide which one to kick next. "And this is a different situation. Tessy was strong-willed. Grown. The decision was hers to make."

I leaned against the building, between the door and the window of our room. "I don't see how this is much different, Conner. Victoria is strong-willed. Grown. The decision is hers to make. Once we get her through this situation, anyway. Her decision could be the same."

Conner stopped distracting himself with the leaves and looked up from the ground. "Hmm. Seems you're right. Except maybe for one thing."

I knew what Conner meant. As much as I'd tried not to, I'd already become a factor with Victoria. "I haven't encouraged—"

"You didn't have to. She's knocking through any walls we put up. She knows. She might not understand, but she knows what we've all figured for years."

"Things are complicated, though. She could still choose a different path, one she's more familiar with." I let out a sigh that filled the air in front of my face with an icy cloud. I didn't want to think of the possibility, though I'd respect it if that was her choice. "Let's concentrate on the now, which is keeping her safe. How far away are the shuttles from here?"

"Right. The now. The shuttles are only a couple of miles from here."

"I agree with the ship's assessment of Brian. He's no threat. As long as the rest of the group stays where they are, we're going to remain here. We can make it to the shuttles long before they could get to us. I need the medical feedback from the ship in order to make the right decisions if things . . ." I hesitated. Tas's words—*worst case*—rang in my ears. "If things take a turn for the worst. We can't rescue Victoria from these people just to have her die on the ship."

Conner clenched his teeth. “Ugh. Why didn’t we anticipate this? Why didn’t any of us feel this possibility?”

“I have no idea. But we’ll work through it. We have to.” I raised my head to the heavens and prayed for the Universe to give Victoria strength. To give us all strength.

# CHAPTER 40 - VICTORIA

My worry morphed from mental to physical, manifesting in a churning sea of uncertainty that raged in my gut. I clutched at my stomach like my hands could keep what little bit of sandwich I'd been able to choke down from coming back up for a visit.

It wasn't working. I made a dash for the bathroom and knelt over the toilet, letting bits of sandwich and stomach acid fly. After a couple of dry heaves, my body was satisfied that it had rid itself of all the food I'd just eaten and my stomach muscles stopped convulsing. My nerves were still twitchy, though.

I plopped onto my bottom and leaned back against the bathroom wall, too weak to stand up, but needing to put some distance between my face and the place where who knew how many strange butts had been. I yanked a strip of toilet paper from the roll and dabbed my mouth. I had to pull myself together before Gaige and Conner came back inside. This *thing* happening to me—the intuition, the sensitivity, the *whatever*—was affecting me more than I cared to admit, zapping my energy and now giving me enough insight and worry to make me physically sick. I'd never been a weak person and didn't want to start now. But if I couldn't be stronger, I had to at least fake it better.

The outside door of the motel room creaked open. I was out of time. Forcing myself up from the floor, I took a quick look in the mirror. With pale skin and bloodshot eyes, I'd definitely had better days, but they would have to do. I pulled the door open and stepped out of the bathroom.

Gaige's brow wrinkled. I'd seen that look before—his worried face. "Are you all right?"

"Yeah, just touching up my makeup. I figured I'd better look good for my mug shot." Concentrating on each step I took, so I'd at least *appear* steady, I tried to make my way across the room.

Gaige put his arm around my back and guided me to the bed. "You're not slick, Earthling."

"I'm a little slick." I sank onto the bed and let the façade float away.

"Maybe a little. You had me fooled earlier. Not an easy task considering Anuans' empathic abilities."

Gaige sat down beside me, placing a hand on my thigh as naturally as if he'd known me forever. I liked the feel of it, of him next to me, of him caring about me.

Conner sat down at the table and went back to eating his sandwich. He kept his attention focused on his food and away from me and Gaige.

Gaige rubbed his hand up and down my thigh. Probably trying to comfort me, but doing so much more. My breath stuttered. He stopped.

"Sorry." He pulled his hand away, but his eyes remained on mine.

"Don't be." I couldn't break from his gaze, nor could I catch my breath.

Conner stood up. "I'm going to take a walk." And Conner was gone in a nanosecond.

Gaige and I both stayed fixed on each other, not bothering to say a word to Conner when he left.

"Victoria . . ." Gaige started to speak, but no more words came.

"Gaige . . ." I could find no words either. Only feelings. Longing, desire, connection—

Gaige shook his head and looked away. The spell was broken.

"I'll be more careful," he said.

"Okay," I answered.

And it was over. Another moment that had grabbed us and didn't want to let go. But Gaige was a gentleman. That was good, since I didn't seem to be able to think straight about *that* kind of thing where he was concerned.

"When Conner and I came back in here, you weren't doing well. How are you feeling now? Tell me what's going on."

Gaige's presence made me feel better. A little discombobulated over the thigh rub, but safer, for the moment, with him there. Overall, though, the running was getting to me and I didn't want to admit that to him. "I thought you were an empath. You tell me."

"My focus is a little *disrupted* right now."

We both knew why and I started laughing. Then crying.

Gaige hugged me. "You don't have to hide things from me, you know."

"I don't need a babysitter. I'll work through it." I sank my face into Gaige's chest, trying to pull myself together.

“Okay, that’s fair. But at least tell me, what are you working through?”

I raised my head and Gaige wiped the tears from below my eyes with his thumbs.

“Tell me,” he said again.

“Stress, I suppose. This situation *is* concerning.”

“Stressful. Yes. I could . . .” Gaige put his head down, thinking, maybe.

“You could what?”

He raised his head. “Hold you. It would help, unless . . .”

“Yes, I’d like that. It’ll be okay, I think.”

He scooted around behind me and pulled me to him. “Still okay?”

I laid my back against his chest, letting my head rest in the crook of his neck. Feeling more comforted than aroused this time, I knew I could handle it. “Yes. Better than okay. I’ll behave. You do the same.”

“I promise,” he said. “I agree, this situation is concerning. And, the fact that you seem to be so open to our energy is not helping you deal with the already stressful situation. That alone can be exhausting for you physically *and* emotionally, even without these people chasing us. But you know, you don’t have to worry about them catching us. We have means you can’t even imagine. If we need to use them, we will. These Kians could never keep up then. Okay?”

Why hadn’t I thought of that? Certainly, they could come up with something more technologically advanced than the car we were using to run from these people. But how long would we run before the Anuans stepped in with their technology? And what would that ultimately mean for me? “You said, if you need to use Anuan means, you will. It seems like maybe . . ." *that time has come.* I couldn't bring myself to say it out loud. But it was there, hanging between us.

"Yeah, maybe," he said. "We're assessing things."

"Your conversation outside just now?"

"Yes. You don't need to worry. Just know we'll keep you safe. One way or another."

I believed Gaige. Still, I wondered how, exactly, all this would work out, starting with what means of escape Gaige had at his disposal. "You melted your space ship. Does Conner have his stashed somewhere?"

"Yes, Conner has his. We call them shuttles. The spaceship is much bigger and is well beyond Earth's atmosphere right now. But shuttles are here on Earth. Everyone on the rescue team has one and they're cloaked not far from here."

"Cloaked?" I sat up and turned in the bed to face Gaige. "Like Klingons?"

Gaige grinned. "Ah, Star Trek. Yes, like Klingons."

One step at a time, I decided. We had a way to escape the cycle of motel hopping. The notion gave me relief for the time being. I wanted to hold onto that just a little while, before letting my mind worry about anything else. "Okay, then." I snuggled back into place, not really feeling the need for comfort at the moment, but not beyond using it as an excuse to stay close. "I think I'll take a little more of this. You know, to keep me calm."

Gaige enclosed me in his arms. "You're scandalous, Earthling."

"I'll accept that, Alien."

# CHAPTER 41 - GAIGE

Having Victoria nestled against me on the bed felt more natural than anything in the universe. I didn't want to move. But Brian was on the way and I needed to explain that. I let her rest while I sent calm energy to her until I couldn't delay any longer.

"Victoria?"

"Yes?"

"We need to talk," I said.

"Do we have to? This is kind of nice."

"Unfortunately, yes. There's something you need to know."

"Okay." She moved to one of the two chairs at the small table and patted the other chair. "Come. Talk."

I joined her at the table. "You know government officials from Wright-Patterson are coming this way?"

"Yes. You said we had a good lead on them, though. I figured since we were still here, they weren't close yet. Right?" She picked at the top of her sandwich bun, but didn't eat anything. Just tossed the bits of bun she'd plucked off back onto her plate.

"Well, not entirely."

She lost interest in picking at her sandwich and turned her focus to me. "What part's not right?"

"We still have a good lead on them. Except for one. Brian."

"Brian?"

"Yes. They've sent him ahead, to try and bring us back. We're going to talk with him. We don't believe he's a threat to us. And he's probably only a part of the group because he's being forced into it."

"No, Brian wouldn't be a threat. But what's the point in talking with him? We're not going back, are we?" Her eye narrowed at me. "You're still assessing things where I'm concerned, right? You're not sending me back yet?"

"No. We're not sending you back. We still haven't figured things out, especially where you're concerned. That's unusual. So, we're buying some time, that's all."

Victoria had found some peace knowing we had means of escape. She didn't need to know their focus had turned to her. If she figured it out on her own—which she might—I'd deal with that then.

I leaned toward the window and cracked the curtain open. "We'll figure it out. In the meantime, we'll keep you safe."

Conner sat on the hood of the car, scanning through the enacted view screen on the sleeve of his suit.

"Okay. I trust you." Victoria pulled the other side of the curtain open so she could see from where she sat. "I think we scared him off."

"Nah, Conner doesn't get scared away easily. He probably wanted to give us some privacy."

Victoria let go of the curtain. "Privacy. Yeah. To talk things out."

"Yeah, to talk things out." I waved Conner in. He nodded and I let the curtain drop.

*Talk things out.* I had to make sure that's all we did. She pulled at me with black hole force, connecting at every level, flipping things on within me that were hard to control. She felt it too. How could she not? I had to be strong—strong enough for both of us.

Victoria peeked behind the curtain to look out the window again. "This is all kind of crazy, you know? I'm holed up in a motel with a couple of space aliens with government agents in hot pursuit."

"Not what you expected when you woke up this morning?"

Victoria tilted her head and stared off for a moment. "Actually, I knew there was something different about this day when I woke, probably even before. I didn't imagine today would be this far removed from the ordinary, though."

Conner opened the door, walked in, and sat on the edge of the bed. "The scientist is almost here."

# CHAPTER 42 - VICTORIA

Gaige and Conner paced the motel room, back and forth in front of the paisley wallpaper, waiting for Brian to arrive.

Gaige broke from his pacing, pulled the edge of the curtain back and peered through the crack. "He's here."

Soon, a knock rattled against the hollow door. Conner stood at the end of the bed, waiting, while Gaige opened the door.

"I'm not here to hurt you." Brian held his hands in the air. "Can we please talk?"

"Come in." Gaige moved back from the door to allow Brian to step inside.

Brian looked like crap with his face slack and his eyes droopy. He thanked Gaige for letting him in and gave me half a wave. He opened his jacket and pointed to the black ink pen sticking out of his shirt pocket. At the same time, he brought his index finger to his lips. Gaige nodded. Brian picked up the complementary motel notepad and pen that lay on the night stand and sat down at the table with me. Gaige sat on the bed opposite Brian.

"As you know . . ." Brian wrote as he spoke to Gaige, holding the paper at an angle so Gaige could see.

Conner moved next to Gaige and the two watched the letters and words form on Brian's paper.

"I work for the U.S. Government on top secret aircraft research," Brian continued, still writing. "Your craft was of great interest to us and I was asked to reverse engineer it. Since the craft is now of limited use, we would like to discuss the matter with you personally."

I leaned forward and stretched my neck to see what Brian was writing. Though upside down from my perspective, I could clearly make out the words.

> *They're about fifteen miles from here. They will come for you if I don't bring you back with me. They want Tori more than they do you. I don't know why. You have to get her out of here! I will stall as long as I can.*

*Me!* So I *was* in trouble for leaving with Gaige. But why would they want me more than an alien?

Gaige nodded and reached his hand out for me as he rose from the bed. "I'm willing to consider having discussions with you and your people," Gaige said. "But first, please tell me more about what kind of arrangement your government would like to offer. I want to hear all the details."

I slid my coat on and took Gaige's hand. Brian gave Gaige a thumbs-up and me a weak smile. He began to ramble off lengthy details, none of which required a response. I followed Gaige and Conner toward the restroom at the back of our room. I supposed they didn't want to take any chances that the entrance was somehow being monitored.

Once we had squeezed into the small bathroom, Gaige closed the door softly behind us. Conner pulled back the curtain and my heart gave a hard thump inside my chest. The window was only a couple feet wide, if that, and not a lot taller. Cut the height in half when considering how much of the window actually opened, and it was questionable whether Gaige or Conner would fit through.

Conner slid the window open, trying not to make any noise. Regardless of his effort, the old metal frame made a high-pitched squeak. Conner didn't let the noise distract him. He looked out into the wooded area behind the motel and checked to the right and the left. He sat on the counter and put his feet through the opening. His legs and hips easily fit, but the right side of his flight suit snagged on the frame. He tugged it loose and angled his shoulders in order to maneuver his way out. Once firmly on the ground, Conner turned back toward the motel to help me out. Gaige picked me up and handed me through the window to Conner, who eased me down onto the ground. I'd fit easily and both Conner and I were free of the motel. Now only Gaige, the biggest of us all, was left inside.

# CHAPTER 43 - GAIGE

"Gaige," Tas blurted into my ear.

"What's wrong, Commander?" I whispered, as I put one leg then the other through the window.

"Pags has identified two other teams closing in on you. We don't know where they came from, but they're not far. You've got to get out of there! The Captain is bringing the ship closer, in case we need to quickly move into transitioning range. Engineering is on standby for a short-term boost of power to the ship's cloak in order to counter the effects of the high solar activity. The Council has been notified. Under the circumstances, they're in agreement with an emergency transition of Victoria to the ship. IF it comes to that."

Tas had given me every bit of information I needed to know, except the most important. "And Zada?" Without her input, I couldn't make a proper decision. "What does she say about any medical issues?" Trying not to panic and get hung up in the window like an animal in a trap, I stretched my arms above my head to make my upper body more streamlined for my exit.

"There's risk, but she thinks it can be mitigated."

"Have her assemble medical teams to deal with anything Victoria might need. I want them on standby in sickbay." I wriggled my body in small increments, one side then the other, as fast as I could in order to get my shoulders through the tight opening. I had to get myself free and get Victoria away from there.

"She's already working on that."

"Good. I want to know as soon as the teams are ready."

"As soon as I know, you'll know. Commander out."

The rough metal frame of the window gouged into my flight suit, but it didn't tear. After a couple more seconds of maneuvering, and with only a minor cut on my hand to show for it, I was free.

# CHAPTER 44 - VICTORIA

Flakes of snow flitted around us, whipping into swirling frenzies when gusts caught them. With Gaige now through the motel window, I could see the look on his face. Conner's expression matched Gaige's. Sheer terror. I knew they'd been fed some new information through their fancy suits.

Gaige grabbed me by the shoulders. "We have to run."

"What's wrong?"

"There are two other teams closing in on us. Brian probably didn't know. We just figured it out ourselves. We have to run!" Gaige spoke fast, his voice panicked.

"Okay, I'll run."

"No, you don't understand. We're much faster than Kians. You'd never be able to keep up. I'm going to have to carry you."

The words hadn't completely left his mouth before he scooped me up as if I weighed nothing, and everything became a blur. Smears of grays and blacks and browns whipped by in the moonlight as we ran through the woods. My stomach rose and fell, dipped and turned. I felt like I was on the most chilling amusement park ride that had ever been made. Only, I didn't like thrill rides. Almost unbearable pain pressed at my temples and behind my eyes, and my stomach grew nauseated.

"Conner, she's not doing well!" Gaige yelled as we slowed to a stop.

I moaned. The pressure in my head felt like it might split my skull in two.

Gaige sat me down on a fallen tree trunk.

I grabbed my head with both hands. "Ow."

"Motion sickness," Conner said. "She's not used to that speed."

I could barely hear him speak through the ringing in my ears. I bent forward and placed my head between my knees to steady the spinning. "My head is killing me and I feel sick."

A quick flash of light put an abrupt stop to my pain and nausea.

"Is that better?" Gaige asked.

I lifted my head and paused for a moment, waiting for the stabbing sensation that had consumed my brain only seconds before to return. It was gone. Not even the smallest twinge of discomfort or nausea remained. "Yes. What did you do?"

Gaige held up a small, thin cylinder about the size of a pocket flashlight. "It can elicit various effects on the human body."

"That's what you used on the guards, isn't it?" I asked.

"Yes, it is." Gaige flipped the side of the cylinder open, pressed a small button inside, then closed it again and handed it to me. "Here, take it."

I took the object from his hand. A soft hum emanated from it and all the muscles in my body relaxed. "What's it doing?"

"It's going to help ease the stress our speed causes your body. Hold on to it tightly." He took my hand and firmly closed my fingers around the object he'd given me. "Are you ready to try again?"

I felt so relaxed with the object in my hand that I would have probably tried anything right then. I noticed the snow, beautiful snow, turning to slivers of tiny ice crystals. Beautiful ice crystal. "Gaige, the snow is so beautiful, isn't it? It's dancing. Dancing and sparkling. Conner, look at the snow. Like tiny little pieces of glitter."

"It's working, Conner. Let's go." With glitter raining down on us, Gaige lifted me into his arms and we were off again.

# CHAPTER 45 - BRIAN

Sitting in the empty motel room, I'd talked as long as I thought I could get by with. I now had to figure out a way to end the charade. I searched the room for ideas as I continued to ramble on. A distant rumble of cars quickly grew louder. *Did they leave early?* I peeked through the crack at the edge of the curtain to see several black SUVs pulling into the parking lot. *Shit!*

"No, don't hurt me!" I picked up a lamp and threw it against the wall. The ceramic base crashed so loudly it covered the noise of the incoming vehicles for a brief second. I grabbed the piece of paper on which I'd written the message to Gaige and put it in my mouth. Spreading myself out amongst the scattered shards of blue glass, I chewed the note into a mushy blob and choked it down.

The door burst off its hinges and launched into the room, nearly landing on top of me. A flow of men—suits and a few military—rushed in with guns drawn, yelling warnings at me not to move. Two of the civilians jerked me off the floor and slammed me against the wall. My hands went out reflexively and caught the wall just in time to prevent a full-blown face plant. The others spread out through the room looking for Tori, Gaige, and their friend.

One of the men who had shoved me against the wall twisted my right arm behind my back. Whether it was the fight-or-flight instinct ingrained in my DNA, old training creeping back from a world I'd left behind, or just plain being fed up with the whole situation, I swung my left elbow backward in the direction of the guy's head. A spray of blood flew from his nose and he grabbed his face with both hands, freeing my right arm. Before the other guy could react, I delivered a right hook to the side of his chin that hit his nighty-night spot perfectly. He dropped to the floor with an *umph.*

Too bad it wasn't me against the two of them. Even with muscles that hadn't been used like that in years, I'd have taken them. A room full of spun-up men—now coming at me with guns aimed at my face—not so much. The last thing I remembered was being knocked on the head.

# CHAPTER 46 - GAIGE

Conner and I zigged and zagged through the woods. We had to be cautious. At our speed, we could easily take a misstep and crash into a tree. Victoria rested peacefully against my chest, oblivious to much of anything, thanks to the medical device she held in her hand.

"Gaige," Tas said. "One of the groups just arrived at your last location, and the other is coming toward you, only about a mile away. They've now been instructed to use any means to keep the three of you from escaping—even shoot to kill, if necessary. Don't chance making it to the shuttles if you're not sure you can."

"The medical teams?" I asked, panting hard. Those teams were critical. If I couldn't keep Victoria safe on Earth, I had to make sure I kept her safe, and alive, on the ship.

"They're in place," Tas answered.

# CHAPTER 47 - VICTORIA

We broke free of the woods and came to a stop in a wide-open field with Gaige and Conner throwing strings of their Anuan garble back and forth. Gaige looked off across the open landscape like a parched man seeing his mirage just out of reach. He put me down, took the device from my hand, and flipped it off. My euphoric state faded and reality settled back in.

"I need you to listen to me very carefully," he said. "We can't risk making it to the shuttles, but I can get you to our ship until we can sort all this—"

"Yes." I didn't need to hear any more.

"I would never leave you in the middle of a mess like this. If you don't want to go, I'll stay here. We'll figure something out."

I grasped his hands and interlaced my fingers with his. "You know that's not the answer."

"I know." He tightened his grip on my hands. "But going to the ship could be a difficult adjustment for you."

Two paths stood before me: the road I'd been on and the road I needed to follow. Even if it was only a temporary reprieve, that path called to me and I *had* to take it.

"That's my choice, Gaige. No matter what that means. Now do what you need to do."

## CHAPTER 48 - GAIGE

There was no more time to discuss. Deep down, I knew it wouldn't matter anyway. Victoria had made her decision. Now I had to act and act *fast*.

"We're a go! All three of us," I said to Mission Control. "Repeat. Three to transition. We're abandoning our attempt to make it to the shuttles. Withdraw the rescue team and have the captain bring the ship close enough for a transition. Coordinate our positions and send us directly to sickbay. Inform Zada to be ready. Put a lock on Bri—the scientist, too. But don't transition him unless his life is in danger. If that happens, transition him to isolation, so I can discuss the situation with him and The Council before doing anything permanent."

"The captain already has the ship in place," Tas said. "Cloak is holding for now. Trigget's coordinating your positions for transition to the ship. Estimated time, five seconds."

Three vehicles skidded to a halt in front of us. Men scrambled from them, guns already drawn. My eyes darted fast as I counted them—thirteen. We couldn't defend ourselves against that many, even as quick as we were. And I couldn't take the chance of leaving Victoria exposed to attempt it.

The fear in Victoria's eyes cried out to me. I stepped in front of her, positioning myself between her and the gunmen. I had to protect her. At any cost.

# CHAPTER 49 - VICTORIA

The shots came fast and loud. So loud. Fear numbed my body, but pain found its way through in one hot blaze. I wanted to remain upright and tried to do so, but my head became light and my body wouldn't obey. Despite my struggle to stay standing, my legs gave way beneath the dead weight of my body. I didn't feel myself hit the ground, but I must have, because I stared up at the stars now. I searched among them, wondering which one Gaige had said was his home sun. The pinpoints of light grew distant and dim. I said goodbye to the path I'd chosen, to everything, and my world faded to black.

# CHAPTER 50 - GAIGE

Shots blasted out in rapid succession, echoing in a soul-vibrating mingle of hollow reverberations through the cold, empty air. Conner dropped to his knees beside me, clutching his stomach. Searing pain ripped at my chest with such force it threw me backwards—into no one. Victoria, who had been behind me, where I thought I'd have her blocked from harm, lay on the ground bleeding.

The ship's weapons system fired in a blinding white flash, putting a quick stop to the shooting. A last resort, but in this case a necessary one. All the men who'd been shooting at us toppled to the ground like toys. Probably only stunned, but stopped nonetheless.

I bent over and picked Victoria up off the hard, frozen earth. Cradling her limp body in my arms, Earth faded away and sickbay formed around us.

"She's been hit!" I yelled, watching Victoria's face for any signs of consciousness. There were none.

"Here, Gaige. This bed." Zada turned quickly, her long, dark ponytail snapping around behind her.

I followed Zada. An entire medical team surrounded us, medical wands already scanning over Victoria. Another team surrounded Conner, lifting him from the floor. The remaining teams waited on standby for whatever Victoria or the rest of us might need.

I laid Victoria on the bed, letting her head down gently. Blood covered her right arm and side. I moved to her left side so I wouldn't be in Zada's way, and held Victoria's hand.

"Please, Zada. Fix her." The words came out so small and distant that they seemed to come from another person. I leaned close to Victoria and whispered in her ear. "I'm here, Victoria. You're going to be all right." I couldn't bring her there to die. I couldn't.

Zada cut Victoria's coat off and tore open the sleeve of her sweater to expose a deep wound that sliced across the side of her arm. Blood flowed from the gash but looked like it may have slowed since soaking her clothing. Or maybe I only hoped it had.

"Zada?"

"We can fix this, Gaige. She's lost some blood, but it all came from this one laceration, nothing else. The shock of the situation was probably harder on her than this injury. She'll be fine."

I found relief in Zada's diagnosis, but only for a moment. "And, aside from the wound?"

"You had already figured out her extrasensory abilities are strong. We've confirmed that. The numbers from our scans for internal-external energy flow are high. Very high. You've only seen a fraction of what she could be capable of, with the right training." Zada stayed focused on Victoria, not looking up at me once while she spoke. She lifted Victoria's arm straight up and shot a blast of cold air onto it from her medical wand. "She'll be soaking in our energies. Trying to manage all of us at once will most likely throw her into an emotional overload. It will be a situation we'll have to watch closely until she adjusts. But first, the laceration. I've got this. You need to get to a bed."

"No. I'm not leaving her."

"Gaige—"

"No. I'm fine." I felt bad cutting Zada off. She'd only been trying to help, but I had no patience for anything at the moment. "I'm sorry, Zada. Just let me see her healed. Then you can do whatever you want with me."

"Can Miccan at least assess you and give you something for the pain while you wait? You won't have to leave that spot."

My next breath sent a sharp pain through my side, causing me to appreciate Zada's persistence. "That's fine."

Zada motioned to Miccan. "Go ahead and do what you can with Gaige while he stands there."

Miccan and her team started scanning me with their medical wands while I stayed with Victoria and watched Zada treat her.

Zada laid Victoria's arm back onto the bed and held her wand over the top side, where the gash began. She ran the device's laser slowly along the cut until she reached the other end, on the backside of the arm. The wound seamed itself together as the ray passed over it and the bleeding stopped.

"Done," Zada said. "It will heal perfectly."

"Thank you, Zada. You don't know how much . . ."

"Yes, I do. I know this has been a long time coming."

Overjoyed that I hadn't lost Victoria, I still couldn't let go of the tension that knotted itself at the base of my neck, knowing the physical injury was only part of her battle.

Miccan and her team finished scanning me. "Nothing life threatening. A few broken ribs are the worst of it. We've stabilized and numbed the areas." Miccan stood silent then, waiting for Zada's instructions.

"Gaige, she's sleeping," Zada said. "Why don't you go ahead and have your injuries healed."

"Just give me a few more minutes with her. Please." I squeezed Victoria's hand. "Then you can do what you need to."

"All right. Let me know when you're ready." Zada released Miccan and her team and then checked Victoria again before moving to another part of the room.

Conner lay in the bed next to us. A full body healing laser was making passes over him, moving slower as it crossed his stomach. The beam receded into the ceiling and the computer announced that his injuries had been healed. His team seemed to be pleased with the results and disbursed after giving him one more scan with their medical wands to check his status.

"Conner, are you okay?" I asked.

"Well, I've had better days. But they tell me I'll live. Is Victoria all right?"

"They're watching her."

"Hello Captain, Commander." I heard Zada say.

I looked back to see my Dad and Tas entering sickbay. Dad's coloring—black hair and tan skin like my own—was usually only slightly darker than Tas's, with his brown hair and similar skin color. Except for today. Today, Tas's coloring held a pale quality about it. And something else was off. The men had been such close friends for so many years that they normally even held themselves with a similar strong, authoritative posture. Probably because they'd been built from many of the same experiences. But today, Tas's sturdy veneer showed a slight crack.

Tas and Conner exchanged nods, a silent *how are you, son* and *I'm okay*, then Tas came to a stop at Victoria's side. "How is she?" Tas asked.

I studied the pink ridge running across the side of her arm. Soon, it would be no more than a thin line. Ultimately it would be gone completely, or close. "Physically fine."

Tas didn't say another word, just stared at Victoria like he was looking at a ghost. I supposed, in a way, he was.

After saying a quick hello to Conner and seeing that he was well, Dad put a hand on my shoulder. "The rest will happen in time."

"You had to deploy the weapons," I said. "I can't believe a simple mission ended up coming to that."

"Yes," Dad said. "I knew you and Conner were protected. And you were doing a good job of shielding Victoria, but—"

"But, not good enough." I looked down at Victoria, lying helpless on the sickbay bed.

"It's superficial, Gaige. Victoria will be fine. But they weren't going to stop. Even in the suits you could have only taken so much. And the plasma shields protecting your heads wouldn't have held up for the repeated blasts they were hitting you with. Their attack had to be stopped to give us time to get you out of there alive."

"How did they track us like that?" I asked, still keeping my eyes on Victoria. "And the other teams? Why didn't we know?"

"We're not sure," Dad answered.

"Kians couldn't have managed that on their own." I said. "We should have been able to easily pick up their transmissions—all of them. They don't have the technology to block our surveillance methods the way they did. And how did they know where we were every step of the way? Do you think someone has broken the accord and assisted the Kians beyond their own abilities?"

As I bombarded my father with questions, Tas stood in silence opposite me, still staring down at Victoria.

"We don't know," Dad said. "Tas has some suspicions, but we can talk about them later."

I gave my father a quick look over my shoulder, remembering that in this situation he was both my father *and* my captain. "Yes, Captain. Did the cloak hold?"

"It waffled some toward the end."

Having been cleared to leave whenever he felt up to it, Conner rose from his bed with good color and sound energy, considering what he'd been through. He stepped next to Tas and placed his arm around his father's shoulder. Conner had his mother's auburn hair and eyes. The height he'd gotten from Tas, though he wasn't quite as broad as his father. "Let's go, Dad, and give Victoria some space."

Still in his ghostly world, Tas nodded. "Let me know if anything changes," he said, and hesitantly walked out with Conner.

Dad squeezed my shoulder. "Focus on Victoria right now. We'll talk about the rest later."

After my father left, I wiped Victoria's blood from my flight suit until the stain lightened enough not to be immediately noticed. I didn't want the sight to scare her when she woke. I looked for signs that she *would* wake. Her pale skin showed the weakness of her body, but her emotional state concerned me more. It was so fragile now, and I had no idea if she could handle what she'd just been thrust into.

# CHAPTER 51 - BRIAN

Lying face down in the rear of one of the SUVs, arms handcuffed behind my back, I struggled to breathe through the heavy blanket that had been thrown over me. A smothering pocket of heat created from my trapped breath caused a layer of sweat to form on my face and neck.

Through the thick material, I strained to hear any clues about where we might be going, and whether or not Tori, Gaige, and their companion had escaped. I couldn't make out anything clearly. Whatever Tori had gotten herself into, I hoped to hell Gaige could get her out, because I couldn't help her now.

After what seemed like hours, the motion of the vehicle stopped. I heard the muffled sound of the rear doors opening. Someone whipped back the blanket that had been covering me and a blast of cold air hit me full force. Five men—all military—hovered outside the back of the SUV. Two of them dragged me out of the car and dropped me on the pavement of a parking lot where I landed firmly on my kneecaps.

In the dark, the men guided me, not so gently, into a building and down a flight of stairs. After one quick turn, they stopped and removed the handcuffs. Before I could make any moves to get away, they gave me a hearty shove that sent me reeling into the back wall of a dimly lit cell. My chin stung from the salty sweat on my face and I knew I'd lost some flesh when I hit the rough brick. Metal bars slammed closed behind me with a damp echo and the men left without a word.

Something told me this facility wasn't a part of any jurisdiction's justice system. Aiding and abetting a fugitive's escape from justice. Guilty. Someone had already played judge, jury, and . . . well, hopefully not executioner.

In less than a day I had gone from the United States' top stealth scientist to prisoner. I'd underestimated the gravity of the situation by a mile. My credentials had given me no protection. I was as expendable as anyone else, and not just in regard to the job. General Ash hadn't been exaggerating to protect his precious rank. What had happened to him? Had he remained in the not-so-good graces of whoever called the shots, or was he in some unofficial, probably even unknown, cell like me? Or worse?

I touched the raw spot on my chin, wondering what else might be coming.

# PART II

# CHAPTER 52 - VICTORIA

Muffled voices somewhere in the distance attempted to seep into my awareness. I didn't know to whom the voices belonged or what they were saying. Nor could I muster enough strength to figure it out. I was there, but I was not, aware merely of my existence . . . somewhere.

I allowed myself to drift in and out of consciousness until I gathered enough energy to open my eyes. Someone sat by my side with his head resting on the edge of my bed. A warmth cradled my hand. And my soul. Though I couldn't completely make out his form in the dim light, I already knew it was Gaige who held my hand. I tried to say his name, but didn't have the strength to form the word.

"Wake slowly, eighty percent Earth illumination," a female said.

The room began to lighten. The walls changed from black to gray, then to pastel orange, and finally a delicate shade of blue. It was as if the sun had risen in the room, though with a gentler light.

The woman approaching my bed was an exotic beauty with a silky black ponytail tied low at the back of her neck. She wore an outfit similar in both style and material to the ones Gaige and

Conner wore, except hers was two-piece. “Hello, Victoria. I’m Zada, your doctor. He just drifted off.”

I looked down at a sleeping Gaige then back at the doctor and the new world that surrounded me. The milky white floors and sky blue walls shined like polished glass. My eyes followed the walls up to where they curved into the same blue ceiling, with no hard corners to mark the transition. A sunshine glow emanated from the walls and ceiling, warming my face like a summer day.

“We made it,” I said.

Gaige stirred. “You okay?” His hand tightened on mine.

“I’m fine.”

Gaige breathed a relieved sigh and said a quiet *thank you* that I thought was meant for someone or something higher than any of us in the room.

“You need anything?” Gaige said.

“I just want to take it all in.” I lifted my head, easing my hand out of Gaige’s to push myself up. The top of the bed rose to meet me and I rested against it.

“This room is our ship’s version of an emergency room,” Gaige said.

The place contained no furniture except my bed and Gaige’s chair, but could have held much more. Scrutinizing the room for every detail, I noticed barely visible lines etched into the luminescent walls and ceiling. The same outlines surrounded the area where my bed and Gaige’s chair extended from the wall. Maybe the place did hold more furniture. We just couldn’t see it right now.

On the far side of the room, a small silver robot about the size of a Frisbee, but thicker, hovered in the air. I studied the smooth curve of its top, its flat bottom, the intricate patterns that marked its surface. It made no movement, just hung there, still and quiet. After a few moments, I gave up on my hopes of seeing the droid in action and followed the gentle curve of the sparsely furnished room back to Gaige. Then I saw them. Three dark circular blotches on the front of his flight suit where the material had been nearly shredded. “Are you hurt?” I reached my hand toward the marks. “Did they do that to you?”

He grasped my hand to keep me from touching him. “I’m fine.”

“Gaige, are you hurt?” The words came out louder than I’d planned.

“Really, I’m fine. They've been healed. I acted on reflex.” Gaige placed my hand on his chest. “You can touch them. They don't hurt.”

I dragged my fingers lightly across one of the coarse marks. He didn’t flinch and didn’t seem to be in pain.

“See.” Gaige said. “Now what about you? Are you *sure* you feel okay?”

I felt no pain, no nausea. Only relief. “I feel good.”

“Let’s give Gaige some peace of mind.” The doctor rolled her eyes toward Gaige and pursed her lips. “Again.” She smiled and pulled something from the wall that, once removed from its hiding place, looked like a bar code scanner. “This will check whether all your systems are functioning properly. You won’t feel a thing.” She held the scanner over me, moving it from my head down the length of my body. Symbols I didn’t recognize flashed on a display screen on the backside of the device. “She’s still doing well. Why don’t I check your status too, Gaige?”

Gaige agreed and the doctor commanded a bed to extend from the wall next to mine. Gaige sat and lowered the top part of his flight suit to his waist. Three large yellow bruises—barely visible—mottled the skin on his chest. Not the color of fresh bruises. Like Gaige had said, they truly had healed. Or nearly so.

"Why don't you lie down, Gaige. This will only take a minute."

Gaige did as the doctor told him and she scanned her medical device over his chest. By the time she pushed the scanner back into the wall, Gaige was fast asleep.

"I thought that might work," she said under her breath.

"Has he been here with me the whole time I've been unconscious?"

"Yes. He refused to leave you. I figured if I had him lie down, he'd fall asleep. I hope you don't mind."

"No. Not at all. Let him sleep. He must be exhausted." I searched for the bruises on his chest. If I hadn't already known they were there, I might have missed them. But, considering the condition of his flight suit, his injuries must have been serious when we arrived here. "Will he be okay?"

"Gaige will be fine. All his injuries have been healed. He just needs rest now."

I sighed and laid my head back against the bed. Gaige was safe, away from the maniacs who'd been after him. And after me too. Gaige felt I wouldn't have been safe if he'd left me in the lab. But why? My mind was so foggy and it all seemed like a dream now. A crazy, unbelievable dream. Yet there I was, on a real, honest-to-goodness spaceship, with Gaige lying next to me. My mind raced through all the things he'd done for me. "He's a good person."

A strange feeling in regard to the doctor drew my attention to her. Our eyes locked in an unspoken conversation . . . or agreement . . . or *knowing*. Gaige *was* a good person. I knew it and she knew it. But she also knew more.

"Doctor?"

She blinked, breaking the trance. "Yes, you're right. Gaige is a good person. For now, let's just say you've come to mean a lot to him." She stood and removed the medical device from the wall. "Why don't I see how your arm is healing?"

"My arm?" For the first time, I realized the sleeve of my sweater had been cut open. I'd remembered the plan to abandon our attempt to make it to the shuttles and instead go to the ship *somehow*. There had been no time for details. But only now did I remember hearing the shots and feeling the pain in my arm.

"Yes, that's right. You were shot in the arm. It's been healed, though. The pinkness will soon fade." The doctor scanned the side of my arm, looked at the readout screen, and then placed the device back into the wall. She eyed the thin scar. "It's mending nicely."

A pink line about four inches long ran horizontally across the side of my arm. I reached my hand through the slit in my sweater and rubbed my fingers across the wound. It didn't hurt and, other than the color, the smooth mark was not at all distinguishable from the area of skin around it. "I can't believe they really shot at us."

"Yes, it's a difficult concept. Your injuries could have been much worse. Fatal even. The flight suits can withstand penetration by most Earth bullets. Gaige knew your clothing could not, so he tried to block you from the bullets. The best he could, anyway."

I remembered Gaige stepping in front of me. "*I'm* the reason for his injuries?"

"No, you're not the reason. The men were aiming for all of you. Even Conner was hit. But, because of the suits, Gaige's and Conner's injuries were only impact wounds from the force of the bullets and were easily treated. Both will be fine."

"Good." There was so much to absorb in the new place. Floating robots, bulletproof suits. They all factored in to remind me that *I* was now the alien in someone else's world.

"Is there anything I can get you? Food? Water? I provided you with hydration. Something like your Earth IVs, but administered by patch rather than needles. I also provided nutrients the same way. But I can get you some real water or food now that you're awake."

My mouth was moist and my stomach satisfied. I could think of nothing *I* needed, but with Gaige lying bare-chested, I wondered if he should have a blanket. "No, I think I'm fine for now. Could I get a blanket for Gaige, though?"

"The room tracks both core and surface body temperatures and will adjust to keep him comfortable. You as well. But if you'd feel better having blankets, I can get you some."

"Oh. No, as long as he's comfortable, that won't be necessary."

"Would you like some more comfortable clothing? Gaige didn't think you'd want to be changed while you slept." The doctor lowered her head, attempting to hide a grin.

Gaige did seem to know me well, and she knew it. I could have used something more comfortable than my jeans to sleep in, but was glad Gaige hadn't allowed them to expose me to the world, or at least the people who happened to be in the room. A yawn fought to break free. I didn't want to be rude by yawning in the doctor's face, so I stifled it, straining to keep my jaw clamped shut until it passed. At that point, I just wanted time alone to process all that had happened. "I know I just woke up, but I think I *could* sleep a while longer. Maybe after I wake again, I could shower and change then?"

"Absolutely. We'll get you a change of clothes whenever you're ready. For now, rest as much as you need to. Being exposed to all of us is a lot to manage if you're not used to it. You'll continue to need time for that. It will be a long, sometimes tough, process."

"Gaige said it might be a difficult adjustment."

"Gaige was right, but things will get easier. Give yourself time." The doctor stood and briefly laid a hand on my shoulder. "Everything will be okay. I'm going to check on a patient in another room. If you need anything, Toji can help you."

She turned to the little droid robot that had been hovering in the air on the other side of the room. It came alive with tiny yellow lights embedded around its disc-shaped body. These lights blinked randomly for a second or two and then stayed solid. The robot glided through the air, smooth and soundless. It stopped a foot or so from me and floated effortlessly down to my eye level.

"This is Toji, my droid assistant," the doctor said. "Toji, this is Victoria."

A few of the tiny lights on the droid turned green and blinked. It extended a jointed arm from its body and reached its small metal hand toward me. Its fingers encased my own hand more gently than I'd expected from the blocky metal digits.

"Pleased to make your acquaintance, Victoria," the droid said in a silky male voice.

"Um, it's nice to meet you, too." I pulled my hand back, wondering if the contraption could actually have a conversation *with* me or if it had been pre-programmed with canned responses, unaware of my actual comment or even my presence. I turned to the doctor. "Does it comprehend what I'm saying?"

"Yes, Toji understands. Though constructed from artificial means, he's an intelligent being. He can have a perfectly coherent conversation, in English or any other language, with completely appropriate responses. In addition to Toji, the room monitors medical needs and will alert us to anything you might not be able to tell us."

"Thank you, doctor."

"Please, call me Zada," she said. "I'll turn the lights down so you can both sleep more easily." She gave a command and the lighting in the room reduced to no more than that of a nightlight. Zada left the room through a section of the wall that opened on its own and then slid silently closed behind her.

A tiny pang of anxiety stirred my stomach. Perhaps it was unease over the *difficult adjustment* I'd been warned about. And perhaps not. I wasn't sure of these new feelings.

With only the two of us in the room, I couldn't keep myself away from Gaige. I slid off my bed and stepped next to him. I studied his face. His brow bore no worry lines now. Stubble from his time on the run and waiting for me to wake covered his firm jaw. The lips that had kissed my forehead rested with their edges curved upward in a slight smile, even as he slept. I let my eyes trace down his body, past his neck and his broad shoulders, to the arms that had carried me so protectively. His chest, once marred with bruises from shielding me, rose and fell beneath perfectly healed, bronzed skin. I stood for a long time watching him sleep. He was the most beautiful being I'd ever laid my eyes on, both inside and out. In that moment I knew, without a doubt, I was undeniably in love with him.

Not thinking, I placed my hand on his cheek and stroked it. His eyes opened ever so slightly. His gentle smile grew and he reached his arm out for me to lie with him. I crawled into the bed and snuggled into the warmth of his body. He fell back to sleep instantly.

Lying next to him, I was more content than I'd ever been in my life. I could have stayed like that forever. With my face resting on his bare chest, I heard every beat of his heart. I felt his chest rise as he breathed in, and then listened for him to slowly exhale. Absorbing every moment of him, I drifted off in his arms, so content. I wanted every night to be exactly like that. But somehow, I knew that whatever had happened back on Earth—it wasn't over.

# CHAPTER 53 - LOME

Deep underground, the smell of earth hung heavy in our thick-walled complex. I snorted the scent of it from my nostrils, sick of the dank, dark dungeon we'd been concealing ourselves in all these years. But daylight and fresh air, finally, were not far from us. For now, we'd remain patient. A skill that only in hiding the Tamanacke had learned to use to our advantage. A skill we'd continue to master, remaining hidden from the prying eyes of the general Earthling population and the range of any surveillance devices from beyond, Anuan or otherwise.

My leaders filed into the meeting room and formed an impeccable line, ready for my orders. This was an army. Well-disciplined, obedient, competent. Nothing like these imbecile leaders we'd had to deal with on Earth, these stupid Anuan offspring. If I said capture, my men captured. If I said kill, they killed. No excuses, no mistakes.

"Squad Leads reporting, ready and eager for your instructions, Candar Lome," Cruck announced.

"Sit, all of you," I said, taking my rightful place at the head of the table.

Of course they did as I, their candar, commanded, and distributed themselves around the large, wooden conference table. Many times through these long years we'd planned our strategies at this very table for the days now close at hand.

Once all others were seated, Cruck lowered himself into the chair to my right and bowed his head to me. "Candar, we await your bidding."

"My bidding would be to annihilate every one of these sss-stupid Earth creatures," I hissed. "Primitive and human. How could we have expected anything but incompetence?"

Raspy sniggers and nods of agreement reinforced the truth of my statement.

"But, not yet." I spoke and my leaders silenced themselves. "For now I will select only one and set an example for more proficient behavior."

"Excellent, Candar Lome. And your plan?" Mant asked, head lowered.

"You will witness it soon enough. The Earth idiots who erroneously considered themselves worthy of bringing me the girl and the two Anuans, and failed even with our help, is flying here now. They'll arrive by morning. *Then* you will see."

# CHAPTER 54 - VICTORIA

"No!" I opened my eyes, disoriented and scared.

A hand grabbed my arm. "Victoria, what's wrong?"

Hearing the sound of Gaige's voice brought everything back. I was safe, on Gaige's spaceship, in its dimly lit sickbay. Just now, the yellow snake eyes—those had only been a dream.

"Victoria." Gaige hovered over me in the bed now. "What is it?"

"Just a dream. No big deal." I put a hand on his chest, gave him a gentle nudge back down onto the bed, and rolled against him. "I'm fine. Go back to sleep."

"You're sure?" He whispered against my forehead.

I didn't speak until the warmth of his breath had drifted over me and away. "Very sure. Please, go back to sleep. It was only a dream. I've never felt safer."

"Okay." The word had barely been formed, soft as air, and Gaige was out again.

"Sleep well," I whispered.

He needed the sleep. I, on the other hand, was now wide-awake. I lay there, letting my eyes adjust to the dim light, trying to wrap my brain around everything. I was on a freaking spaceship, lying in the arms of an alien. How had it all happened, and so fast? What had drawn me into the lab? Gaige, of course, though he hadn't meant to. But how had he attracted me like that? The similar intuition thing? Maybe. Whatever the reason, it felt right. All of it.

Still wrestling with my thoughts, I noticed Toji float up beside me, his green lights blinking.

"Victoria," he said in a low voice. "Is there anything I can assist you with?"

If nothing else, the little guy could keep me company while Gaige slept. I eased myself from beneath Gaige's arm. He didn't move.

"You can help keep me company," I whispered, searching for the chair. "And, I suppose you could also help me find a chair."

"Yes, I can assist with both. Chair ten," he said.

A chair unfolded quietly from the wall on the far end of the room. I went to it with the little droid following behind me. The chair's surface matched the hard, sleek look of the rest of the room. But when I sat, I sank down like I'd settled into a cloud.

The droid came to a stop a couple feet from me and dropped down to my level. "How may I assist in keeping you company, Victoria?"

Being cuddled into the soft chair gave me second thoughts about how wide-awake I truly was. I figured I might as well get right to it. "So Toji, do you know how I came to be here?"

"Yes, I'm privy to that information." Green lights flickered on Toji's disc body each time he communicated.

"It's kind of crazy. Not something an Earthling, I mean Kian, runs into every day. Well, any day, for that matter."

"True. The Kians don't know of the Anuans. It might disrupt their natural course."

I yawned, placing a hand over my mouth until the yawn passed. "Hmm. Yes, I get that. But the Anuans still go to Earth."

"Secretly, yes. Primarily for scientific missions."

Something told me Gaige wasn't just peacefully collecting samples or making observations when he was captured. "And Gaige? Why, exactly, was Gaige there?"

Toji's lights went dark then gradually came back to life. "I'm sorry, Victoria, but that information is restricted."

"Well, Toji, I'm going to guess that if Gaige had been on a purely scientific mission, that information would not be restricted."

Toji's lights dimmed again then lit back up. "That would be a logical deduction."

"Victoria?" Gaige spoke from his bed on the other side of the room.

"I'm here, Gaige, talking with Toji." I yawned again, ready to be back in bed. I pulled myself from the cloud. It had nothing on lying next to Gaige. "Toji, thank you for the conversation. I think I'll go back to bed now."

"You're very welcome, Victoria," Toji replied, remaining where we'd been talking.

When I slid back into Gaige's bed, he put his arms around me. I lay there for a long while, fully awake, working to hone the intuition thing Gaige and the Anuans used so well. Perhaps *it* could help me find the reason Gaige had been on Earth.

# CHAPTER 55 - LOME

In the bowels of our complex, I sat at the conference table with my most trusted Tamanacke warriors. The incompetent group of U.S. government Earthlings filed into the room. Each of the members entered looking more stupid than the one before. The scientist had already been deposited in a holding cell back in their Midwest. These Earthlings may have considered that sufficient punishment. I, however, did not. But I'd deal with him later. That could be counted on.

The blank stares on their worthless faces, like lost children not sure of their fates, annoyed me. But these were not children. Perhaps I could have shown some pity if they had been. *Perhaps.*

Soon we would no longer have to concern ourselves with being seen and exposing our existence. If that had already been the case, we would not have had to rely on these inferior Earthlings and would not have been parted from the girl. Why, after all these years, had they come for her, just as our numbers were finally reaching an acceptable level to re-engage with the Anuan murderers? Without her, our revenge would not be as sweet.

Mant closed the door. Everyone stood waiting—seventeen members of the supposedly specialized team, hand selected by General Ash to do our bidding. Each had considered himself a superior human, deserving of a place on the team. I wondered how they judged themselves now. I knew how I judged them all—idiots.

I stroked the vial sitting on the table next to me and swiveled my chair in their direction. They were, however, not worthy to look upon, so I fixed my gaze on the wall above them. "We help you maintain superiority over your enemies and you, in turn, cannot complete a simple task for us."

Not one of the pathetic creatures spoke a word.

"Hmm. What to do?" I rose from my seat and paced back and forth in front of them, pausing at each one to stare him down. "I'm afraid I'm going to have to set an example."

While the lesser beings watched, I returned to my seat and held my right hand out in front of me. Turning it from front to back, I admired my claws, paying close attention to their sharp points. "Yes, I must set an example."

Some trembled. Some began to sweat. Some swallowed hard and tensed, bracing for what might befall them. All were terrified. *Good, they will learn from this example.*

"You." I pointed to General Ash, their leader.

"Yes sir, I . . . I take full responsibility. We will do whatever we can to correct the problem."

"I'm afraid it's too late for that," I said, calmly. "Unless you Earthlings have developed rapid space travel, they will be well out of your reach by now."

Sweat began to form on the general's brow. "We can still salvage some data from the remains of the spacecraft—"

"I care nothing about the craft." I waved my hand in the air, dismissing his offering. "Your people can play with the machines. We don't need them. It was the *beings* I wanted."

Clueless. I'd spoken to the imbecile long enough. "Take off your clothes."

"What?" General Ash asked in a wispy, almost inaudible voice.

"Yes, take them off."

I had stated my wish, yet he stood motionless.

"Now!" I yelled. "Everything!"

He began disrobing and didn't stop until his clothes lay in a heap in front of him. The general's manhood dangled for the entire room to see. His colleagues averted their eyes in silence, but the Tamanacke hissed heartily at the amusement the display offered.

"Now bring them to me," I said.

He gathered the clothes from the floor and carried them to where I sat.

"Put them down." I waved toward the table in front of me. "And step back."

He obeyed. When he was well clear of the clothes so as not to stain them, I stood and stepped toward him. The smell of fear clung to his naked body. I let him wonder for a moment what lay ahead for him. I let them all wonder. Then with one quick, smooth stroke, I opened his throat with my claws. The Earthlings gasped as their leader dropped to the floor like a boneless doll, blood pulsing rich and red from his gaping neck.

I handed Cruck the vial. "Fill this with his blood. Quickly! Before it's all on the floor."

Cruck finished filling the vial in seconds while the death stare fixed itself firmly upon the general's face.

# CHAPTER 56 - GAIGE

Awakened by Victoria's voice, I opened my eyes. She still slept safely tucked under my arm, but flailed. Turning her head one way then the other, she continued to mumble incoherently.

"Victoria?" I whispered.

"Gaige, help!"

"Victoria, it's okay." I sat up and pulled her against me so she'd feel secure.

"No!" she screamed, clutching at her throat.

"You're safe, Victoria." I pulled her arm away from her neck. "It's just a dream."

Panting like she'd been running all night, she opened her eyes. "Gaige?"

"Yes, it's me. You were having another dream."

She scanned the room and her breathing slowed. "We're on the ship."

"That's right, we're on the ship. You're safe." I stroked her hair, trying to do something I thought might calm her.

She let out a deep sigh and her body relaxed.

"What were you dreaming?" I asked.

She pulled away from me and ran her fingers through her hair, brushing back the loose waves that had fallen over her face. "I'm fine, Gaige. It was just a stupid dream."

"The second in one night."

"I've had them before, these dreams. Maybe not two in one night, but—"

"When? When have you had them?"

"Around the time my parents died. They stopped for a while, but seem to have started again."

Both times around major upheavals in her life. Her skills had been with her all along. She didn't need us to arouse them. Our presence would surely increase their intensity, though.

"These dreams, what are they about?"

"Thank you, Gaige." She gave me a gentle kiss on the check. "For everything."

"Always. But—"

"And you don't need to worry about me, or these dreams," she said. "I'll manage."

Toji floated up next to us. "Good morning, Gaige, Victoria. Can I help you with anything?"

I wanted to know more about these dreams. Were they just jumbled thoughts brought on by unsettling events in her life, or was her intuition trying to tell her something? She obviously didn't want to dwell on them, though. So, for now, I'd let the matter go.

"No, Toji. Victoria just had a nightmare. What time is it at home port?"

"0916, day 313," Toji said.

"Perfect. It's morning at home. Wake, one hundred percent Earth illumination."

The walls lightened, cycling through the sunrise I thought Victoria would like so much, until they reached the crystal-clear blue of her favorite summer sky. I rose from the bed and stretched away the night's long hold on my body. Reaching high into the air, I twisted right, then left. The top of my flight suit still hung at my waist where Zada had checked my impact wounds. I slid my hands through the arms of the suit and fastened the front.

"Gaige." Victoria's voice sounded troubled. She sat up and perched herself on the edge of the bed.

"What is it?"

"Brian. What do you think will happen to Brian?"

I'd expected this question eventually, and hated to tell Victoria about her friend's situation. I knelt down in front of her. "Brian has been jailed. We don't plan to leave him there, but his life is not in immediate danger. So, we'll just monitor his situation for now."

"And if his life should become endangered?"

"Considering what we recently dealt with on Earth, we can't risk going back in the shuttles, but we'd do what we could to allow me to transition down and help him."

"Transition?" She tapped her chin and her eyes wandered upward as if searching. "Oh, yes." She nodded and looked back at me. "That word is one of the last things I remember hearing before I woke on the ship. What exactly does *transitioning* entail?"

I searched for the best way to explain the process to someone who'd never been exposed to such technology. It would sound terribly unsafe to her to hear the details described. *We completely deconstruct a person at the cellular level in one place then reconstruct all the cells somewhere else in virtually no time.*

"Gaige?"

"Uh . . . Beam. You know, beam me up . . . Scottie."

Victoria laughed. "Did you seriously just quote Star Trek?"

"I guess I did. Did that explain it?"

She laughed again. "That explains it. I'm sure there's a more technical answer but you can fill me in later." She stopped smiling about my adventure into her cinema-land. "You were nearly killed trying to leave Earth, and now you may go back?"

"Don't worry. Using transitioning, I'll be in and out before anybody even realizes I've been there. I'd go now so we wouldn't have to leave Brian's situation unresolved, but your sun is experiencing high flare activity that would cause problems with cloaking a large vessel like this ship. We're currently hidden by Earth's moon, so we don't need to be cloaked. To get into a good transitioning position, we'd have to move within full view of Earth, where we'd been seen. However, if things get bad for Brian, we'll divert as much energy as we can to maintain the cloak, despite the flare interference, and move forward with a rescue. If not, the flare activity will subside in a few days and we'll go down to deal with the situation then."

"Thank you, Gaige, for not abandoning Brian."

"He helped us. We could never disrupt his life like this and then leave him to sort it out on his own."

Victoria thanked me again with a hug, but drew back too slowly, leaving her lips to linger near mine.

Everything in me wanted to kiss her, and more. But I couldn't. I pulled away before she did what I was afraid I might do myself. "Are you hungry?" I stood and extended my hand to help her off the edge of the bed.

She squinted her eyes critically at me, and then took my hand. "Actually, I am pretty hungry."

"May I assist you with breakfast?" Toji said.

"Yes, Toji. Thank you. Victoria and I are ready to eat."

"Table eight, two chairs," Toji called out.

I took Victoria's hand and followed Toji. He reached the table quickly and hovered next to it, waiting for us to catch up.

"This furniture thing. Very efficient," she said. "What do you Anuans eat, anyway?"

"You don't have to limit yourself to Anuan food. We can construct anything you wish."

Victoria sat down and wrinkled her nose, causing a little crease to form across its bridge. "Construct? Do you mean *make*?"

I loved finally having the chance to share my world with her. I sat, too, ready to answer her question. "Constructing is not quite as simple as *making* something the way you're used to. Though we can do that as well. When we construct something, we use technology to manipulate simple atoms into whatever we want, including food. Though it's not *grown* or *raised*, it will still have all the same properties—taste, texture, nutritional value. You can try something Anuan or have one of your favorite Earth foods. Or, you can try something from another planet."

"Other planets? Inhabited ones?" The wrinkle across her nose relaxed and a smile grew on her face. "Of course. Why wouldn't there be?"

I had to remember that until a few days ago, she had no idea anything existed beyond her own Earth world. Everything outside of that was brand new to her. "Yes, that's right. There are many other planets, and lots of them are inhabited."

With curiosity beaming from her face, she leaned toward me, resting her elbows on the table. "How many?"

I found myself drawing nearer to her, our foreheads almost touching. Her excitement electrified me. I wanted to soak in every ounce of it. "There are hundreds that have the ability for space travel. We associate with many of them on a regular basis. There are thousands more, like Earth, that are not as advanced and are not aware of Anu or the others. We won't influence their development, but we will observe them from time to time to see how they're progressing."

"Amazing," she said, looking off into the room at nothing in particular.

I watched as her world expanded, wondering what she thought about it all. I could tell so much by the awed look on her face, and the feel of her energy, but I wanted to hear *exactly* what was going through her mind. "What are you thinking?"

Her eyes came back to me. "I find it amazing that there are so many worlds beyond my own. Earth and its people have just been reduced in both size and significance. I feel almost guilty that I've been allowed to step through a door and out into the universe when everyone I've ever known is still closed up in their tiny little existences. But, at the same time, I'm thrilled to have escaped the place where I'd felt so smothered."

She was enthralled by my world and I was enthralled by her. Neither of us moved. Our energies held fixed to each other like magnets with no outside force to pull us apart. I had to be that force.

I straightened up in my seat, putting distance between us. "It's a lot to take in. Let's not overwhelm you. Why don't we have Earth food this morning? You can learn all about the rest later. Maybe something chocolate? You like chocolate."

A silent void filled the space between us, like the air had suddenly been sucked from the room and sound no longer had a medium in which to travel. I realized my blunder too late to take it back and by the tone of the energy between us, Victoria realized it too.

"How did you know I like chocolate?"

She did like chocolate. But how would I explain why I knew that? "Hmm. Don't you? Most people do."

"Is that so?" She squinted her eyes at me again. "I thought you Anuans weren't voyeurs?"

"Don't worry." I tapped the tip of her nose with my finger. "Your pink bedclothes are still safe."

"Mm-hmm. I'm glad to hear it. Now, why do I feel like you're keeping something from me, Alien?"

I bowed my head, thinking, trying to figure out how to handle this. I wouldn't be able to hide what I knew from her for long. I might as well be honest. As honest as I could be, anyway.

"Gaige?"

"Well." I looked her in the eye. "Because I am. Keeping something from you. But I'll tell you everything once you've settled in and feel steady."

"Gaige, I feel steady now, so tell me."

"You only think you feel steady. Remember back in the motel, I told you that your exposure to our energy would not only be taxing on you physically, but emotionally as well. You saw a little of that then. As you continue to absorb our energies here, including all our emotions, you're going to become overwhelmed by what you receive until you learn how to process everything. After that, I'll tell you what you want to know."

She stared at me for a few seconds. Those seconds moved like hours while I hoped she'd agree.

"How about a chocolate croissant then?" she said. "Can your atom machine come up with one of those? And hot chocolate?"

"Absolutely." I turned to Toji, who still hovered quietly next to us. "Toji, two chocolate croissants and two hot chocolates." I exhaled a breath I hadn't realized I'd been holding. I'd bought a little time, but knew my reprieve would only be temporary. Sooner or later, she'd have to be told why I was really on Earth that day and what it had to do with her.

# CHAPTER 57 - GAIGE

Victoria slowly pulled loose a piece of the flaky pastry and put it in her mouth.

"You like it?" I asked, watching her lips move with every chew.

"Yes, it's really good." She tore off another piece. "In fact, it's the best chocolate croissant I've ever tasted."

"I'm glad you like it. The constructors do a pretty good job. We can even construct some Earth clothing for you, if you'd like."

She tugged on the arm of my flight suit. "Well, actually, I like your clothes. Can I get some of those? I mean, built-in heaters and phones, bullet-resistant fabric, and who knows what other cool features. You can't get clothes like that on Earth." She put another piece of croissant in her mouth.

I smiled at her wide-eyed enthusiasm for the things this world had to offer her. "You can have anything you want."

"Anything, huh." She grinned.

I knew where her mind had gone. I knew because it was the same place my mind went as soon as the words left my mouth, too late to stop them. I needed to be more careful about what I said now that we were here, together. If she already knew all there was to know and I could be positive she understood her feelings, I'd have bonded with her right there. But she didn't. There was so much we were keeping from her. And her emotions, her feelings, they couldn't be trusted yet. I had to backpedal—quickly.

I swiped my untouched plate aside and took her hands in mine. "Look, Victoria, you know you shouldn't be in a hurry for . . . well . . . anything. We have no idea what the next few days will bring. You could be back in your home before you know it or you could . . ." I paused, wondering if I should even say the words.

"Or I could stay, permanently? Is that a possibility?"

I groped for something to say. Something that would satisfy but not influence her. "It's too soon to contemplate a decision that significant. There's too much to consider first."

"But it would be a possibility?"

It was a possibility. One I hoped would come to pass. That was the problem. I feared that telling her *yes* with my hopeful intentions behind it might lead her in that direction. I couldn't impact her decisions so I decided I should change the subject and steer clear of the topic all together. "I need to meet with the captain and mission commander. Are you ready to see your quarters? I'll show you to them—"

"What? Wait a minute. My own quarters? I won't be staying with you?"

"I'd just complicate things for you. You need time to adjust before thinking about anything else, including me. But I'll be here for you, for anything you need."

Victoria's energy dropped, along with her head. Her emotions grew heavy.

"It won't be so bad. I have a surprise for you. And there's someone who will help you get settled while I'm in my meeting. I think you'll like talking with her." I put my finger under Victoria's chin and raised her bowed head. "Okay? And I'll be back as soon as I can."

"Of course. I don't want to keep you from your meeting. And who could pass on a surprise?" Victoria smiled, the corners of her mouth rebelling against her sagging emotions. "Take me to my quarters and go. I'll be fine."

You *will* be fine, I thought. I had to make sure she knew that. The barrage of our energies might have been starting to affect her emotions. I had to send positive, calming energy to her, to override the avalanche of feelings she might be experiencing. They would only create confusion, doubts, fears. There was no need for them. *Everything will be okay. Everything will be okay. Everything will be okay.*

"I know it will."

I snapped out of my thoughts. "What?"

"I know it'll be okay. You don't have to worry about me. I'll settle in while you go to your meeting."

"You heard me?"

Victoria wrinkled her brow, no doubt as confused as I was surprised. "Yes. You said everything will be okay."

"No, I didn't. Well, I did, but not out loud."

The wrinkle in Victoria's brow grew deeper. She dropped the piece of croissant that she'd been holding during our conversation. "What are you saying?"

"I'm saying you read my thoughts. I *was* projecting them. But I was just trying to send you the positive, calm energy of those thoughts. Not the thoughts themselves. I can't believe you heard them."

Victoria sat, mouth agape. "Are you sure you didn't say it out loud without realizing?"

Her presence did have a way of distracting me. But I was certain that I'd only sent the intention. "No, I'm pretty sure I only thought it."

"How could I read your mind? I'm not Anuan."

"It's a human trait. It's just that most Kians don't attempt to develop it the way Anuans do. Therefore, it lies dormant. You're a special case, though. As you've already seen with the intuition." Getting into more than that could open up topics she wasn't ready for. I had to put some separation between us so I could think. "Why don't I escort you to your quarters?"

# CHAPTER 58 - VICTORIA

"Shall we?" Gaige waved an arm toward the door, obviously not wanting to get into a big discussion about the fact that I'd just read his mind.

I could make out the outline of a door in the area of the wall Gaige indicated. When we got near enough, it slid open.

"Floor 5, Sector 2, Earth gravity," Gaige said, still standing on the sickbay side of the open door.

Yellow lights located within the upper portion of the hallway walls blinked twice then stopped. They blinked twice again and stopped again. The pattern continued to repeat.

"Is the rest of the ship set to Anuan gravity?" I asked.

"Yes, but we can adjust it. I'm doing that now. We'll change the settings to Earth gravity wherever you'll be."

I didn't want to be treated differently. I wanted to blend in here as easily as Gaige had on Earth. Aside from the space-alien flight suit he'd had on, that is. "But I'll have to get used to Anuan gravity eventually. Why not start now?"

Gaige kept his eyes on the lights. "It would be a pretty noticeable difference for you. Zada wants to assess your tolerance levels first. If you end up staying here . . . That is, if you need to stay here for any length of time . . . depending on the situation . . ." Gaige sighed. "It's just better to acclimate slowly."

I *could* stay here, beyond this "situation," if I wanted. I could tell. Anuans respected personal choice. Was Gaige being hesitant about it, and us, so as not to interfere with my choice? Or the revelation he had to tell me when he thought I was stable enough, could that affect whatever decisions I might make?

I tried to picture myself back on Earth and couldn't. But I saw myself with Gaige and the Anuans. Their draw had gripped me and didn't want to let go. Could I let go of them? What might I find out that could make that a possibility? On the other hand, could I so easily let go of Earth, if that time really came? I wasn't so sure I could if fantasy turned to reality.

The lights stopped repeating their pattern and remained a solid yellow.

"Are you ready?" Gaige asked.

"I'm ready."

I stepped into the hall with Gaige. The glassy, pale-blue corridor stretched out smooth and long before us like some futuristic tunnel. While walking through the new alien surroundings, thoughts spurred by the foreign place weighed on me. I continued to think about the secret Gaige had to tell me and whether I'd end up staying with these people after all was said and done. It seemed to be a possibility. But would I choose it? *Could* I choose it and leave all that I'd ever known behind? Being able to read Gaige's mind also weighed heavily in my thoughts. Had he, maybe, spoken the words out loud after all and not realized it? There was one way to find out. If it worked in one direction, it must work in the other as well. I concentrated hard, reaching out to him with my thoughts.

*"Gaige, can you hear me?"*

Gaige stopped. "Did you say something?"

"No, but I thought it."

Gaige forced a weak, troubled smile. "Maybe you should go slowly with that. At least until we understand how your acclimation here will go."

My energy level had dropped in that short moment of *thinking* to him and I doubted I could have managed much more anyway. "Agreed."

Gaige started walking again and I stayed close by his side. The lighting in the hall warmed my face like sunshine. "It's like we're outsidc on a sunny day."

"It's designed that way," he said. "It's not good for a body to go without sunlight for long periods of time. So the lighting throughout the ship simulates the light of a main sequence star, like your sun or ours. The cycle of light and darkness throughout the common areas is coordinated with Anu's days and nights at our home port."

I stopped and closed my eyes, reveling in the rays of light as if they were shots of happiness. Even a hallway here made me feel good. Winters in Ohio were cold and gray. I missed the Florida sunshine and the warmth. "That explains it."

"Explains what?" Gaige asked, waiting patiently.

"Why this light is so energizing. It's like real sunshine."

"The properties are identical."

"And does it always seem like the sun is rising whenever the lights are turned on?"

"It's one option. I thought you'd like it."

"Yes, I do."

Though I could have stretched out right there on the floor and soaked up that "sun" like I was spending a day at the beach, I knew Gaige had to get to his meeting. So, I started walking again through the eerily empty halls.

"Where are all the people?" I asked.

"Your quarters are in a converted well room. You'd call it a hospital room. But don't worry, it won't seem like one. We don't use them very often, but need to have them in case there's a major accident on the ship or on one of the missions. Since they stay unoccupied, we were able to block off a whole section for you. We can keep the entire area at Earth gravity so you'll have plenty of room to safely roam around."

"I'll be glad when I don't need all this special treatment."

"You need time to—"

"Time to adjust." I spit the words out like that could rid me of them. I knew better. "Sorry to interrupt."

Gaige took me by the arm to stop me, and turned me toward him. "I know you don't like that you have to go through this. I don't either. But please, try to be patient. It is for your own good to take things cautiously."

"I just don't think all this caution is necessary. But I'll try to be patient about it."

"That's all I can ask." Gaige took me by the hand and led me down the corridor. "There's no one who will be happier than I if all our caution ends up being unnecessary." He squeezed my hand and I reciprocated.

Up ahead, I saw what looked like a window, but it couldn't have been since there were rooms on both sides of the hallway. Whatever it was, it seemed to be a good distraction from the impatience I'd have to learn to tame. "What's that?" I asked, walking up to it.

"It's a virtual window that shows a projection from Anu." Gaige stopped next to me. "They're scattered throughout the corridors to give people a glimpse of home."

A field of tall, fuchsia-colored wisps of vegetation spread out as far as the eye could see. Breezes blew majestic patterns across the bright pink carpet, swirling the thin stalks one way then another. The patterns morphed and overtook each other, continuing their dance until they disappeared over the horizon, only to be replaced by another wave, and another.

"So, this is a live feed from Anu? This is happening right now?"

"There may be a few seconds of lag, but it's close."

I placed my hands against the window, wanting so badly to run my fingers across the wispy flowers. "What is this place?"

"You're looking at the Plains of Tonken."

I followed a breeze as it danced across the field, almost hypnotized by it. "It's so beautiful."

"Yes, it is."

"Does every window show a different location on Anu?"

"The windows in the corridors, yes. You'll be able to see many of our scenic sites—the White Mountains of Kadesh, the Merimose Falls, the golden rocks of the Taskeel Valley—and some of our more populated areas, too. The exterior windows are real. From them you'll see the space that surrounds this ship."

I kept my hands pressed against the glass, trying to be closer to the place that seemed to call me to touch and hear and breathe it. After a few moments, I pulled my hands away from the window and began walking again in the same direction we'd been going. These windows would give me a glimpse of Anu, the place. But what of its people? "Who is the person you're having me meet?"

We turned down a new corridor that looked the same as the one we'd just been in.

"She's Conner's mother. I thought she could help you with some of the things you might be going through as you try to adjust here."

"More than you could?"

"Yes, she's an expert on Earth and is a consultant for the ground missions. She and Conner's father are both assigned to this ship. They have been for years."

"Ah, an expert on Earth. So that's why you thought she could be helpful to me?"

"Not necessarily because she's an expert, but *why* she's an expert." Gaige gave me a sideways look with a grin like he was about to hand me the keys to the universe.

"Okay, I'll bite. *Why* is she an expert?"

"She's a Kian. She'll be able to truly understand what you're going through."

I stopped in my tracks. "She's what?" I'd heard what he said, but could hardly believe it.

"Kian. It means from Earth. She's from Earth."

"I know what Kian means—Earthling. Like me. But, there's another one here?" The pitch of my voice had risen noticeably.

"Yes, there is." Gaige wore a broad smile, obviously happy to see me so ecstatic.

"Is Conner's father Kian, too?"

"No, he's Anuan." Gaige took my hand. "We should keep moving, if you want to meet Conner's mother."

"Oh, yes. Of course I do!" I noticed a little extra bounce in my step after hearing the news. I might have been an alien in an alien world, but I was no longer one of a kind, left to wonder how I'd fit in. Not only had Conner's mother made the transition to Anuan life, but she'd done so with an Anuan man. Spending time with her made perfect sense.

So engrossed in what Conner's mother and I had in common, it took a moment to realize what else that meant. "Wait! That makes Conner half-Earthling."

"Yes, that's right."

"I would have never guessed he wasn't a full-blooded Anuan, what with the speed and all. He seems to have the same abilities as you. You're all Anuan, right?"

"Yes, I'm fully Anuan. He inherited the Anuan speed and strength. They seem to be dominant traits. Our gravity also helps in developing those traits. So, he does as well with that as any full-blooded Anuan. You'd never know unless somebody told you."

"And his mother? She gets along fine here? She doesn't stand out?"

"Anuans and Kians *are* both humans, so there's no reason she'd stand out. Her speed, strength and extrasensory abilities may not be quite as strong, but any human can improve those abilities to varying degrees. Anuans have just been honing their skills longer, for generations. She works hard to catch up, though."

"I have a million questions. How did she end up here? And how did she meet Conner's father? And—"

“We’re here.” Gaige stopped and motioned with his head to the door to our right. “She’ll be able to tell you everything. Conner should be here, too.”

It was comforting to know that being part Earthling hadn’t caused Conner any disadvantages. I would soon find out how difficult it had been for a full Earthling to acclimate to this life without the benefit of even one drop of Anuan blood to dominate in any way—a glimpse at my future, for whatever length of time it would exist here. Maybe only a day or two. Maybe longer.

# CHAPTER 59 - VICTORIA

When the door opened to my quarters, I took one step inside but could move no farther. My eyes scanned the entire room, looking for anything identifiable as a spaceship. There was nothing. I glanced behind me at the door we'd entered, which looked like it belonged in a spaceship, but that was all. Aside from the door, if I hadn't known better, I would have sworn we were standing in my bedroom back home in Florida. I ran my hands along the wall. The smooth surface with the customary glow had been replaced by dull, rough drywall, painted in the light rose color of my bedroom. I stepped to the bed and pressed my hands into the soft comforter that covered the thick pillow-topped mattress. The bedding sank, engulfing my hands until they disappeared into an ocean of pink and gray mosaics. Lifting the comforter to my face with both fists, I closed my eyes and inhaled a long, lingering breath through my nose. The aroma of my favorite detergent scent, spring rain, filled my memories with nights snuggled in bed, reading until the early morning hours. Everything in the room was exactly the same as at home, right down to the two photos on the dresser—one of me with my real parents and one of me with my aunt and uncle.

"This is your surprise. But we can change it if you don't like it," Gaige said.

"No, this is perfect." Something familiar in a future of unfamiliar was exactly what I needed. Releasing the comforter, I walked over to the window and looked out, expecting to see the space in which we floated. Instead, my eyes were met with my sunny backyard in Florida.

"You can change it to either of your homes." Gaige slapped the wall next to the window and the scene changed to the yard outside my apartment in Ohio, dead and frozen with a skip of fresh snow barely coating the brown grass.

"How did you do this?" I asked.

"We worked the angles on some of our surveillance satellites," a female voice said. "They're live feeds."

I turned toward the new voice and saw a woman standing next to Conner, bearing the same features and coloring. I only topped her by an inch or so, but next to her tall son, she appeared relatively petite. She wore a pale yellow outfit similar to Zada's, and had on very little makeup. Her natural beauty made even that much unnecessary.

Conner couldn't have been any older than me, but when he smiled, soft little crow's feet formed at the edges of his eyes. His mother's smile could have melted butter, and I saw the same crinkles at the corners of her eyes. Standing in the room with her made me think of my mothers, both of them. I missed them more than I realized.

"They've been helping get your room ready," Gaige said.

"Thank you," I said. "I'm sorry I didn't realize that you were here. I mean, I knew you would be, but I forgot when I saw the room. It's really amazing."

The kind smile remained on her face. "It's okay. So you like your room? We wanted you to feel at home."

"Yes, I like it very much. It's perfect."

Conner raised a hand toward his mother. "As you've probably already figured out, this is my mother, Bec."

"I'm so glad to meet you, Victoria." Bec put her arms around me and gave me a surprisingly firm hug. Her efforts in building strength had paid off.

Still enveloped in her embrace, I spoke into the soft cascade of auburn hair that lay against her shoulder. "I'm so happy to meet *you*. And thank you for the room."

Bec released me, still smiling. "You're very welcome."

"Victoria," Gaige said. "Would you like me to stay for a while?"

I knew I'd be comfortable with this new person, this Earthling. "No. Thank you, Gaige. Go ahead to your meeting. I'll be fine."

"Well, you ladies probably have a lot to talk about." Conner kissed his mother on the cheek then made his way toward the door. "Gaige, I'm grabbing a sandwich, and then I'll see you on the bridge. You're in good hands, Victoria. Love you, Mom." And Conner was out the door.

Gaige placed his hands on my shoulders, leaned down, and kissed me on the forehead. "I'll see you soon. Okay?"

"I'll be fine, Gaige."

"Yes, I'll help her get settled and we'll have a nice talk," Bec told him.

Gaige left the room, looking back over his shoulder. I waved to him and smiled until the door closed between us. I wanted him to know I'd be okay. With Gaige and Conner both gone, the answers to my gnawing and endless questions stood before me, with just the right perspective behind them.

# CHAPTER 60 - TAS

Daigon remained on the bridge performing his captain's duties while I waited for Gaige in Daigon's private planning room, off one side of the bridge. I needed time alone to speak with Gaige both as commander and as friend before we moved on to the other business that needed to be addressed.

Chairs lined the large oval conference table that dominated the center of the room. One also sat behind Daigon's desk. I knew sitting would not squelch my anxiety, so I stood at the center of the space-view window, staring out. The window took up most of the outer wall, from floor to ceiling. The vastness of that view helped keep everything in perspective and helped me remember I was not alone. I had the entire universe to draw from. One could shut off any connection and become an insignificant grain of sand, like the Kians chose to do, or tap into it and become as expansive as the whole. One with it all.

Silencing my rampant thoughts, I reached out, pulling in strength from the universe to help me deal with whatever lay ahead. Gaige and Victoria had grown too close, too fast. It wasn't supposed to happen that way, but her senses were keen. If my intuition was right about the other potential problem, the issues with Victoria may pale in comparison.

"Gaige requesting permission to enter," the computer said.

“Grant permission.”

The door slid open and Gaige passed through. His color was good, eyes bright, energy high. If it hadn’t been for his tattered flight suit, I would have never guessed the ordeal he’d been through.

“Gaige. How are you doing?”

He looked down at his flight suit and grinned. “Better than I look. I’ll change after our meeting. I didn’t want to hold anything up.” He gazed past me at the view, probably searching for help from the universe, just as I had. “Victoria’s doing really well, too.” The grin melted from his face, leaving a hollow sadness behind.

He knew, but I had to say it anyway. “Gaige, you and Victoria are becoming too close.”

“Yeah,” he said, quietly. “I didn’t mean for her to attach like she has.” He paused. “And like I have. She’s so much more open to energy exchanges than I’d expected. I tried to filter myself, to block her. But I haven’t been very successful.”

“Conner said the same thing. And the shuttle crash threw you together too soon. If she’d been approached more gradually, like we’d planned, we might have been able to assess everything better and adjust.”

It wasn’t Gaige’s fault, we’d all underestimated her. But, still, a correction needed to be made.

Gaige lowered his head. “I’m sorry, Tas. I know how important the mission was—is—to you, and that you didn’t want her decisions clouded by me.” He looked me in the eyes then. “She’s just amazing. Her skills, I mean. There’s no way she wouldn’t want to be here, with us, all of us. She belongs here.

She has to know that, regardless of how much she may or may not be attached to me."

I stretched my neck from side to side, trying to work out the tension. The situation sounded simple enough when Gaige put it like that, but was far from it. "Or is that just our interpretation, because we want her to stay?" I approached the conference table and willed a chair out far enough for me to sit down.

"Well," Gaige said, taking a seat across the table from me. "Maybe. Maybe I *am* seeing what I want to see. I have to admit, she has me muddled. I suppose I probably have her muddled, too."

"That's the problem." Dreading what I had to say, I paused, borrowing a few extra seconds before telling Gaige what *had* to be done. "I have to pull you from the mission."

Gaige nervously tapped his finger on the table. I knew he'd resist. He had to be choosing his words. After some time, he appeared to notice his nervous habit and clenched his hand into a fist. "Look, Tas, I understand why you would want to do that, but she trusts me. She's comfortable with me."

"*Too* comfortable. Things can't progress with you and her. She has to know the truth *first*. She has other decisions to make *first*."

"I know that. And, under these circumstances, I would *never* cross any lines with her."

"What if *she* pursues *you*? If any kind of connection is there, regardless of whether she can interpret it properly or not, she'll be compelled to follow it."

"Yes, she will." Gaige pounded his fist on the edge of the table and pushed himself back. "And has," he added, under his breath. He made a few laps around the room then sat back down.

"But, I can be strong. For her. She'll be confused and upset if you pull me away from her. It could set her emotions spinning. She's far from adjusted yet. I'll accept your decision as commander, of course, but *please*, Tas, think about what I'm saying."

He did have a point, especially considering what Zada had told me about her. Gaige waited for my response with so much pent-up, anxious energy that he looked like a caged animal ready to burst free. Before I could answer, or even know what my answer would be, the door slid open and Daigon walked into the room.

"Is there anything I can help with in here?" he asked.

"Seems your son and I have a difference of opinion, Daigon," I said.

Daigon sat down at the table with us. "I can imagine."

He couldn't be surprised. We both knew how much Gaige already cared for Victoria, long before the mission.

"Could you use a neutral viewpoint?" Daigon asked.

"I think you could be of some assistance here," I said. "Your son has made a good case, but you know my concerns. Both Gaige and I are somewhat vested, though, and perhaps clouded. So, old friend, I *would* be interested in your opinion."

"Of course," Daigon said. "All right, Gaige, I know what Tas is worried about—you and Victoria getting too close, of her becoming the other half of you, before she can comprehend the whole of who she is and before she can decide where her future lies. Perhaps it's somewhere else. Being tied to you before she can sort all that out wouldn't be fair to her."

"I agree. But, keeping me away from her could disrupt the stability she currently has. She'll need that when all the Anuan energy finally overwhelms her. She's soaking us in quickly. It's amazing. She's even communicated with me telepathically. I didn't mean for it to happen." Gaige shook his head and sighed. "It just did." He put his head down, apparently regrouping his thoughts, and then continued. "But I think it's a comfort to her. Everything and everybody here are still strange to her. I think it helps to know she can connect to me whenever she might need to. You know, and not feel alone. Don't take that away from her. It's only a matter of time before she's absorbed more energy than she knows how to manage. She needs to be in as steady a place as possible when that happens. I'm that place for her. It wouldn't be good to change what she's used to right now. I can be strong. For her. For both of us. I won't let things go any further with us."

Daigon's eyes searched mine. *"He doesn't know?"*

"No, he doesn't know," I answered aloud. "I haven't gotten to that yet."

"Know what?" The fear in Gaige's eyes contradicted the strength of his voice. "Is something wrong with Victoria?"

"Victoria is doing as well as you think—right now," Daigon answered. "But her transition may be much more difficult than you think, and her future somewhat predestined, *if* she stays here."

Gaige looked from Daigon to me, trying to read us. "I don't understand."

"Do you know of my great-grandmother?" I asked.

"Yes, she was Head of the Supreme Council." The realization flooded Gaige's face. "Wait. You're not saying . . ."

I nodded my head. "Yes, we are. Her levels of awareness are higher than any we've seen in decades. As high as my great-grandmother's."

"The Council will want her to serve with them." Gaige left us sitting by ourselves and lost himself in front of the space-view window. "They can't. It's too much," Gaige muttered, more to himself than to us. "She'd be overwhelmed to be approached with this—" Gaige spun around from the window then. "Did you know this? Before the mission, did you know?"

"No, Gaige," I said. "All we knew was that she had abilities beyond a typical Kian. With her being closed to her potential on Earth, we only saw small indicators that she probably wasn't even aware of. We had no idea they'd end up being so strong. When she started opening up around you, we saw signs of what she might be capable of, but didn't realize the magnitude until she got here and Zada ran her numbers. Apparently, The Council suspected, but only told us once Zada's tests confirmed it."

"Gaige, sit back down with us," Daigon said. "And relax, for Victoria's sake. She doesn't need your tense energy. The Council will not approach her with this now. They realize it would be too much for her to handle at this point. It's a decision that will be far in her future, after she's completely acclimated and her skills are trustworthy. And only if she would decide to stay with us. But you can understand Tas's concern that her decision about where her future lies has to be made without your influence—in any way. Staying here with us could lead to big responsibilities at some point, if she should choose to accept that honor."

Gaige sat back down and breathed slowly, in and out. His anxiety began to dissipate, but only a little. "I worry about her taking on too much, that's all."

"And that's why you were chosen for the mission to begin with," I said. "I knew you'd take great care with her. But now . . ."

"So, Gaige," Daigon interjected. "You thought you could be strong enough for the both of you. Knowing the potential strength of Victoria's connections, are you still sure you'd be able to do that?"

Gaige was quiet at first, not saying yes or no. It would be an incredible challenge. One I wasn't sure he, or anyone, would be able to handle. And good reason to pull him from the mission.

"Yes. Yes, I can do it." Gaige said, firmly. "I'm not saying it will be easy. But I can do it. For her sake, I *will* do it."

Daigon didn't say another word. He closed his eyes and sat quietly for a long while. It was a difficult decision, made between two of the closest people in his life—his son and his best friend. We'd grown up together as children, raised our own together, and had many wonderful times throughout the years. There were the tough times, too—a war no Anuan wanted, the rebuilding of our planet, and such a personal loss I thought I'd never recover from it. Maybe I hadn't. That made the outcome of this mission, and this decision, all the more important. But Daigon was a master at removing emotions and making his decisions based purely on the facts. That's what made him such an exceptional captain.

Daigon finally opened his eyes. "You both have some very valid concerns, but we have to look at the most critical issue for Victoria right now. Damage caused from an emotional energy overload could be as devastating to her as any physical injury. Maybe worse. If it's too much, she may not recover from it. What might have been in her future wouldn't matter if that happens. I think it's best for her environment to stay as steady as possible and Gaige is a part of that environment. She already relies on his support. He's going to have to be strong, no doubt. But I think what's most important right now, and over the next few days, is to keep Victoria's new world as stable as we can."

Gaige didn't say a word, just waited for my decision. After hearing Daigon lay things out so simply, I knew there was only one decision I could make.

"Gaigc," I said. "Can you really manage this?"

"Yes, absolutely. Knowing the consequences will keep me strong."

So many scenarios had floated through my mind. I hadn't been able to be objective enough to grasp the most likely. But Daigon had made things clear. If Victoria didn't survive her transition, it didn't matter where, how, or with whom she would have wanted to spend her future. She would have no future. "Then stay with her. Help her adjust. But *nothing* else, Gaige."

Gaige reached his hand out to me. I gripped it and shook. An Earth gesture for this girl from Earth who meant so much to both of us.

"Thank you, Commander," Gaige said. "I won't let you down. Or Victoria."

# CHAPTER 61 - BRIAN

One small, bare light bulb hung down from the center of the cell's ceiling. It didn't emit enough light to make much of an impact, even on the floor directly below it. There were no windows to tell day from night. No sounds to let me know the world still existed. It was enough to drive anyone mad. Though with no food in my stomach, I didn't have the energy to go anywhere, even crazy.

Worn out from trying to find a way to escape, I sat below the light bulb to give myself some illusion of heat. Bloody scrapes—from feeling over the brick walls for passageways—crisscrossed my palms. I closed my hands into fists, only to quickly release them when my nails, jagged and torn to the quick from trying to open the lock, scratched the tender skin of my palms. I could have opened the lock with any number of items, but my pockets had been emptied when I was unconscious. I had nothing but my body and my clothes. Thankfully, they'd left me with those.

Wondering how much time had passed, I rubbed the less tender back of my hand across my face, careful to avoid the scab on my chin. Two days growth of stubble, maybe three, had covered my jaw. It might already be Monday by now. Did anybody wonder where I was? And Tori, had she and Gaige escaped?

I let my head loll forward, too weak to hold it upright anymore. I wanted to lie down and sleep, but the floor of the cell was so cold. *Did they plan to ever let me out of this place?* Without water soon, it wouldn't matter.

# CHAPTER 62 - VICTORIA

With Gaige and Conner gone, I stood alone with Bec, wondering what to say. I didn't have to think long before she broke the silence.

"Gaige had an outfit sent for you," Bec said. "It's in the closet."

I went to the closet and opened the door. Inside, on an Earth hanger and next to my Earth clothes, hung a light pink, two-piece Anuan outfit. My old and new worlds colliding right there in front of me.

"It's a ship suit," she explained. "The style and material are the same as the flight suits that Gaige and Conner wear. But the flight suits are reinforced and one-piece to make sure the body is always protected. We don't need that kind of protection on the ship. Your suit is fully loaded. Gaige insisted on all the accessories, medical and otherwise. There was enough data from your sickbay scans that the fit, both for the suit itself and the accessories, should be right."

"I love it!" I pulled the ship suit out of the closet and, being lighter than I'd expected, almost jerked it over my shoulder. If I hadn't been looking directly at it, I'd have sworn the hanger was empty. I held the suit out in front of me to examine it, rubbing the sleeve between my left thumb and forefinger. The soft material reminded me of a horse's velvety nose.

While looking the suit over, the light caught the front of it at just the right angle and the pink surface glistened ever so slightly with pale rainbow swirls, as if it were coated in oil. I ran my finger across the spot. The colors shifted, but my finger remained perfectly dry. *Not oil then.* Holding the outfit this way and that revealed the barely visible coloring everywhere.

"It's a property of the material," Bec said. "It's very resilient, even when it's not reinforced. Gaige said you liked pink, so that's what he sent you. You can get other colors, too."

"This one's perfect." I pulled the suit close to me and visualized Gaige in his—tearing out of that cage and taking me by the hand, stretching out on the motel bed so calm, lifting me into his arms when things became too much for me—

"You're fond of him," Bec said. "Gaige, I mean."

I hung the suit back in the closet and closed the door. There was no use trying to hide what I felt. My affection for Gaige filled me to the point I thought I might burst. That was impossible to cover up. "Yes, I'm very fond of him. I've never been drawn to anyone like this. He's thoughtful, and kind. Understanding, protective, gracious. And ornery. Yes, and when he's being ornery he gets this mischievous grin, with dimples that turn me to absolute putty."

Bec stood listening to my every rambling word, a warm smile on her face. The warmth didn't stop at her smile, either, but radiated into her eyes and beyond. Even her body stance—relaxed, head slightly tilted—said *talk all you want, I'm listening and I care.* But I was being rude, leaving her standing there while I went on and on.

"I'm sorry, Bec. Would you like to sit down?"

"If you'd be more comfortable, we could sit."

"It seems I'm a bit long-winded today. Maybe we should."

I dragged the tan parsons chair from the corner of my room and placed it next to my bed. "Here you go, Bec."

Bec sat, crossed one leg over the other, and folded her hands on her knees like she was ready for a long conversation.

I crawled to the center of my bed and settled in, wondering what I must sound like rambling on about someone I'd only just met. "I guess I sound pretty silly, huh?"

"No, not silly at all. I know exactly how you feel."

I didn't want to pry, but I had to know how she ended up with the Anuans. "Can you tell me your story? You know, about how you came to be here and how you met your husband?"

"Yes, I can tell you everything. Everything I remember, that is. I was home from college visiting my parents. We were going for a drive one day, a simple drive. Somehow, the car went off the road into a river. Tas, my husband, was a young ground mission team member at the time—he's commander of the missions now. He had been collecting samples on the bank of the river and was able to save me before the car sank. My parents . . ." Bec paused and closed her eyes for a moment, then began again. "My parents were in the front seat and died on impact. I don't remember anything about the accident itself. The first memory I have of that time is opening my eyes in sickbay and seeing Tas sitting next to me. I sobbed in his arms when he told me my parents were dead. Even through all the pain—both physical and emotional—I felt something for him that first time he held me. Though the Anuans' had advanced medical means, my recovery took a long time. He helped me through every minute of it. During the process, he was so patient and strong and encouraging. I couldn't have done it without him."

The dreamy smile on Bec's face said it all. She loved him with her entire being. She *did* understand how I felt.

"And the thought of you going back to Earth?" I asked.

She shook her head. "There was no way. To us, my leaving would have been like ripping one complete being into two separate halves. The mere thought of doing that was beyond comprehension."

"Yeah, I understand. But how does that happen, so fast and so intense?"

"Kians might call it love at first sight. That happens with Anuans quite regularly. Kians are typically only aware of the superficial at first, yet they base lifelong decisions on that. It can be a disaster for them. Anuans, on the other hand, feel and connect on much deeper levels than the humans on Earth allow or are even aware. At those levels, they're able to have a more accurate sense of compatibility. True and lasting compatibility. They can feel the core of a person and know right away whether it resonates with their own. When a connection like that is made, at the very center of a being, it evolves very rapidly and deeply. There is no separating it once it's established."

I clasped my hands together. "But Bec, if there is no separating the connection once it's established, then with Gaige and me, why can't our fate already be accepted?"

Bec let out a quiet sigh. "Your situation is very complicated, dear. Do you trust Gaige?"

"Yes, of course."

"Then trust that he's handling things in the way he feels is best for you. Isn't that what someone who cares for you would do?"

She'd responded perfectly. The details of why Gaige was being so overly cautious didn't seem quite as important anymore. "Yes, it is."

"Would you like to take a shower and change now?" Bec asked.

"Yes, I think I would." I scooted myself off the bed, retrieved the ship suit from the closet, and hung it in the bathroom. Reaching through the neck of my sweater, I grabbed the chain that held my real parents' wedding rings and pulled it over my head. Before placing the rings in the tiny silver jewelry box that sat on top of my dresser, I held them tight in my hand. I could almost feel my parents' presence. I missed them. The void their deaths had created felt fresher here, yet at the same time, it seemed to find something adequate enough to begin to fill it. This place had created so many ways of seeing and feeling, such a swirl of everything within me all at once.

"You miss them," Bec said.

I wasn't sure what was more prevalent in Bec's expression, the sadness or the compassion. I realized at that moment we had more in common than just being displaced from Earth or being in love with an Anuan. I'd been so focused on those things that I had allowed the fact she'd also lost both of her parents to fade into the background. She really could understand so much of my situation and the emotions I would be experiencing. Gaige was right to have me meet her.

"Yes, I miss them very much," I admitted. "I feel their loss more now than I have in a long time."

Bec approached me and wrapped her delicate hands around the closed fist in which I held my parents' rings. "Being here with the Anuans will stir things in you that you won't understand. You'll be much more sensitive to your own thoughts and emotions, and those of others as well. You may be on an emotional rollercoaster for a while, but in time, you will learn how to manage what you're experiencing, and everything will make sense." She removed her hands from mine and brushed them lightly over my hair, smoothing it—a comforting gesture my aunt had done so many times when I was young.

I opened my hand to study my parents' rings. The light in the room twinkled off the gold, just like the day my aunt and uncle had given them to me on my thirteenth birthday. I'd cherished them ever since. They were the only personal items of my parents that my family had. The only connection left to them. Bec said I would be more sensitive and I could tell that was true. After all these years, my parents were on my mind almost as much as Gaige and this new place.

I put the rings back in the jewelry box. Nestled down in the red velvet, they looked cozy, at home. Everything was in its place now. In that duplicated room, it was as if I'd never left home. But I had. I ran my finger across the black and white photo of me with my real parents, and then touched the one with my aunt and uncle. "I wish I'd have been able to talk to my family before I left. But things happened so fast." Only now did I consider what my staying there might do to them. Would it be like I just disappeared? Or would I be able to tell them goodbye?

"Arrangements could be made for you to see them," Bec said.

"Oh, that would be so great." Though this place tugged at the deepest part of my soul, I couldn't hurt my parents. I missed them already and wondered how long it would be before they realized I wasn't in Ohio anymore. I didn't want them to worry.

Bec looked toward the picture of my biological parents. "You look very much like your mother."

"Yes, my aunt always said that."

"She was very beautiful, as are you."

"Thank you, Bec." Drained from our talk and the memories, I had nothing left for more conversation. "I think I'll take that shower."

"Okay, dear. We thought you'd prefer water for now, so we've reproduced your bathroom exactly as it is in your home."

"Prefer water? How else would I take a shower?"

"The Anuan's have developed a form of ion beam that cleanses the body very well. It conserves water and is much faster than the traditional shower or bath."

"Really? No water and you still get clean?"

"Yes, your bathroom has that option, if you'd like to try it."

"I think I'll take a water shower this time," I said. "The ion thing is tempting, though."

I opened one of my dresser drawers to get clean underclothes. The drawer was full of familiar items, just as the closet had been. It was an eerie feeling, yet comforting at the same time, to have such an exact replica of my old life laid out in the middle of my new one. It pulled the future I saw for myself from this place to home, this place, home. They were right about the emotions. At the moment, they swung from longing to the emptiness of loss. Which emotion would be assigned to which place? I had no idea yet. What I did know is that the emotional swings drained me. Other than that, it really wasn't that big of a deal.

So far.

# CHAPTER 63 - GAIGE

When Conner arrived at my Dad's private planning room, he approached a seat several down from me, my dad, and Tas. The chair glided back from the table when he neared it and he sat. After the three of us caught Conner up on Victoria's potential, Tas was ready to move on to the next topic.

Tas had a hardness about him I'd never felt before all this happened with Victoria. I could understand it, considering Victoria's situation. But something told me there was more. I couldn't read his emotions beyond the hardness, though, or my Dad's. They were both pros at blocking others from the ship's business.

Tas's posture looked as hard as his emotions felt. The crease in his brow had to be the size of Valles Marineris. And my Dad had his arms crossed and his jaw tight, like a captain with a very big problem to manage.

My dad moved to the front of the room, with everyone turning in his direction. "Tas has some concerns. I'll let him start." Dad held his arm in Tas's direction.

Tas nodded to him and, remaining seated, began. "I received a recent update from the monitoring room. Pags has been tracking the Kian team that pursued you. They flew to the government's remote area in Nevada. Since that's deep underground and so well-reinforced, we weren't able to penetrate the facility for visual or audio. To try and take a team in just for information wouldn't be worth the risk. Everyone is safe on the ship and in no danger from them now." Tas looked down, shook his head, and looked back up at us. "Still, I'd like to know why we had issues picking up some of their communications and how they were able to keep up with you so easily."

"Communication issues . . . maybe the solar flares?" Conner's eyes searched the ceiling as he thought. "As far as tracking is concerned, we had satellite feeds from the crucial areas blocked, so they couldn't have used satellite data. Kians have drones, though."

"But no drones were anywhere near you," Dad said.

"True," Conner agreed. "We'd have spotted them from the ship's monitoring room, no matter how small."

Tas rose from his seat and moved to the window. He stood with his back to us, silhouetted by the star-studded blackness he looked upon. "This has the marks of the Tamanacke. No other known beings with the necessary technology would interfere with a fledgling race like this."

"We don't know the Kians had help," Dad said. "Besides, the Tamanacke are supposed to be extinct, due in large measure to us." Dad sat then and gazed at the wall opposite him. With a deep sigh, his presence drifted away from us, no doubt to the time of the Tam-Anuan war.

With Tas reaching to the universe for guidance and Dad lost in his memories, the air in the room grew heavy. I only knew of the war through our history, but our ground mission commander and our captain had actually participated in their younger days and played a major role in the obliteration of the Tamanacke race. If they hadn't succeeded, the Anuans wouldn't exist today.

"But the Anuans had no choice," I said.

Tas turned from the window and crossed his arms. "There's always a choice, and we chose to defend ourselves."

# CHAPTER 64 - VICTORIA

After showering, I slid into the new outfit. There were no buttons, snaps, or Velcro. The outfit closed on its own as if magnets within the material drew each side to the other. I gave the opening of my top a tug to make sure I could trust the hidden devices. It held strong.

Once I was dressed, Bec and I resumed our conversation in my duplicated Earth bedroom. She sat in the chair and I sat in the center of my bed, as before. I didn't ask any more questions about me and Gaige. He had set a slow and cautious pace for me, for us, whether I had the patience for it or not. Bothering Bec about it wasn't going to change anything. I'd deal directly with Gaige about that. So, Bec and I discussed the ship, the planet, the language, the food—anything Anuan.

Suddenly, a strong feeling came over me that Gaige was close. I could sense his presence becoming stronger and knew without a doubt he was approaching my room. "Gaige is coming."

"Hmm." Bec closed her eyes and took a slow breath. "I believe you're right."

A soft chime sounded. The door became transparent and I could see Gaige standing outside in the corridor, though he didn't seem to be able to see me. Since there were no knobs or handles on the door, I wasn't sure how to let him in.

I turned to Bec. "What do I do?"

"Well, since I assume you want to let him in, just say *open* or *allow.* Anything along those lines will work."

"Yes, I do. Open."

The door slid open. Gaige walked through, looking refreshed and clean-shaven in a casual outfit—a loose fitting tan V-neck pullover and brown pants, both made of something like relaxed linen. When he cleared the door, it automatically closed behind him and appeared solid again. On his face he wore a smile a little too stiff to be believed.

"Hello ladies." He sat down on the edge of the bed and scanned my clothes. His smile grew bigger, truer. "I like the outfit. You like it? It's what you wanted, right?"

"I love the outfit. Thank you, Gaige."

I wanted to hug him, to *really* thank him. I looked to Bec, wanting to ask *should I or shouldn't I?*

She gave me her warm smile and stood up. "I think this room has one person too many right now. I'm sure you two have a lot to talk about. I'm going to check in on Tas."

Gaige walked Bec to the door like a gentleman. He gave her a kiss on the cheek and thanked her for helping me get settled. When he returned, he paused at the edge of the bed but sat in the chair. He squirmed for a moment, like he couldn't get comfortable, and stood up again. "You like Bec?"

"Yes, very much. I'm glad you had us meet."

"I thought you'd like her. So, are you ready for a tour of the ship?"

He held his hand out to me, but I didn't take it. A tour could wait. I wanted to talk to him about his timeline for my adjustment.

"Actually, can we talk first?"

"Talk?" His hand dropped to his side. His eyes scanned my empty room, stopping at my bed. "Here?"

"Yes, here. I want to talk to you about my adjustment period." I patted the bed for him to sit down. "I don't think I need it."

He watched my hand for a moment, which patted the spot right next to me, and then sat in the chair. "Okay, we can talk."

I stilled my hand. "Gaige, I'm not going to bite you."

"But I might bite you." His ornery dimples flashed for a second, then disappeared. "I think it's best if I sit here."

"Fine." The word came out as sour as a lemon. I hampered my attitude and continued. "Sit wherever you'd like."

I scooted myself to the edge of the bed opposite his chair and hung my legs over the side. His knees nearly touched mine. The muscles in his neck tightened and his eyes wandered to the wall, the ceiling, the floor—anywhere but mine.

I snapped my fingers in front of my face. "Gaige, I'm right here."

His eyes found mine and fixed themselves in a mesmerized stare. "Yes, you are." He reached a hand toward me, but quickly pulled it back. He got up and went to the window. "Looks cold out there."

I followed and stood behind him, stretching to look over his shoulder at the frozen Ohio yard I was sure he cared nothing about. "Gaige, you're killing me here."

He turned to me with his worry face—the same furrowed brow I'd seen on Earth when things weren't going well. "What do you mean?"

"It's about this . . . you . . . me . . . everything. I don't know." I bowed my head, gritted my teeth, and then stood tall, determined to say what I needed to say. "I know there's something between us. I feel it in every fiber of my being. I can't fight it. I don't *want* to fight it."

Gaige tensed, but stayed silent, not jumping in to argue or change the subject like I thought he might.

"You want me. I know you do." I took his face in my hands. He stiffened even more, but didn't pull away. "On Earth, the way you touched me, caressed me. You'd barely been able to stop yourself. And here. I slept in your arms last night. You walked me to this room hand-in-hand. And the forehead kisses you give me. Your words are cautious, especially since we arrived here. Your body and your energy are not in agreement with the words, though. Even now, it's like you're afraid to be in the same room with me. But your body is still reaching out to me. What is causing you to fight that? I know—the adjustment, something you're going to tell me, blah, blah, blah—"

"You don't even know how long you'll be here. I told you what that means to an Anuan. It's a life-long commitment."

I dropped my hands from his face. My draw to him had taken over my brain and I hadn't thought about that part. Was I ready to leave everything I'd ever known behind? Forever? I hadn't quite reconciled that. "We wouldn't have to take things that far."

"Could you stop short, Victoria? Because I couldn't. It's best we not tempt it."

"I could stay here if I wanted to, couldn't I? Permanently, I mean. It's more than some far-out possibility, isn't it?"

Gaige closed his eyes and took a breath. I wondered for a moment if he would answer at all. But his eyes opened and he spoke. "Yes. You could."

"Do you not want me here? Do you not want to be with me?"

The worried lines in Gaige's face had been replaced with a weary softness. "I didn't say that. I just don't want to be the reason you stay. I want you to take time to figure out what *you* want."

I looked at the picture of my parents sitting on the dresser. Before long, they'd realize I wasn't in Ohio anymore. Bec said I could see them again, but would it only be to tell them goodbye? Could I walk out of their lives and into another world? Could I hurt them like that?

Then there was Gaige, standing in front of me. How could I walk away from *him*? Or this place that tugged at me to stay? I wanted to go home, to tell my parents I was okay, that I loved them and would never leave them. But I also wanted to wrap myself in Gaige's arms, that very second, and stay forever. "What I *want* is for you to stop putting distance between us." I balled my hands into tight fists. "I hate it!"

"I know you do." Gaige raised a hand to my face. His fingers hovered just over my cheek for a brief second before he pulled his hand away without touching me.

I didn't want understanding at that moment. I wanted a resolution. I couldn't take another minute of the way things were. I had to get through to him.

"Gaige . . . I love you!" I froze. The words had tumbled out on their own. I'd meant them. But to actually hear myself say them out loud, to him, scared me to death. How would he respond? Had I been delusional?

Gaige's mouth searched for words but said nothing. His eyes glazed over, like they didn't recognize I stood in front of him. The longer I waited, the more I felt like a fool, pouring my heart out to him and getting nothing in return. Tears welled up in my eyes that matched the anger boiling inside me.

"Say something!"

I slammed my palms into his chest. A tingle ran up my arms like I'd grabbed a live wire. Faster than I could track what was happening, Gaige had me pressed against the wall with his lips on mine. I clung to his shirt, never wanting to let go.

"No." He mumbled between kisses but didn't stop.

I gripped his shirt tighter, fighting against the *no* that teetered on a fine edge of indecision.

"No!" He broke from our kiss and embraced me so firmly I couldn't move. "I love you, too," he whispered. The words mingled with his breath, almost too indistinguishable to hear. But they were there.

He pulled away and held me at arm's length. "That's why I won't do this to you. I love you enough to stop myself and give you time to understand what you're feeling. If it's real and if it's meant to be, it will be. But not now."

# CHAPTER 65 - GAIGE

Victoria touched her lips, "You . . . you . . ." Then she held her hands out in front of her like they were two foreign objects. "I, I pushed you. I only meant to touch you. But I was so angry. Gaige, I'm sorry."

Tears pooled in her eyes as one of her hands went to her lips again. Still feeling my kiss there, I was sure. *What had I done?* I could feel the passion and the longing and the guilt and the anger, and a hundred other emotions in Victoria. Every single one of those emotions played out on her face, ready for the wrong touch or the wrong word to give them the microscopic nudge they needed to shatter her into a million pieces.

"I don't know what I'm feeling, Gaige. I love you and I hate you. I want you and I want to punch you. I want to cry and I want to scream. I don't know what to do."

Her tears broke free, streaming down her face. She gasped for air through her sobs. I couldn't help myself. I pulled her to me, to comfort her. *Only to comfort*, I repeated to myself. *Only to comfort.*

"There's not a lot you *can* do. I'll show you how to relax and put things in a proper perspective. But mostly, you just need to give yourself time to learn how to manage all the extra emotional energy you're picking up here."

"Okay," she said, her voiced muffled against my chest. Sniffing uncontrollably and still trying to catch her breath, she raised her head and wiped her cheeks. "I really am sorry, Gaige."

"It's okay. I know you didn't mean it. And I'm the one who should be sorry. I should never have kissed you. That only made things worse."

"Don't be sorry." She touched my lips with her fingers and became calmer.

I didn't say a word, and just let her work things out. After a moment her breathing steadied, with only an occasional sniff to disrupt her stillness.

"You love me?" she said.

I nodded. "I do. I still shouldn't have kissed you. You're not ready. You understand that now, right?"

"Yes, I do." She lowered her hand from my lips and wiped away the remaining tears from her cheeks. "So how about we call things even and start over?"

"That sounds like a good plan." I released my hold on her but we didn't move otherwise.

After a moment, Victoria spoke. "So, what now?"

What now? A good question. "Uh. Well." *If this was any other person in the universe, what would I do?* "We'll see the ship. Yes, our tour. And we'll introduce you to some people. But *gradually.* We need to take things very slowly. Okay?"

"Okay." She laid her head back against my chest. "And thank you."

"For what?"

"For saying it."

I wasn't sure telling her I loved her was the best thing. At least I'd been able to give her some peace. "You're welcome."

She took my hand. "So who do I get to meet first?"

"I think we should see the ship first, and give it a few days before I introduce you to any more people than you've already met."

Victoria's shoulders slumped. "Maybe you're right. But I have already met you, and Conner, and Zada, and Bec. Maybe one or two new people at a time would be all right. Since it has been so far." Victoria looked up at me through her long dark lashes. "What do you think?"

I didn't like the idea, but I wanted to be fair to Victoria and consider her question. Meeting me and Conner had affected her, but not catastrophically. I wasn't sure Zada and Bec were good cases by which to judge. Victoria had had time to adjust to Zada in sickbay before they'd formally met, and Bec's abilities most likely weren't strong enough to have much of an effect on Victoria. What little exposure Victoria had had to us, wasn't sufficient to predict how well she'd acclimate to a ship full of Anuans.

The right pace would be a guessing game and I wanted to stay well on the cautious side. Logic told me I should keep her isolated from as much energy as possible for a while. Not that energy wasn't already present everywhere, but it wasn't necessarily at the same concentration that would be associated with a person. One thing I did know: she wouldn't be happy wrapped up in a cocoon and hidden away from the world.

Victoria waited patiently for my answer, with her puppy dog eyes urging me to agree with her. If she really wanted to meet somebody, I could think of only one safe prospect. My Dad was so good at blocking his energies from others, meeting him would be almost like meeting no one. It seemed like a good compromise right now. A way to keep Victoria happy *and* protected. Whether she would be comfortable meeting my *father* in her current, shaky state was another matter. That piece of information, perhaps, should wait.

"Okay. Maybe just one."

Victoria's face brightened. Making her happy made me happy. But I couldn't let myself get caught up in her excitement and forget that the slightest wrong decision could send her spinning out of control.

# CHAPTER 66 - BRIAN

A clang echoed through my cell, waking me with the familiar sound from the night they slammed me into that place—cold metal bars locking hard and firm. Only this time, the sound came from farther away.

Too weak to move, I stayed in my fetal position on the cold concrete floor trying to hold in what little heat I could. I waited, hoping someone was finally bringing me food.

Footsteps came closer, reverberating off the walls the same way the din of the clanking doors had. I assumed I must be the target of the visitor. As far as I could tell, no one else shared my fate in that dreary place. I hadn't heard a sound from man nor beast since I'd arrived. I considered the latter to be a good thing, though.

The footsteps stopped right in front of my cell. I dragged myself off the floor—barely—and stood. Squinting, I tried to make out the person's form in the dark area beyond my light bulb. Nothing differentiated it from the rest of the blackness.

"You're not very smart for a scientist, are you? It doesn't pay to try and be a hero."

The voice belonged to a male, but I still couldn't tell what the man looked like or whether he wore civilian or military clothes.

"Here," he said.

Something bounced across the floor of my cell and ricocheted off the wall behind me, just to my right. Then another item landed with a soft thud in front of me. Within the small circle of light, the sight of a few precious slices of bread in a clear storage bag made my mouth water.

"That'll buy you enough time for your visitor to arrive," he said. "He'd be pretty upset with us if we let you die before he had a chance to *deal* with you himself."

*My visitor?* The footsteps receded and the clang echoed again through the silence left behind. I dropped to my knees and tore open the bag of bread, stuffing a piece into my mouth. The cheap white bread tasted better than any food I'd ever had. Still chewing, I groped the floor behind me with raw palms, looking for the other object. My hands finally met a plastic bottle. I swung it around under the light. Exactly as I'd thought—a bottle of water. I twisted off the top and began to gulp the precious substance.

I stopped suddenly, realizing it might have to last for a while.

# CHAPTER 67 - VICTORIA

Gaige stopped where my corridor fed into another. "Right here is where Earth gravity ends. Except today. Today I have the whole ship set to Earth gravity. The children love it. But normally, you will need to stop right here." He swung his arm back and forth like a pendulum at the end of my corridor.

"Okay. I get it, Gaige. Right here. I won't go past this point." I took his hand and stepped across the normally forbidden line.

Gaige didn't reciprocate my grip, deciding, I supposed, whether or not handholding would stress any *adjustment period* boundaries. Apparently concluding it to be manageable, he tightened his fingers. He pointed with his other hand to the lights lining the top of both sides of the corridor. "These yellow lights indicate something other than Anuan gravity. In this case, Earth gravity. If you forget, just look for the lights. No lights mean our normal Anuan gravity is present. You shouldn't go there. I don't want you to get over-stressed."

Gaige turned left down another corridor with the same solid yellow lights lining its walls. The halls all looked alike to me, so I paid close attention to when we turned and which way we went.

"Is your gravity really that bad?" I asked.

"It could cause you difficulty."

"Okay, I'll take your word for it. Where are we going first?"

"We're going to the bridge. You wanted to meet somebody and I thought the captain would be a good person to start with. He's been a mentor to me my whole life."

"So, he's important to you?"

"Yes, he's very important to me."

"Then that's a perfect place to start."

Gaige and I came to a stop in front of a door that slid open upon registering our presence.

"This is an ibbs, uh, I mean elevator," Gaige said. "Our equivalent of an elevator, anyway."

"I can call it an ibbs. That's what it is here."

Letting go of my hand, he waved his arm toward its interior. "After you."

Gaige followed me inside the smooth-walled pod, shaped more like an egg than the box configuration of an Earth elevator. Our reflections looked back at us, uninhibited by any buttons or other obstructions on the wall's shiny metallic finish. My bloodshot eyes reminded me how upset I'd been back in my room. Embarrassed at even the thought of my behavior, I looked away. I couldn't be reminded of that other me. The one in turmoil. The one I'd break free of as soon as I could.

Gaige told the pod to go to the main bridge and asked permission to see the captain. A silky female voice confirmed his request. When we began our descent, symbols lit up behind what I thought had been a solid metal wall. I noticed the familiar clanking noises associated with Earth elevators were strangely absent.

"It's quiet," I said.

"It runs on pressure rather than cables. We're floating to our floor."

As the ibbs glided down, my stomach drifted up within my body like it wasn't sure it wanted to stay with me. I wrung my hands together, intertwining my fingers, untwirling them again, and then repeating the actions. My nerves ramped up higher and higher with each step we progressed toward the bridge and its captain. I jumped when the door opened to a large room with several corridors leading from it.

Gaige took my hand again. "You okay?"

"Mm-hm." I focused on living up to my answer by putting one foot in front of the other as we stepped out of the ibbs. I figured I could manage meeting the captain if I broke it down to one step at a time. "Was that a real person speaking in the ibbs?" I asked, thinking some kind of conversation might be a good distraction from the nerves that didn't want to settle down.

"No, it's the computer system."

I barely heard Gaige's answer. My mind started rethinking whether I *should* have waited a few days before meeting any more people. *No*, I thought, convincing myself of the answer more than actually reaching a decision. I could do this. I *would* do this.

Gaige stopped. "Don't forget, you're dealing with an empath. You're good at covering, I'll give you that. But I'm reading loud and clear that you're nervous about this. I'm taking you back to your room."

"No!" I panicked at the thought of missing an opportunity to make progress. The only way I'd beat my nerves was to control these feelings by learning to manage them. These emotions would not win. I took a breath and started again, more calmly. "Okay, Gaige, here's the deal. I will conquer this transition. So, how about instead of hiding me in my room, you pour some of that calm you have on me. Help me accomplish this?"

Gaige pressed his lips together in a thin line. To help me or protect me by hiding me away in some little box of a room? Which would he choose?

"Being stifled would feel worse to me than dealing with my nerves, Gaige. Much more frustrating for me and therefore more of an emotional strain."

Gaige's jaw tensed and the muscles and tendons in his neck corded into thin ribbons beneath his skin. I could almost see the wheels in his head spinning, trying to decide what would be less emotional for me. After what seemed like a long time, the tension in his neck released. "You're determined to do this?"

"Yes. I am. I will beat this, and not by hiding from it."

"Okay," he said. "I could be enough of a buffer to help you through." He rolled his eyes. "And I could be giving myself way too much credit. Either way, if you're going to go full-on at this, I'm going to give you every advantage I can."

He took a few slow, deep breaths and held his arms out to embrace me, but stopped. I hadn't thought about how difficult this could be for a person determined to stay within platonic boundaries. He put his arms down and started over again with the deep breaths then pulled me against him, staying quiet and still. I let myself relax and be open to whatever he was sending my way. Within minutes, my nerves had settled and I was ready to take on the world. Or at least the captain of a spaceship.

"You're good?" he asked.

"I'm good. You?"

"Yeah. Good."

With both our statuses *good* and boundaries maintained, we proceeded hand in hand down the long corridor, passing several doors along the way.

"The bridge is through there," Gaige said, as we passed one of the larger doors. "And this is the captain's private planning room." He pointed to the next, smaller, door. "That's where he'll be. We could cut through the bridge, but I think it would be best to save that for later. Are you sure you're ready?"

I thought for only a second. "Yes, I'm ready."

We stepped up to the door. "One moment, Gaige," the computer voice said, and then the door slid open.

"Come in. I've been anxious to meet our new arrival." Confidence boomed from the captain's voice. It filled the entire room with his presence. His tall, muscular frame reminded me of a warrior. But his eyes twinkled with an ornery streak, just like the mischievous glint I'd seen in Gaige's eyes. The captain's playful personality gleamed from brown irises instead of aqua-blue, though. "Welcome aboard our ship, Victoria."

Gaige gave my shaky hand a squeeze, bolstering my courage.

"Thank you for allowing me on board, sir," I said.

At that moment, the computer voice permeated the room. "Sir, Chessa is requesting permission to see you."

Gaige and the captain looked at each other in silence, like they were having some Anuan mind-meld conversation. I wondered who this Chessa was and why she was worthy of a conversation behind my back, so to speak. A jealous twinge panged my gut.

Gaige pulled me aside. "Victoria, I should have told you something. It's just so hard to know exactly how to manage things right now."

My heart sank. "You said you weren't married." Had he lied? Would he do that? *Could* he do that?

"No, I'm not married. Why would you think—?"

"Girlfriend? You have a girlfriend?"

"No! Oh. Chessa?" Gaige smiled. "No it's nothing like that."

"Ex-girlfriend, then?" My voice seemed distant. Scared.

"Gaige." The captain interrupted. "Why don't we let Chessa in? I think you'll love her, Victoria. It's not what you think."

I could handle anything but what I was thinking. I had to know for sure and the sooner, the better. "Yes, please, let her in."

"Gaige?" The captain said.

"Uh . . ." Gaige looked at my do-as-I-say face and sighed. "Let her in."

"Allow Chessa back," the captain responded to the computer.

After a moment, the door slid open and a little girl with long, brown pigtails bouncing with each step, bounded into the room. Jumping into the Captain's arms, she hugged his neck and began talking to him in Anuan.

A loud sigh escape my lips. Definitely not a girlfriend, present or past. But why did Gaige think he had to tell me something about this girl? "She's not . . ." The tiny words, so small I could barely hear them myself, came out unintended.

"No. Not mine." Gaige whispered. "Remember. Bonding, life commitment."

"Right. Yes. I remember." Remembering was something I could manage to do, apparently with some help. In this situation, the unstable emotions were playing against logic and whatever ability I'd developed to tap into my intuition, and I still couldn't make sense of why Gaige felt he needed to tell me something about this girl.

The captain placed her on the floor and squatted down to her level. "Yes, Chessa, it is bouncy in here today. That's because we have a Kian in our presence. How is your English?"

"Good, I think, Grandpa," she answered, as she looked around the room, searching out the stranger.

"Uncle Gaige!" shc shouted and ran to Gaige with her arms outstretched. "I heard you were back."

Gaige lifted her up when she reached him and gave her a big hug, spinning around with her as he did. "How's my pretty girl?"

"I'm good. We learned about Earth elephants this morning. But I would rather hear about your trip."

"I'll tell you all about it. First I'd like for you to meet Victoria." Gaige turned the little girl, still in his arms, in my direction.

"I know all about you," she said, examining me.

"We'll talk about that later," the captain interrupted. "Shouldn't you be getting back to school?"

"Yes, Grandpa."

Gaige placed the little girl onto the floor. She ran for the door, pigtails swirling.

"Love you, Grandpa. Love you, Uncle Gaige. Nice to meet you, Victoria."

With the little girl gone as quickly as she'd arrived, I was left to catch up on their relationships. If Gaige was this girl's uncle, and the captain was her grandfather, that meant the captain was Gaige's father. Everything made sense now. Gaige was right. He should have told me I was meeting his *father*. Probably the most important man in Gaige's life, and likely to have a critical eye on whomever Gaige might have an interest in. I felt the blood drain from my face and my anxiety level skyrocketed.

"It's okay," Gaige whispered in my ear.

"I hope my son is taking good care of you," the captain said.

He had to realize my painful awareness of their relationship and seemed to be trying to smooth things along. But I couldn't find any words to respond.

"Yes, I'm trying," Gaige said. "I'll be showing her around the ship today."

"Good. Everyone on the ship will help you get acclimated," the captain said.

"Yes, sir. Thank you, sir." My response sounded more like a robot than myself.

"You can call me Daigon."

"Yes, sir. Yes, Daigon." I wanted nothing more than to get out of there. I would have melted into the floor like the Wicked Witch of the West if I could have.

"Gaige why don't you finish showing Victoria around?" The captain sat down behind his desk and appeared to busy himself with something.

Taking his attention away from us helped my skyrocketing nerves a little. The fact that he no longer stood so tall and intimidating helped, too.

"Yes, we have a lot to see," Gaige said. "I'll talk to you later."

"Nice to meet you captain, sir, uh, I mean Daigon . . ."

Gaige guided me, still stammering, from the room. But I was sure I'd be able to find a few choice words for Gaige as soon as I recovered myself.

# CHAPTER 68 - GAIGE

With each step we took away from my father's private planning room, I felt Victoria's anxieties turning to rage, and I prepared myself for what would come. I should have insisted on taking her back to her room when I sensed her nervousness elevating. But forcing her to do something she didn't want to do—no, that wouldn't have gone over well. Instead, I should have told her who she was meeting and let her decide if she wanted to go. Knowing how to best manage Victoria's situation was not easy.

"Why didn't you tell me?" she demanded through clenched teeth.

"I understand meeting someone's family can be a significant and nerve-wracking event to a Kian. I didn't want to stress you with that. I planned to tell you after you met him. I'm sorry. I realize now that was a horrible decision." I tried to take her hand in mine.

"Don't touch me!" She jerked away and moved to the opposite side of the corridor, planting her feet hard with each step she took.

I didn't follow her, trying to give her space. But I kept pace with her on my side. "You wanted to meet someone and he's the most skilled person I know at blocking his energies. I thought that would be the best thing for you right now."

"You should have told me who he was." She continued to stomp down the corridor.

"I should have. I know that now. But I was trying to protect you."

"I don't *need* to be protected. I want to face this. I want to beat it and be done with it!"

"You *do* need protecting. I know you're anxious to get past your transition, but you have to be careful. If you become too emotionally overloaded, the damage could be irrevocable. I won't let that happen!" I had to make her understand. I crossed the corridor and grasped her arm. "Victoria, please stop. Stop and look at me."

She came to a halt and turned in my direction, but her eyes didn't meet mine.

"Please look at me."

Her fists tightened so firmly that blood trickled from her palms where her nails dug into them. She had to go through this, but I couldn't let her hurt herself. I had to find a way to calm her down. The closest door led to the smallest planning room in the bridge corridor. As a mission lead, I had access.

"Access," I said.

Thankfully, the computer system recognized my stress-filled voice and opened. I gently pulled Victoria by the arm into the room so we'd have privacy.

"Why are we going in here?"

"Gaige, it's Zada," I heard through the communication device in my clothing. "We're picking up readings from

Victoria's ship suit that her blood pressure is rising pretty rapidly."

"Got it, Zada," I said.

"Zada? You're talking to Zada?" She ran to the conference table and slammed her fists down on its top over and over. "I don't need a doctor. I can do this myself! I have to learn to control this!" Tears streamed down her flushed face.

I didn't know whether to stop her and comfort her or let her work through her turmoil. But what if it was too much? She dropped to her knees, sobbing. I knelt down next to her. Pulling her against me as tightly as I could without hurting her, I rocked her gently.

"I want to manage this. I *have* to manage this." She sputtered through her sobs.

"You will. Human minds adapt. Right now, yours is working through what's happening to it and learning how to process the new things coming at it. We just have to be careful not to expose you to more than you can handle until that adjustment is complete."

"You said it could be difficult. But . . ." She buried her face in my chest, her hands now relaxed. "I don't want to be like this."

"I know you don't."

She raised her bloodshot eyes. "What if this is who I'll be here?"

"It's not. I can separate your true essence from the turmoil you're going through. This is only temporary. You *will* have peace."

She put her arms around my waist and laid her head back against my chest. “Oh God, how could I have ever been mad at you?”

“You weren’t. Not really.”

Not loosening her grip on me, she sniffed and rubbed her cheek against her shoulder to wipe away the tears. “Gaige?”

“Yes.”

“What you’re keeping from me—it’s big, isn’t it?”

I had to be honest with her, she knew anyway. Her intuition was strong. “Yes, it’s something big.”

She closed her eyes, causing another tear to roll down her cheek. After a moment, she patted my chest, eyes still closed. “And Gaige?”

“Yes, I’m here.”

“You weren’t on Earth for any scientific mission, were you?”

“No. I wasn’t.”

“Okay,” she said, quietly.

Exhausted by her episode, she peacefully fell asleep in my arms. I’d hoped she would. The incident had taken a lot out of her. Her essence was at peace, for now. I still wanted Zada to check her, though. At the very least, her hands needed mending.

“Zada?” I said, quietly.

“I’m here, Gaige.”

“Can you come to Bridge Planning Room #3, please? Victoria is sleeping now, but I’d like for you to examine her.”

When Zada arrived, she scanned Victoria, still in my arms, with her medical wand. She found that no damage had been done, but thought Victoria would sleep for a while. Zada then passed the wand over the gouges on Victoria’s palms. The caked blood disintegrated and the moist, open wounds dried and closed. The pink, crescent-shaped lines lightened, and then disappeared completely. Maybe Victoria would never realize she'd been quite so upset. Even so, she was now one step closer to the peace she deserved, and knowledge of the secret that had been kept from her for so long.

# CHAPTER 69 - LOME

Having pushed the furniture back to give me plenty of room, I sat in the middle of the floor of my dark quarters. I examined the vial of blood in my hand—my means to take General Ash's identity and deal with the scientist as an Earthling. I did not relish the thought of taking on such a disgusting form. But it was imperative to protect my true identity. The existence of the Tamanacke had to be guarded from the Anuans or any others who might be monitoring this primitive planet.

The incompetent general's clothes sat waiting in a neat stack on a chair. Next to that, on a small side table within quick reach, lay a mirror. I laughed at the memory of the general's colleagues dragging his worthless body away to think about what they had seen. Definitely an example set.

I drank the vial of blood. Spreading the residue around in my mouth, I willed the change to begin. The taste of human blood was one of my favorites. I savored every second of the fluid's coppery tang while I waited for the sweet pain to overtake me.

The first twitch struck my right arm, followed by another in my left leg. My body began to spasm, flailing about on the floor. Cramps gripped my muscles, stretching and contorting them. I clutched and massaged every writhing part of my body, trying to work through the pain of transformation. My skin burned, morphing from the tough hide that protected us so well to the soft frailty of human flesh. I raised my hand in time to see my claws shrink and flatten into thin, useless sheets of keratin. After several more excruciating minutes of thrashing around on the floor in full-blown agony, the pain subsided. The metamorphosis was complete. I picked up the mirror to inspect the results and was pleased.

"Well, hello there, General Ash."

# CHAPTER 70 - VICTORIA

After my meltdown over meeting Gaige's father, Gaige insisted we go to the observation deck. He thought he could help me there.

When the ibbs's doors opened, I stepped into the depths of space and floated among its stars. Or so it seemed. Undetectable windows—no framing, no reflections—encircled the entire observation deck. They curved up across the high ceiling to the center of the room where we stood. Nothing but the glass separated us from the universe. Gaige said the room comprised the entire top floor of the ship and was nearly a half-mile wide. Dwarfed by the universe in which I stood, the heavens called to me, pulling me forward.

"Wait a minute," Gaige said.

"What?"

"Just one minute." Gaige stood at a chest-level, square cubbyhole near the ibbs. He spoke a few words and, as if by magic, a blanket appeared within the hole. He removed the blanket and turned toward me. "Okay, now I'm ready. We'll need this."

I reached a finger toward the hole, but stopped before getting too close. "Is that a constructor?"

"Yes, this is a constructor."

"On TV, they would call that a replicator." I grinned up at Gaige.

"You and your television." Gaige laughed. "Well, constructor was my translation from Anuan to English. I suppose replicator will work just as well."

"Or your Anuan word. I can learn some more of those."

I wondered why we needed a blanket, but with the universe calling to me I didn't take time to ask. Nor did I care anymore what we called the cubbyhole. I moved forward, toward the edge of the room, pulling Gaige along by the hand.

As my vision adjusted to the dim light, I began to see people here and there in the darkness. Some of them gazed out into space. Some chatted with others. Some strolled around like the place belonged only to them. The massive expanse of the room allowed everyone to have their own private space, spread out far away from each other. I doubted Gaige would have brought me otherwise.

We reached the edge of the room and I stopped without a word. The pinpoints of starlight shined bright against the black backdrop—not only in whites, but yellows, oranges, reds, and even blues. Distant galaxies glowed among them, radiating their pale-yellow auras. Some lay flat, their discs no more than thin lines in the darkness. Others reached out with spiral arms like tiny pinwheels in the night. Across the scene, as if it had been swiped through with a paintbrush full of glitter, the Milky Way sparkled with grandeur.

"I've never seen anything so breathtaking." I placed my hand on the window, feeling the beauty of it like I'd touched a living being.

Gaige let me stare into space for a long while. I could feel him watching me. Finally, I turned around. “I love this place. Thank you for bringing me here.”

“I knew you’d love it. It’s my favorite place.” Gaige spread the blanket on the floor. “If the ship changes position, we’ll be able to see some of the planets in your system, too.” Gaige gestured toward the blanket on the floor. “Here, lie down.”

I lay down and looked up into the heavens above. Gaige quietly stretched out next to me. Before either of us could speak a word, I became dizzy and my vision blurred.

“Relax,” Gaige said. “Just let it happen.”

*It?*

“Relax,” Gaige said, again. “It’s okay.” He took my hands and opened my clenched fists. “Let your body relax. Let the tension flow through your body from its core to your hands and feet. Let it escape out into the universe through your fingers and toes. Visualize it flowing away from you.”

I pretended to push the tension from my stomach, my heart, and my gut to my extremities. Releasing it from my body, I saw it float away like errant shreds of paper on a windy day. My muscles loosened and my body rested light on the blanket. “That worked. My body’s relaxed.”

“Now your thoughts. Close your eyes and relax your mind. Let go of any worries, any thoughts. Pretend they fly off, like birds. Or butterflies. However you want to imagine it. Giving your feelings a visual component can help when you’re learning.”

I closed my eyes and imagined all my worries drifting away. They became lightning bugs—no, not fast enough. They became humming birds, darting quickly away. The weight of all the thoughts they represented left me. Lighter now than the air I breathed, I felt as if I were floating up, rising higher and higher. The observation deck no longer confined me. My world expanded to the edges of the universe. I hovered, suspended in the middle of everything that existed. I felt the stars, and the planets, and the people. They were a part of me, and I was a part of them. My consciousness melded with it all. I felt an inherent belonging, a connection. I was one with the universe. It took my breath away and I gasped to catch it.

"It's okay," Gaige said, softly.

The sound of his voice resonated throughout my body and mixed with a euphoria I'd never felt before.

"*What's happening?*" I asked him in my thoughts. Too overwhelmed to speak, I knew he'd still hear.

Silently, he responded. *"You're learning what you're capable of."*

I didn't try to fight the experience. It was too overpowering to resist. I allowed my soul to float peacefully, mingling with the heavenly bodies of the universe.

After some time in the pure bliss, I opened my eyes again. Though my mind had been drifting through the heavens, I still lay in the observation deck, with the stars looking down upon me and Gaige by my side.

He propped himself up on an elbow and leaned over me. He affectionately ran his finger down the side of my face. "You're ability to connect is extraordinary. What do you think?"

I looked up into Gaige's aqua eyes. Their beauty equaled the majesty of the stars behind him. "That was . . . it was incredible."

"There is an interconnectedness between the universe and all beings in it, beyond that of the physical senses. You have a significant gift in your ability to connect with that."

"*All* beings? So all humans have *this* potential, too? Like with the other traits I have?"

"Not only humans, but every living thing. Not all beings choose to develop it, though, which can be unfortunate. Especially for the ones who become technologically advanced, but who don't gain the broader mindset needed to respect what they have, and each other."

I thought of Earth's murders and wars. Its people disrespected each other on both small and large scales. Tears welled up in my eyes and a lump formed in my throat. I tried to swallow it down.

"I'm sorry, Victoria." Gaige wiped a tear away, catching it as it escaped over my lashes. "I shouldn't have said that."

"No, it's true. Not saying it doesn't make it go away."

"Let's focus on this place," Gaige said. "It's too beautiful to waste talking about such things."

"You're right. Lie back down with me."

Gaige shifted his weight off his elbow and lay next to me. I snuggled into the crease of his arm and rested my head on his chest. He tensed. His breathing became shallow, like he was afraid to move enough to even take a breath. Gaige's muscles relaxed a little more with each second that passed. When he no longer felt like a coil ready to spring loose, he curled his arm around me.

"It is beautiful," I said. "I could stay forever."

"The universe can help you through your transition. And anything else. I'll teach you to use it to find peace and guidance.

All you have to do is reach out to it. Go to that place you just were. There, you'll understand things in a broader perspective. You'll find the balance you need and your exposure to us will eventually become effortless."

"Do you really think so?"

"I know so. It won't happen all at once, but it *will* happen. You just have to be patient."

# CHAPTER 71 - LOME

Cruck entered my quarters. Without a word, he walked up to me, within inches of the face. He leaned forward and peered into the eyes. Taking a step back, he scanned the figure all the way down to the floor and back up again. He shook his head like he was trying to shatter the vision. "Ugh, you're difficult to look at right now, Lome,"

"Yes, I know. Ugly creatures aren't they?"

"The shift was perfect," Cruck said, gawking and angling his head this way and that to get every perspective. "I can't tell the difference. But they all look alike to me." He touched the hair, and then pressed the smooth backside of his claw into the cheek.

"Be careful, you'll tear it. They're fragile creatures." I stumbled away from Cruck, still trying to learn how to maneuver the human body. He'd examined enough. The shift had gone well. There would be no questions.

"Why do this, Lome? These humans will handle the scientist with only a word from you. Why do it *personally*?"

"Because, it is personal! And because these stupid Earthlings botch everything they touch. You were young when we arrived here, Cruck, but listen to my words. They provided us refuge, but that's about all they've managed to do correctly. We have watched their mistakes time and again. The mess they made with the mother, for one. Granted, the refugees were still weak, but they made a poor decision enlisting the Earthlings' help with that. Even in our crippled state, we'd have done a better job alone."

"They are exceedingly incompetent," Cruck said, still ogling the human form to which I'd reduced myself.

"When I took control of what was left of our kind, I vowed to be patient until our population and our armies could rebuild. That time is drawing near, and now these perpetually incompetent Earthlings have let the girl—the most precious piece of my revenge—transition off Earth right in front of their faces! I will have no more mistakes. *That* is why I'm doing this *personally*. The scientist will pay for interfering with the girl, and he will pay at *my* hands."

# CHAPTER 72 - VICTORIA

Gaige scooped the blanket from the floor of the observation deck while I, once more, scanned the countless stars and galaxies suspended around us. Even with the scene spread out in front of me, it was hard to believe such breathtaking beauty actually existed. My imagination could never have come up with such a vision. But now I had it, etched in my mind forever.

Gaige hesitantly put his arm around my shoulder. His gesture could only be supportive right now—adjustment first. He'd made that clear. After a couple uncomfortable emotional episodes, I understood better why it had to be that way. I was grateful he hadn't completely stepped away from me, and that he was trying to manage touching me again. Even if it had to stay on a small scale. Not experiencing his touch at all would have been like living in a desert without water. I put my arm around his waist and patted his side. A silent *thank you* for his effort.

"This is my favorite place on the entire ship." He'd told me that already, but it was worth hearing again.

"I think it will be mine, too," I said.

I hated to leave. That place reached in and touched the soul. But there was so much more to see. When we reached the constructor cubby near the ibbs, I watched Gaige place the blanket inside, where it disappeared as magically as it had appeared.

"Come here," Gaige said. "I want to show you how to use this." He positioned me in front of the constructor and dictated instructions over my shoulder for me to carry out.

With Gaige's help, I brought the blanket back then sent it away again. "It's easier than I thought it would be."

"Yes. Now you can order whatever you want—clothes, food, anything—whenever you want."

Gaige and I left the observation deck to see the rest of the ship, but moved through almost-empty corridors. No doubt a part of Gaige's strategy to keep me tucked away in a safe little bubble. I didn't want to remain in a bubble, though. More and more, I felt like I'd wither up and die if I couldn't mix with these people. Convincing Gaige to allow that would be like moving a mountain. But I had to try.

"Gaige, I want to see the people. Meeting your Dad didn't upset me, beyond a little nervousness. It was the fact that you lied about it that affected me so much. I handled the *people* part fine."

He shook his head. "It's not a good idea."

Anger started to build inside of me, like dynamite nearing detonation. I told myself to be rational, to stay calm. Gaige had his reason—protecting me. But my fury burned, ready to consume me in a hot flash.

"Victoria, you're angry with me, aren't you?"

I gritted my teeth and tried to reason with myself that I shouldn't be this upset. He was only trying to help me. I should be grateful and appreciative. And I was. But at the same time, I was also damn mad. "Yes, Gaige. I'm angry with you. But I'm really trying not to be."

"Seating," Gaige said, and a bench rotated out from the wall. "You can't help how you feel. Sit with me and let's see if we can work through this." Gaige sat and waited patiently for me to join him.

I didn't want to sit or talk. I wanted to be allowed to blend in.

Gaige held his hand out to me. "Please, Victoria."

I ignored his hand, but sat. "I don't want to be isolated. I don't want to be the alien. I want to be a part of this world. Please let me be with the people. Help mc fit in here."

"Victoria, I understand how you feel—"

"Oh, you're a displaced Earthling? I didn't realize that."

"That's not what I meant."

The hurt in his eyes reached inside me, like someone had stabbed me in the heart. My anger dissipated immediately and I hugged him. "I'm sorry."

He stroked my back. "It's okay. I know you can't help it."

"It's so strange that I can't control these irrational feelings. I know they don't make sense."

"That's part of adjusting to us. These emotional extremes seem completely illogical, but they're not. Not really. You're trying to sort out the higher levels of emotional energy the Anuans emit. The illogical extremes are just a part of that process. You're making progress, though, even if it doesn't seem like it yet. Look how much shorter this episode was than the last. You're putting your new environment in order, slowly but surely."

While I snuggled against Gaige, he continued to rub my back, smooth my hair, and massage my neck. All of it soothed me. I loved him. I wanted him. But no amount of wanting could bring us together. I had to get through the rest first—whatever that entailed. He'd made that clear.

I raised my head. "I'll do whatever you think is best."

"I have an idea," he said. "What if I show you some of the places where many people go? But for now you'd have to promise to watch from a distance."

I jumped up. "Yes! I promise."

A smile spread across his face. "Okay, I'll show you one of our binmars."

I grabbed him by the arm, pulling him up. "Yes, a binmar. I want to see a binmar. What's a binmar?"

He laughed. "I'll show you."

We reached the end of a corridor that opened up into a large gathering area filled with shops, restaurants, galleries, and a number of more dynamic activities to keep the Anuans entertained during their off hours. The Anuans and Earthlings had taken different paths many centuries before, but it appeared both craved the same social connections.

I moved forward, drawn to the people.

Gaige grabbed my arm and pulled me back into the corridor. "This is close enough."

"But I feel fine."

Gaige didn't let go. "You're fine now, but remember how quickly that can change."

I relaxed, resigning myself to watch the people from where we stood. "Okay, I did promise."

Almost an hour later, I still stood in the same place, leaning a shoulder against the corridor wall, peering out into the binmar. Gaige sat on a bench, holding a display tablet he'd retrieved from the wall. He was supposed to be reviewing information regarding his mission to see Brian—who he'd assured me was still fine—but every time I looked at him, he was watching me.

"Would you like to see some other things now?" Gaige finally asked.

"Oh. Okay. Do we have to go through nearly empty hallways? Look at all the people at the binmar. We're not that far away and I'm doing fine."

He pushed himself up from the bench and returned the tablet to the wall, where it blended in smoothly. "Well . . ."

"Please, Gaige?" I locked my hands together and held them under my chin in a praying—or begging—posture. "Please?"

He rolled his eyes and tilted his head back. "Uh, how can I say no to that?" He put his face in his hands, let out a groan, and then looked back at me with a sigh. "All right, maybe we can take a route that's not *quite* so isolated."

On our new route, we only saw a few more people than we'd seen in the other mostly desolate hallways. It was progress, though, and I was doing so well, Gaige had even started introducing me to people we passed. He knew them all and had something personal to say to each one. *How is this project? How is that relative?* The Anuans were like one big, happy family. I had no idea how many people were on the ship. I guessed it must have been hundreds, because I could feel the presence of each and every one of them.

We were about to pass a young couple. I happily prepared myself for another introduction. As the couple came closer, they seemed to blur, divide, and come back together again, before waffling wildly. My chest tightened and I couldn't get air.

"Victoria, what's wrong?" Gaige asked.

"I can't breathe. I can't breathe." I sucked in empty breaths that couldn't satisfy the need of my lungs. My body weakened, as if every ounce of energy I possessed had been sucked out all at once. I couldn't keep Gaige in my sight as a single individual. He shattered then re-formed, only to break apart again, just as the couple had. I tried hard to pull in air, but nothing came.

"Liiiiiink tooooo Zaaaaadaaaaa." I heard Gaige say in a slow, deep slur as my surroundings dimmed.

# CHAPTER 73 - GAIGE

I reached my arm out just in time to catch Victoria before she hit the floor. I clutched her to me. Her head rolled against my chest and her hair fell across her face. She inhaled a long breath and exhaled peacefully. At least she could breathe now.

Zada's voice resonated in my ear. "We picked up the readings from Victoria's monitors. Her condition deteriorated quickly. We didn't have a chance to warn you. Is she still unconscious?"

"Yes. I'm bringing her to sickbay."

I held her close, hoping she wouldn't suffer any negative effects from her episode. The couple I was about to introduce Victoria to offered to help. I knew there was nothing they could do, so they went on their way, continuing to send Victoria positive thoughts for recovery.

The corridors we'd been traveling through weren't that busy. And I'd only introduced her to one or two people at a time. Maybe she'd reached a level where distance was no longer a boundary. The numbers Zada recorded showed she had that potential. If she'd reached that level already, I wouldn't be able to protect her from being bombarded by the energy of everybody on the ship at once, regardless of how isolated I kept her.

I rushed into sickbay. Zada stood waiting, a bed already extended for Victoria.

"She didn't have any emotional upset," I said. "She seemed happy, and then she just collapsed."

I laid Victoria on the bed, then took her limp hand in mine. I brushed the hair away from her face and watched her, still breathing comfortably.

"No damage has been done," Zada said, after scanning Victoria's entire body. She shut off her medical wand and leaned back against the edge of the bed. "We saw a quick spike in her numbers and then they leveled back out immediately. Instead of struggling against her new environment, it appears her system is reaching out to it now, but shutting itself down before it gets too overwhelmed. Her body has learned to protect itself, buffering any overloads before they-become harmful."

Victoria's hand seemed so small and fragile in mine. "She shouldn't have had to protect herself. *I* should have been doing that for her. Instead, I let her do too much."

"No, Gaige. She needs to learn to live among us and flow with our consciousness. It appears her being is craving that anyway, and reaching out for it. We couldn't stop it if we wanted to, no matter how isolated we tried to keep her. Stifling her need to connect to us could only make matters worse."

"So what do I need to do now?"

"Now that we know her system is beginning to manage itself, and won't allow too much, we can let her dictate the pace. It will be best for her that way. Just know there's a potential for these kinds of episodes, where she shuts down to give herself a break. They'll last as long as they need to. She could be past the worst of her adjustment—here on the ship anyway."

I pinched the bridge of my nose, forcing back the tension in my forehead. “And beyond that?”

“If she stays, she may have some more adjusting to do when we get to Anu. For now, just watch her closely and let her manage this exactly how she wants.”

# CHAPTER 74 - TAS

I threw the stress orb hard across Daigon's office. It slammed into the wall and quickly rebounded. By the time it reached me, it had slowed itself enough to float into my hand. "I'm telling you, Daigon, this is not sitting well with me. I cannot think of any technologically advanced beings other than the Tamanacke who would interfere with an emerging civilization. And it *does* seem that the Kians had help." I flung the orb again, at the opposite wall this time.

Daigon sprung from his chair and seized the sphere out of its flight path. "Tas, I hope you're wrong." He tossed the orb back to me, walked around to the front of his desk, and leaned back against its edge. "But we can't take any chances. Gaige will be down there soon. If the Tamanacke do still exist and are influencing the Kians, Gaige needs to be informed of exactly what that could mean. Not just hear about the possibility of their involvement as a passing reference. The Council should be told as well. This is one time they wouldn't be able to warn us. The Tamanacke are dead to us whether they live or not. But maybe The Council has felt things *around* the Tamanacke that they couldn't interpret. Knowing our suspicions might help them paint a complete picture of what they may be sensing."

"Yes, I agree. The Council should be informed, as should Gaige." I squeezed the orb in my fist. "Daigon, if there were Tamanacke refugees, and they took shelter on Earth, that means Victoria has been at terrible risk all these years—"

Daigon clasped a hand on my shoulder. "Tas, don't do this to yourself."

"And what if she wants to stay on Earth?"

"Victoria is here and she's doing well. Let's move forward for now and take this one day at a time. I'll talk to Gaige and The Council."

Daigon spoke with calm reason, but his eyes had grown stern and his energy had hardened. He knew as well as I did, if the Tamanacke still existed, they'd want revenge. It would only be a matter of time before we were met with their violence again.

# CHAPTER 75 - VICTORIA

I opened my eyes and saw Gaige leaning over me. "How do you feel?" he asked.

I squinted at him until he came into solid focus. "You're intact. No waffling or breaking apart now. What happened?"

"You're adjusting, that's all."

I closed my eyes. "I'm sorry."

"There's nothing to be sorry for."

I opened one eye partway, not quite sure I was really ready to wake. "Sickbay?"

"Yes."

The familiar smell of spring rain lingered close. I fully opened both eyes. My comforter lay over me, tucked snuggly under my chin. "You brought my comforter?"

"Constructed. I thought it would make you feel more comfortable."

"It does." I pushed the comforter down enough to free my arms. "I thought things were getting better."

"They are. You were only out for a couple of hours. Not nearly as long as the last time. And you didn't have any emotional episode first. You're learning to process what's coming at you instead of struggle with it."

"I am?"

"Yes, but it's still a lot to manage. So your system will take breaks, like it just did, when things get to be too much. Your adjustment isn't over for you yet, but you've taken a step in the right direction."

"So you won't have to be quite so protective, then?" I said, doubtful my progress would make a difference in Gaige's overseeing.

Still hovering over me like a mother hen, he stepped back to give me room to sit up. "Well, maybe not *quite* so protective."

I smiled, thinking how much I appreciated him being there. I ran my fingers through my hair to straighten out any waves that might have gone astray while I slept.

"Are you ready to go back to your room? Zada said you're fine to leave whenever you want."

"I'm more than ready."

Gaige helped me from the bed and we left sickbay. Though I'd spent a good part of the day sleeping off the episodes I'd had, I plodded along, exhausted. Gaige had to pause every few steps to keep from leaving me behind.

"I know today wore you out," Gaige said.

"Yes, it did. I'm really tired."

"Well, not only does Anu have longer days, it also has longer nights. You'll be able to get plenty of sleep. We'll do some more things tomorrow, but we'll take it slow."

"Are you off-duty tomorrow, too?"

Gaige had stopped again, waiting on me to catch up. "Yes, I'll be with you tomorrow, too. I want to make sure you're familiar with the ship before I leave you on your own. But even when I'm not with you, Bec can help you, or Conner, or anyone else on the ship. And I'm always just a link away."

"Link?"

"Yes, our communication devices."

"Oh, that's what you call them."

Gaige watched our feet as we walked now, making an effort to keep pace with my small, slow stride. "Yes. All you have to do is say *link to Gaige* or *Victoria to Gaige* or even just *Gaige.* If I'm not with you and my name is not part of a conversation the computer will recognize that and *link* you to me. It works the same for others, too."

"Or I could just talk to you in my thoughts," I said, rather proud of myself for already managing that skill.

"Yes, you could. As well as you're coming along, we could probably start practicing that some. *But,* in case you can't manage it for whatever reason—too tired, upset, whatever—you have the link."

"Okay, I have the link. But I'm sure I'll be fine. I'm used to being by myself. You don't have to worry about me."

Gaige interlocked his arm in mine to help me along, apparently giving up on trying to reduce his pace. "I want to make sure you're safe. There's nothing wrong with that. While we're on the topic, don't forget about the difference in gravity. You don't want to end up in distress. And don't get around large groups of people by yourself until we're sure about how you're progressing, in case numbers and proximity are still a factor. You may be beyond guarding against that, but let's be safe."

"I know, I know, Gaige. I'll be careful. Stop worrying so much."

After a few more subtle cautions and warnings, we arrived at my quarters. The door opened on its own, letting us back into my virtual bedroom. Gaige explained how common rooms opened to anybody, but my private room would only open automatically to my presence. Accessorized suits, transitioning, constructors, floating elevators, doors that recognized their owners. How much more remained for me to discover? I couldn't wait to learn about every last detail.

"Well, goodnight. I'll stop back in the morning. Don't forget—all you have to do is say *link to Gaige* if you need anything."

Gaige removed his arm from mine, but I grabbed it back, almost panicked. "Wait! Aren't you coming in?"

"I thought you were tired?"

"I'm not tired enough to want you to leave. You can come in for a minute, can't you?"

A dimpled grin crept onto Gaige's face and I knew he was about to say something ornery. "Well, okay. I suppose you're too tired to misbehave."

"*Me*?"

Gaige gave me a playful poke in the stomach and sat down in my parson's chair.

As affronted as I'd feigned, I'd have misbehaved with him in a heartbeat. But for the time being, I'd settle for just having him with me. I kicked off my shoes and sprawled face up on the bed, so glad to be in for the night. "Ah, I could lie here for a week."

"If that's what you want to do."

I rolled onto my side, facing Gaige. "No, not really. I'd go stir-crazy by noon."

Gaige eyed me suspiciously, his brow wrinkled. Not quite his worried face, but something stirred in that brain of his.

"While you're lying there, take a deep breath and try to clear your head."

"I don't want to clear my head. It's full of all the nice things I saw today."

"Just for a minute," Gaige said.

"Why?"

"There may come a time when your head is full of not so nice things. Remember in the observation deck, we talked about letting the universe help you through all this?"

"Yes, I remember."

"So let's practice."

"Okay." I flopped onto my back again and rooted myself into a comfortable position. "What do I need to do?"

"Start by taking several slow, deep breaths. Then try and clear your mind. Relax, like before. Visualize any stress, or worries, any random thoughts, floating away from you."

Closing my eyes, I slowly inhaled and then exhaled. I repeated the actions several times, while trying to push everything away. All the worries—the running, the acclimation—began to leave me in streaming ribbons of blacks and grays, until only lightness remained and I floated away into a bliss of everything that existed.

"Perfect. Keep your eyes closed and keep doing what you're doing. Breathe. Stay relaxed. Keep your thoughts calm." The legs of my parson's chair scuffed briefly on my hardwood floor, being lessened of their burden. Then the edge of my mattress slanted toward the weight of Gaige's body seated next to me. "We call this finding balance. It gives us perspective in order to deal with some of the tougher things in life."

Back amongst the stars, the planets, the beings, I understood exactly what Gaige meant. "The hate and the pain and the ugliness, it's so small here. Like it doesn't even exist."

"That's right," he whispered.

Keeping my eyes closed so as not to break the spell, I reached for Gaige and, finding his hand, gripped it tight. I wanted him there with me. Not on the bed in my room, but away from our bodies and together in the bliss.

And now Gaige was with me. The two of us hovered weightlessly in the center of the universe with nothing else—no problems, no differences, no secret. He wove through me and me through him, fuzzing—

"No!" Gaige jerked his hand from mine and stood up, stumbling into the chair. "Um, I'm sorry. It's just that . . . it's late." Gaige's breath came in ragged gasps. With his eyes closed, he inhaled long and deep and blew the air out slowly. He opened his eyes again, having only marginally regained his composure. "You . . . you'd better get ready for bed." He forced a smile onto his face that didn't match the strain in his eyes or the trembling of his hands.

I blinked, confused. I couldn't quite orient myself after being jolted from the peaceful place where *something* had started to happen between us.

"I'll stay until I know you're settled." Gaige's smile had faded, but he brought it back to life in an even less successful attempt than the first to act like nothing had happened.

"No!" I scrambled off the bed in a fury, leaving my comforter in a wad. Puffed up like a peacock ready to fight, I faced Gaige nose to nose, or rather, nose to chest. "Something was happening, with us, between us. Why did you stop it?"

Gaige ran a hand through his hair and fidgeted like a child in church. “I’m sorry. I shouldn’t have let you touch me. I didn’t think it could . . . you could . . . you’re . . . I need to keep in mind what you could be capable of.”

“What was happening, Gaige?”

“Nothing.” He looked away when he spoke the words, but *only* when he spoke the words. His eyes were back on me right afterward. He was lying.

“It wasn’t nothing. Back at the motel, you told me your people bonded on levels I wasn’t even aware of. That, a minute ago, that was part of it, wasn’t it?”

Gaige didn’t answer. His mouth hung open with nothing coming out.

“Wasn’t it!” I screamed.

“No.” He looked away again when he spoke.

“Look at me when you speak. So you can’t lie to me again.”

He looked me dead in the eyes, his face set firm. “All right! Yes. That was part of it. The beginnings of it, anyway. We not only bond physically, we bond mentally, emotionally, at the soul level. But it’s not happening, with us. Not right now, at least. I won’t let it happen. I have to go.”

He moved toward the door and I could have sworn a piece of my heart physically tore loose to follow him out. The pain of it dropped me to my knees. “No! Don’t go.” I clutched at my chest, expecting to see an open, bleeding wound beneath my hands.

Gaige turned back, wincing, with his fist over his own heart. “I won’t.” He pulled me to my feet and held me, easing the pain in my chest. “I won’t go. I *can’t*. At least not right now.” He shook his head. “Tas was right,” he mumbled.

"Tas? Conner's Dad? Your mission commander?" I looked up at Gaige. "Right about what?"

"Never mind," he said. "I'm trying so hard not to complicate your life until you can get it all sorted out. Can we please put this on pause? *Please?* Can you do that for me, because I'm trying so hard to do that for you? We need to be strong for each other. Can we do that?"

I lifted my head from his chest enough to look up at him. Moisture gathered in his eyes, not quite tears, but close enough. How could I not do anything possible to ease his pain—a pain I felt right along with him?

"Pause. I can do that. *For us*. I don't like it. I don't even think I agree with it anymore. But I'll trust you. For *us*, I'll trust you."

We stood looking at each other, wondering what followed pause.

"So . . .," Gaige said.

"So . . .," I said.

"I think you were going to get ready for bed. You're tired, right?"

"Yes, exhausted. I'll get ready for bed." I took one slow step toward my bathroom and stopped, checking. No pain. A residual ache, but no pain. I took another step. Still no pain.

"I think it will be okay, now," Gaige said. "I'm not leaving and you know that. It should be okay."

I walked, not too fast, to my bathroom to change. I grabbed a nightgown out of my drawer on the way. Still no pain. When I'd finished changing and came out of the bathroom, Gaige stood staring out the window at my Ohio yard—a frozen landscape on a pause of its own. The view of space would have been a much more beautiful sight. But as much as I wanted to be there and wanted to be with Gaige, I wasn't ready to let go of my Earth world.

"Gaige?"

He turned. "Good, you're ready for bed. You've had a long day."

"Are you going to leave now? *Can* you leave? Not that I want you to."

Dark circles smudged the skin under his eyes. His coloring had faded by at least a shade or two. "I could now, *maybe*. But I won't. I don't want to leave you upset. I'll sleep on the floor. But only sleep, Victoria. Nothing else."

"Nothing else," I agreed.

"Okay, I'll order some blankets for the floor."

A constructor—the perfect distraction. "I have a constructor? Where is it?"

Gaige raised his eyebrows. He probably recognized the same opportunity for distraction as I had. "Yes, you have one. It should be over here somewhere." He went to the wall on the opposite side of my bed, near the corner, and squatted down. "It's right here." He tapped the wall twice and a drawer popped open. "This constructor will work like the one I taught you to use in the observation deck."

Gaige let me practice constructing by having me order several more ship suits in various colors and his blankets for the night. My constructor gave me exactly what I'd asked for each time. We'd found something to follow pause.

Gaige looked at the new ship suits draped over my arm and grinned. "You'll look like an alien in those."

I remembered him looking so out of place on Earth in his alien flight suit and me saying the same thing to him. "That's okay, Anuan. I'm not trying to blend in on Earth, so I'm allowed to."

He had a way of breaking tension that I always appreciated. This time was no exception. I hung my new ship suits in my closet while Gaige spread the blankets on the floor. He stretched out, settling into his makeshift bed.

Without thinking, I knelt down where he lay to give him a quick goodnight kiss, but caught myself in time. "Uh . . ." Only inches from him, I lost myself in his face. The aqua of his eyes. The straight edge of his nose. The square cut of his jawline—

"Goodnight, Victoria."

"Oh. Yes. Goodnight, Gaige," I whispered. "And thank you for staying."

"You're welcome. Sleep well." Gaige turned away from me and pulled a cover I knew he didn't need over his shoulder.

I climbed underneath my rumpled comforter and ordered the lights to lower. They did. I wanted to be with Gaige, but did the next best thing instead. *"Good night, Gaige,"* I said in my thoughts.

*"Good night, Victoria,"* he answered.

A few seconds passed, and then Gaige added something more. *"By the way, you amaze me."*

I lay in my bed, grinning from ear to ear over his compliment. When Gaige's breathing turned to the slow, rhythmic pattern of deep sleep, I quietly eased out of bed. An invisible rope pulled me toward him. He wanted me. Even as he slept, his body summoned me and I couldn't deny him. Dragging my comforter with me, I crawled up next to him on the floor. I lay down as carefully as I could so as not to wake him. I had to be with him on so many levels. But lying there still and silent as he slept, so close I could feel his body heat, was all I would allow that night. I'd given him my word—we were on pause—and I'd keep it.

# CHAPTER 76 - LOME

Surrounded by nothing but wasted open fields, I pressed the gas pedal to the floor. My effort gained only a negligible increase in speed. Typical for such a primitive vehicle. Cruck, now in a human form that he despised, sat beside me, seething with impatience over the trip, though he dare not voice it. The inefficient mode of transport *was* cause for frustration. More than Cruck could even fully comprehend, being too young to remember the Tamanacke in our glory days when we had unprecedented technologies these Earthlings couldn't even imagine. He'd seen enough of what we'd recovered, though, to understand that an automobile was a ridiculous method of getting anywhere. Thus, the reason I brought him. We could alternate driving the inadequate hunk of metal in order to make better time.

For a moment, I had rethought my decision to drive to this *Ohio*. But, no. A plane would have been too risky. The general was not a pilot and my intolerance of humans would not have allowed for any of those imbeciles to shuttle me in one of their flying cans.

"How much longer?" Cruck asked, shifting in his seat.

"We've barely started, Cruck. Be patient!"

“Are you sure we couldn’t use the transition pod? We’d be there in seconds. It would be helpful with keeping our equipment tested, too.”

I gritted the flat excuses for teeth together, annoyed. “We cannot expose our presence on Earth. Especially now. We’ve managed to stay hidden from the Anuan science teams all these years, but after the Anuan’s less than flawless escape with the girl, they’ll be watching Earth closely. They’ll understand the Earth-humans could never have managed to track them the way we did. Unless we get lazy and do things like exposing ourselves by using Tamanacke transport technology for this incidental retribution, they’ll have no reason to suspect us—an extinct race. Or so they think.”

“Whatever you think is best, Lome.” Cruck leaned his head against the door and closed his thin, single eyelids.

Better he sleep than annoy me. Whether either of us liked it or not, things had to be this way. We had to remain patient, something the Tamanacke inherently lacked. Even with my guidance, they still struggled to endure anything short of immediate action. I’d be vigilant about keeping them on track, though. The element of surprise was crucial for our ultimate plan.

# CHAPTER 77 - VICTORIA

I screamed and sat bolt upright from the floor, where I'd fallen asleep next to Gaige. The snake eyes faded and my room came into focus.

Gaige was on his feet in a split second. "What is it? What's wrong?"

A thin layer of sweat covered my body. I balled my hands into fists to steady their uncontrollable shaking. "Nothing."

"Nothing?" Gaige knelt down beside me. "You're scared. I can feel it. What is it? Another dream?"

"I'm okay."

"What was it about?"

"I don't want to talk about it." I drew my legs up against my body and rested my forehead on my knees, wanting more than anything *not* to remember those eyes. "I don't. I don't want to talk about it."

"Okay." Gaige ran his hand up and down my back. "You don't have to talk about it. If it's too traumatic, maybe it's best you not, until you're ready."

I raised my head and saw Gaige's worried look etched into his brow. "Gaige, your face is going to freeze like that. Stop worrying. It was only a dream. I'll be fine."

He brushed his fingers across my check so gently it was hard to believe the same hand had torn open a cage back at the lab. I leaned into his touch. He pulled his hand back, like the exchange was more than his willpower could withstand. I didn't realize how much I needed his comfort until he pulled it away. I remembered how my father used to rock me in his arms after these kinds of dreams. I needed that connection and missed it now more than ever.

"Gaige, I miss them."

"Who?"

"My parents. My biological ones. It's been years. Why do I miss them so much now?"

"I'm sorry, Victoria."

Gaige slid his arms around the back of my neck and pulled me against him. He rocked me back and forth in that familiar way. I rested my head on his shoulder, remembering my father. Memories of my adoptive parents—my aunt and uncle—came to me as well. They'd always protected me, kissed the boo-boos, and made me feel better. Just like my father—and mother—had done. Just like Gaige was doing now.

"I miss my aunt and uncle, too. What if they realize I'm gone and they're worried sick?" Could I leave them behind like they meant nothing to me? I felt as if the two worlds might tear me apart—Gaige and this place or my family and my home. How could I come out of this experience whole regardless of which side I chose?

"Would you like to talk to them?" he said.

I raised my head from Gaige's shoulder. "I could talk to them right now?"

"I think I could make that happen."

"Yes! I'd love to."

Gaige released me and started a link conversation with someone named Pags. I could only hear Gaige's side of the conversation, of course, but after a moment he nodded to me and smiled. "Pags is connecting to them now. It will look like they're receiving a call from your cell phone."

The familiar sound of a ringing phone came into the room and then the sound of my mother's sweet voice. "Tori! It's so good to hear from you."

"Hi, Mom!"

"Dad's on, too."

"Hi, Honey," Dad said.

"Hi, Dad. How are you two?"

"We're good," Mom answered first. "How's . . . Ohio?"

"Ohio's, uh." I glanced at the window. Since I was still sitting on the floor with Gaige, I couldn't see out, but knew how to answer. "Ohio's cold."

We chatted for a while about nothing particularly important. Just hearing their voices and knowing they weren't on a nationwide manhunt to find me made me feel better.

After I'd finished talking to them, I had the strangest feeling.

"What's wrong?" Gaige asked. "I thought you'd be too excited to sit still after talking with your parents."

"Oh, I am. I feel so much better knowing they don't think I've been kidnapped or something. It's just . . . I don't know. Maybe it's that they weren't worried at all. That's the first time I've spoken to my dad since I left for college that he hasn't given me some kind of warning or precaution to take. Keep your doors locked, don't go out after dark, don't drive on icy roads. You know."

Gaige nodded. He did know. He was just like him.

"Reminds me of you, as a matter of fact."

"People who care for you are allowed to worry about you." Gaige stood up and scooped the blankets off the floor. He deposited them in the constructor and sent them away. "I think now is a good time for your surprise."

"Another one?" I said, standing up.

"People who care about you can also surprise you as many times and as often as they want." He returned from the constructor. "So are you ready?"

"Sure. Let's have it."

"Say, 'Access Victoria's personal files.' It has to be your voice."

"Access Victoria's personal files," I said.

"Accessing," the computer voice responded.

"Now say, 'Photos,' " Gaige told me.

"Photos," I said.

"Specify," the computer replied.

I looked at Gaige. "What now?"

"I had all your phone information uploaded to the ship. All your pictures are here. Which one would you like to see? Just describe it—the people, the date, anything to start narrowing it down. The computer will find what you're looking for."

"My pictures? Are here?"

"Yes. Which one would you like to see?" Gaige asked.

"All of them! I want to see all photos!" I told the computer.

Hundreds of photos materialized in the air, filling my entire room with projected images. I ran through the scenes of my life, touching my families' faces in scene after scene. I stopped in front of one of the many old pictures I'd scanned and uploaded before I left for college. It was of me as a toddler with my birth parents. I looked into the face of my mother and my emotions started to crumble.

Gaige stepped up behind me. “Breathe,” he said.

“What?”

“Balance yourself, like I showed you.”

I sat down on the floor where I could be more relaxed. Gaige sat next to me.

“Go ahead. Breathe,” he said.

With all my pictures hanging over my head, I inhaled deeply several times. My mind cleared. My nerves calmed. I drifted away. I could feel the energies of all the beings of the universe, including my parents. “I can feel them, Gaige.”

“They’ll always be with you. Death is not an end. It’s just a transition.”

“Then I can always have them with me?”

“Yes, always.”

“Thank you, Gaige.” I scooted as close to him as I could and laid my head on his shoulder. “I love you.”

He put his arms around me and tilted his head down against mine. “And I love you.”

We were as close to each other as we could possibly be without crossing any boundaries. We sat. And we held each other. And we loved. No *bonding* was necessary for that.

# CHAPTER 78 - GAIGE

Sitting in front of my space-view window, waiting on Victoria to get ready for the day, I wondered about the dreams she was having. She'd had them around the time of her parents' deaths and now during another upheaval in her life. The timing and the level of her abilities told me they may be more than mere dreams.

"Link request from Pags," the computer said.

"Allow. Go ahead, Pags."

"The general, the one they call Ash, left the desert complex. He's heading in the direction of where they have the scientist incarcerated. Right now, it's only speculation that that's where he's going. Nobody has been able to get a read on his intentions, but Kians can be difficult sometimes. If that *is* where he's going, he shouldn't arrive until well after your mission."

"Okay, thanks, Pags. Sounds like we'll have Brian someplace safe before the general gets to him, but keep me posted. Link out."

On my way back to Victoria's quarters, she filled my thoughts—her smile, the fresh, floral scent of her hair, the softness of her lips. I didn't like being away from her now and didn't look forward to being away from her during my mission to see Brian.

Midstep, a darkness fell on me. It wrapped itself around my gut and squeezed it hard, stopping me in the middle of the corridor. I didn't know where the feeling belonged—with the mission, with Victoria, or somewhere else entirely? I broke into a run, as fast as I could go, to Victoria's door. The few seconds it took her to allow me in seemed like forever. I wanted to break the door down. When it opened, she stood smiling, looking perfectly safe and well in another pink ship suit. The brighter shade of this one brought out the blush of her cheeks.

Still catching my breath, I hugged her, opening myself to anything that might be going on with her. I felt nothing but happiness and excitement. My eyes searched the room for anything that could cause her harm. Nothing looked out of the ordinary. "Are you okay?" I asked, releasing her.

Victoria put her hands on her hips. "Gaige, I may not be an Anuan empath, but with you, I don't need to be."

She took me by the hand and led me to her bed. "Sit down."

I sat. Victoria placed her hands on the sides of my face and planted her thumbs squarely in the center of my forehead. She pushed her thumbs across my brow, away from each other, toward my temples. The muscles relaxed and so did my worry.

"I told you what would happen if you don't stop making that face. It was only a dream. I'm fine now." She tilted her head, examining my brow. "That's better." She dropped her hands to her sides. "*And*, I'm not going to have any more overload episodes. I feel strong and settled."

Her tenacious attitude made me smile. Everything about her made me smile. "You might just be right," I said.

She seemed fine. The troubled feeling I'd had must not have been connected to her.

"I am." She sat down next to me. "So, what do you have planned for us today?"

I rattled off some of the places we'd go and things we'd do. I included taking her to get her physical so she could begin her gravity acclimation. I knew that was something she wanted to do. We'd decided, even if she didn't end up staying, it would be good exercise. It would also keep her mind occupied while we figured out why things had gone so wrong on Earth and whether it would be safe for her to go back. If she chose to.

She had leaned into every word I'd said, her smile getting bigger each time I named another stop. With her mood being so solid, I wondered . . . Zada seemed to think it was okay to let her be more involved with the people here—

"Gaige, did you hear me?" She patted my arm to get my attention. "Do you have anything else planned?"

"Well." I paused, not wanting her to take on too much. Since Zada said to let Victoria set her own pace, I'd leave it up to her this time. "You met my father and I was wondering if you might be comfortable meeting my mother today."

"Your mother?" The enthusiasm in her voice waned and her shoulders slumped.

"She's very kind," I said. "You'll like her."

"But will she like me?"

"She'll love you. Remember where you are. Anuans are open-minded, loving beings."

She paused, but only for a moment. "You're right, Gaige. Yes, I would like to meet your mother."

I felt no nervousness at all from Victoria. A good sign. Her emotions *were* settling. Her system would soon level out completely. I would once again have my strong-willed, kind-hearted, loving, selfless Victoria, without the nervous fears and insecurities, the quick anger, and the easy tears. And Victoria would have peace from her struggle.

# CHAPTER 79 - VICTORIA

We arrived at the spaceship's park to meet Gaige's mother and Bec for a walk. With real dirt under our feet and a virtual, blue sky overhead—complete with puffy, white clouds—nothing gave away the true nature of the place in which we stood. The gently rolling park stretched out for acres. Children played and couples picnicked, just like in any Earth park. It took a person zipping by above our heads on what looked to be an airborne Jet Ski to remind me that this wasn't Earth.

A breeze blew past, rustling the leaves of some nearby trees. The colors of the leaves and trunks varied slightly from those on Earth. But all had the same majestic feel, towering tall and strong.

I leaned into Gaige. "Is this what Anu looks like?"

"It's exactly what Anu looks like. Some parts of it, anyway."

I squatted down and ran my hand across the grass, only to find it wasn't like Earth grass after all, but a blue-green ground covering bursting forth with tiny flowers of the same color. My touch released a floral scent so sweet I wanted to bathe myself in it.

Gaige knelt down next me. "It's called asper." He plucked a bloom no bigger than my pinky nail and handed it to me.

I twirled it between my fingers where it left a green smudge. "Grass stain."

"Yes, it will stain, just like grass, though our clothing is resistant to that. But Asper is tough. It won't easily wear thin."

Another sky skier completed a sideways loop over some elaborate play equipment not far from us. We stood to watch. I couldn't wait to join in on some of the Anuan recreational activities myself. But today I was there for another reason.

"Are your mother and Bec here yet?"

"They're here." Gaige nodded.

"Are you going to link to them?"

"No, let's enjoy the trails. We'll run into them soon enough."

As we walked to the edge of the woods, the simple, everyday things that surrounded us—things that tended to be ignored in the shuffle of life—became so apparent to me. The simulated sun shone on my skin. I tilted my face to the sky, soaking in the warm rays. The smaller, flowering trees at the wood's edge and the wild flowers sprinkled among them bloomed with so many vivid colors they put my childhood box of crayons to shame. Carried on a breeze, the fresh fragrances of the flora around us wafted by, smelling sweeter than any I'd ever noticed before. A couple passed us. I smiled at them, and they smiled back. Life was good and I was aware of every precious morsel of it. The balancing exercise the Anuans believed in so strongly really did help put things in a better perspective. It kept the bad from overshadowing all else and helped me see even the simple, everyday things for the blessings they were.

It made me sad that so many times, I could have appreciated the sunshine, and recognized the beauty of nature, and smiled at another human being, but I hadn't. Such opportunities had been well within my power to grasp, yet I'd wasted them. I wished all Earthlings could spend time with the Anuans and learn to see things as they did, with balance and perspective. I was vowing to myself never to be so wasteful again with these kinds of simple gifts when I saw them—Bec and another woman with dark hair, porcelain skin, and full red lips, who walked with the grace of a gazelle.

"Hi Mom, Bec. You two look beautiful today." Gaige kissed each woman on the cheek. "Mom, I'd like for you to meet Victoria. Victoria, this is my mother, Sena."

I stepped forward and extended a hand toward her, no more nervous than I'd have been on Earth meeting a boyfriend's mother. I knew my acclimation was almost over. "It's an honor to meet you, ma'am."

She took my hand in both of hers and dipped her head toward me in a slight bow. "The honor is mine. And please, call me Sena."

We all walked along the peaceful trails that snaked through the woods, dipping our heads beneath a low branch every now and then, or rounding a meandering curve. They told me stories of Gaige as a child and how their families had always been close, long before Gaige and Conner were born. I had a wonderful time talking and laughing with them.

After a while, Daigon joined us during a break from the bridge. I felt completely comfortable around Gaige's father this time. I wondered why I hadn't realized their relationship the first time I saw him. He and Gaige looked so alike—except for the eyes. Gaige had inherited his aqua eyes from his mother, but hers were even more piercing against her fair skin.

As Daigon and Sena walked side by side in front of us, I watched how attentive Daigon was with her. Being captain, he must have had ship's business on his mind, but one would have never guessed during our walk that he was anything other than Sena's husband or Gaige's father. Sena, I had learned, had a stellar career of her own as a cutting-edge engineer, leading much of the research in the advancement of nanotechnology. But, like Daigon, at that moment, her family had her complete focus.

On the other hand, Bec looked adrift bringing up the rear. Her eyes and her attention were off in another world, like one half of a whole, yearning to be complete again. I wondered why her husband, Tas, hadn't joined us. I had a strong, though irrational, feeling it was because of me.

When our trail curved near the edge of the woods, Daigon paused. "I need to get back to the bridge. Gaige, can I speak with you in private?"

Sena tipped her head and eyed Daigon.

Daigon winked at her. "I won't keep him long. I promise."

"Do you mind, Victoria?" Gaige asked.

"No, not at all."

Gaige leaned forward possibly to kiss me goodbye, I thought, then stopped himself and patted my shoulder instead. "I'll hurry back."

I'd felt fine when I'd told Gaige I didn't mind him leaving, but when I watched him and Daigon walk out of sight, a panicked feeling came over me. With Gaige gone, I feared Sena would use the opportunity to interrogate the *girlfriend*. I took a deep breath, the way Gaige had taught me, and searched for balance. I realized then, I had no reason to worry. I was in control of my emotions now and not the other way around. I would soon find out what Gaige had been keeping from me. I would soon be able to decide my future.

# CHAPTER 80 - BRIAN

I'd hoped to hold in heat better by nudging myself against one of the interior corners of the cell. My success remained debatable, but it had been worth a shot. The person who'd brought the bread and water had spoken of a visitor. I waited and listened, wondering exactly what the *visitor* planned to do with me.

My stomach rumbled, begging for another slice of bread. With only one slice left, I wouldn't give in. Not yet. Who knew how long it would have to last? After my initial chug of water, I'd rationed the rest out by the capfuls. Less than half remained. I licked my dry lips and daydreamed of more water, and food, and heat, and my home. *Would I ever see any of those things again?*

# CHAPTER 81 - GAIGE

My father and I walked through the halls on the way to his planning room. Other than exchanging greetings with people we passed along the way, he remained quiet. I couldn't read exactly what emotions he kept hidden, only that he guarded a heavy burden.

When we reached his office, Dad headed straight for the window. I joined him, but stayed silent, giving him whatever time he needed before talking with me. His eyes stayed fixed, looking out the window for only a short while, and then he turned to me.

"Gaige, you know Tas has some concerns about what you experienced on Earth. We both do."

"Yes, I know."

"He feels the Tamanacke could have been involved in the Kian's pursuit of you and Victoria." He called up a virtual image of a Tamanacke and stood next to it. "This is what the Tamanacke look like."

The reptilian creature stood taller than my six-feet-four-inch father by several inches, and broader, too. With the slightly protruding fringe that ran across the sides and top of the head, it reminded me a little of the Earth's ancient *Triceratops*. The mouth and nose weren't much more than slits in the olive-green hide of the face, but the eyes held me. I looked deep into the thin black strips of pupil that ran down the middle of its yellow eyes and wondered if the creature still existed and what it might have planned.

"If Tas is right, this is what you could face on Earth," Dad said. "They're strong, with skin as tough as Anuan roat vine. They're difficult to defeat. Always protect your neck. They'll go for the jugular every time. It's their classic move."

"You think they might really still exist?"

He let out a trouble-laden sigh. "They might. It's impossible for us to know for sure. The Tamanacke's energy resonates much lower than ours, too low for us to sense. At all. Even when they were inundating our planet, our inner senses couldn't tell they were there."

The Tam-Anuan war had taken place when I was a baby. I'd heard the stories and seen the images. It had been years ago, though, before I knew I might have to face one of them. Looking at the projected Tamanacke with that knowledge put a whole different perspective on things.

"Then I'll use my other senses to watch out for them," I said.

"That's a problem too, Gaige. They have the ability to shape-shift."

"Hmm." I rubbed my chin, processing the challenges I might face if I ran into one of these beasts on Earth. "That *is* a problem."

"Gaige, you have to be careful when you go down for Brian. I know we have difficulty reading some of the more closed-minded Kians, but if you come across anyone you can't sense—even Brian—get out. Don't take the chance of battling one of these." He pointed to the image towering over him.

"The person in that cell is no shifted Tamanacke. I spent enough time with Brian on Earth that I can sense him from here. If we don't get him out of that cell as soon as possible, he'll starve to death. I won't let that happen. The second the solar levels are low enough not to interfere with the ship's cloak, I'm going in for him. But I'll be careful."

"Gaige, you have to be. There are no second chances with the Tamanacke."

# CHAPTER 82 - VICTORIA

Gaige had left the park, smiling and socializing. He returned with a hollow face and heavy eyes.

I didn't want to pry into what might have been ship's business, but I had to know what weighed on him so heavily. After we'd said our goodbyes to Bec and Sena, and were far enough away from the park to have a private conversation, I looped my arm around his and moved closer to him as we walked. "Is everything okay?"

Gaige bent his arm at the elbow to give me an easier grasp. "Sure, everything's fine. The captain and I just had some things to discuss about my mission."

I suppressed a grin. I found it funny that he sometimes referred to his own father as captain. In that context, I supposed he was acting as Gaige's captain and not his father. The amusing, yet respectful gesture didn't distract from the pang in my stomach that told me Gaige hadn't shared the whole story. "Your mission? The one to see Brian?"

"Yes, that's right."

"You're sure there are no problems?" I asked. "And Brian is still okay?"

"Don't worry. Brian is still hanging in there and we'll have him out soon. This should be a quick, easy mission."

"*Should* be?"

He pulled his arm loose from mine and put it around my shoulder. "I won't lie to you, but there's no need to worry you unnecessarily either. There are always unknowns. We have to think through all the possible problems so we're not surprised by anything. That's what we were doing."

I could tell he wasn't going to elaborate on the *possible problems*, so I assured myself Gaige knew what he was doing and that I needed to trust him. I wrapped my now-freed arm around his waist. "Okay, it's good that you're prepared."

***

After spending the rest of the day seeing more of the ship, we returned to my quarters. Gaige sat in the chair, leaned his head back, and closed his eyes. I lay on the bed and watched him for a long while. He remained so still, I thought he may have drifted off to sleep. I wanted to tell him to lie in the bed with me. I knew he wouldn't, so I let him rest peacefully in the chair while I thought about all the new things I'd seen that day.

Gaige's quarters had been our first stop after we left the park. Family photos covered the walls. But the pictures didn't hang *on* the walls, they emanated from *within* them. In one photo, he and his father stood, dressed in climbing gear, in front of a rocky outcrop. Matching smiles graced their faces and their arms hung draped over each other's shoulders. Another photo caught Gaige in a moment of laughter with his sister Geeah, Chessa's mother. Other photos showed him with Chessa, Sena, and Conner. There was even a group photo that included Bec and her husband. An odd feeling struck me when I saw the picture of Tas. He looked so familiar, like I knew him from somewhere. But that was silly.

The modest-sized room didn't contain much furniture. It didn't need to. Just like the rest of the ship, extra furniture could flip from the walls as needed. A couple of chairs and a table sat fixed in front of his floor-to-ceiling, space-view window. No doubt he spent a lot of time there gazing at the spectacular scene. There was no better view to settle one's soul.

A small bookshelf tucked in the corner contained trinkets from Gaige's life, including my favorite thing in the whole room—a sparkly chunk of rock about the size of my fist that Gaige had brought back from his first ground mission to Earth: the beginning of a journey that would eventually lead him to me.

Seeing where Gaige lived, with pieces of his life proudly displayed around the room, made me feel closer to him. I couldn't wait to hear the stories behind every item and every photo—the events that had built the Gaige I now knew.

After we left Gaige's quarters, he showed me Engineering. Brian would have loved that place, with its partially assembled droids, light beams, electronic devices, and other gadgets and gizmos the likes of which I'd never seen before. Everywhere, readouts hung in midair, lighting up the room with Anuan symbols I didn't understand. Amongst it all, engineers—male, female, and droid—worked diligently. Some of the droids had features so lifelike it was hard to tell them from the real people.

I knew the situation with Brian would be resolved soon. Maybe he'd one day see Engineering for himself. I had a feeling if he stayed on Earth, he'd never have peace again. Would I, if I stayed?

I didn't want to worry about what might happen on Earth after having such a nice day on the ship, so I let my mind drift back to that. I'd received my physical and got the okay to start a routine that would help me adjust to Anuan gravity—in case I decided to stay. I'd walked in place within a spinning metal frame about seven feet tall. It emitted a grid pattern of purple lights across my body that made the frame look like a screen door. The lights collected data while I walked in increasingly higher gravity levels within the spinning frame. I quickly learned that Gaige hadn't been exaggerating about how difficult Anu's gravity might be for me.

Zada and the trainer used the data to come up with a workout routine for me. Gaige graciously agreed to start my sessions immediately and took me to one of their virtual simulators for a walk in slightly increased gravity. The place first appeared to be a plain, white room, but Gaige entered some commands into its system and it soon came alive as my favorite Florida beach. My feet, which had been firmly planted on solid ground, sank into the sand, and the silence turned to surf crashing against the beach in the distance.

I smiled, thinking of our time there.

> *"Come on. Last one in is a rotten egg!" Hoping to gain an advantage catching Gaige by surprise, I took off running as fast as I could toward the water. With my head down, I concentrated and pushed hard against the loose, sandy surface. Almost there, I looked up to see Gaige already standing ankle-deep in the water with a bored look on his face.*
>
> *"Glad you could finally make it." He faked a yawn. "You don't look much like an egg—rotten or otherwise."*

*"Very funny, Gaige. It's just a saying."*

*"I figured. Kian sayings can be quite odd."*

*"I think I should have had a head start." I bent down, scooped up a handful of water, and splashed it at him.*

*He jumped out of the way, the water missing him completely. "I don't recall any such rule being established." In one fluid motion, he swiped his hand through the water and flung it in my direction, hitting me directly in the chest.*

*I gasped, water dripping down my clothes.*

*He grinned. "You started it."*

I laughed quietly, not wanting to wake Gaige. He was right. I had started it.

At the end of that session, the virtual process had reversed and the scene had evaporated, along with the water on our clothes. Gone just like that. Would I be gone, just like that, too? I would. But from where? Here or Earth? Whatever the answer, I knew I'd have it soon.

Gaige stirred. "Did you have a good day?"

"Yes, I had a terrific day. I was just thinking about it. Thank you for everything."

"You're welcome. I want you to be happy."

"I am. You make me very happy." I walked over and sat down on the floor next to his chair.

He ran his hand across my hair and looked at me with his worried look.

"You're ready to tell me?" I asked.

"Almost."

"It won't change anything."

"I hope not." He leaned forward, kissed the top of my head, and then stood up. "I'd like to try something."

"Okay. What?"

"Remember how I destroyed your phone?"

"Yes, you toasted it with your Jedi mind powers."

Gaige grinned, shaking his head. "Yes, I guess you could describe it that way. I did it with mere thought." He went to my dresser and picked up my hairbrush. "I'd like you to try it." He laid the brush on the palm of his hand. "Try and move this hairbrush using only your thoughts."

"I can't do that."

"Have you ever tried?"

"Well, no."

"Try now." He wiggled his hand, encouraging me. "Just relax and clear your thoughts like when you balance yourself. Then *think* this to you."

It seemed unlikely that my mind could achieve such a feat. But if Gaige thought I might be able to move it, I'd at least try. I focused on the brush. Nothing happened. I tried harder, squinting and straining until I thought I might burst a blood vessel.

"You have to relax," Gaige said. "Don't *fight* to do it, *know* you can do it. Don't doubt yourself."

I relaxed, took a deep breath, and blew it out slowly. I imagined I really could do it. *Come to me*, I told the brush in my thoughts and envisioned it doing exactly that. It wiggled in Gaige's palm. *Come to me now!* The hairbrush quickly slid out of his hand and flew across the room right at me. I held my hands up to keep it from hitting me in the face. It slapped me across my palms and fell to the floor.

"Ouch." I shook my hands to shake the sting from them.

"Nice!" Gaige said, smiling wide.

"I did it! I *really* did it!"

"Yes, you did," he said. "I knew you could!"

"But how was I able to do that?"

"Your abilities are strong."

I rubbed my sore palms with my thumbs. "I had no idea that was even possible. For Earthlings, anyway."

"I've told you, Kians have potentials they never touch. Maybe not potential like yours, but most have something they could build upon."

"So I've had these abilities all along?"

"Your whole life," Gaige said. "You just didn't know it. So, like other Kians, you weren't using or developing them. Here you're able to feed off our energies, too. That's helping to strengthen your abilities. I can't even guess what you'd be able to accomplish right now if you'd have grown up around us on Anu, developing these skills your entire life."

"I want to move something else!" I scanned the room for anything small and loose.

"You shouldn't overdo it." A full-dimple smile spread across Gaige's face, the kind that formed when he was about to be ornery. "Though your timing could use some work."

"Funny, Gaige. I wasn't expecting it to come so fast. So let's practice." I opened my top drawer and pulled out a sock. "We'll use this."

"Hmmm. A better choice." Gaige took it from my hand and placed it back in the drawer. "Tomorrow. I promise."

"Oh, all right. But first thing."

"First thing," he agreed. "For now, we should get some sleep. You wear me out." He laughed and walked to the constructor. "I'll sleep on the floor again in case you have another bad dream. I don't want you to wake up alone after one of those."

I wanted to tell him to sleep in the bed with me. We'd slept together every night since we'd known each other and nothing had happened. Did it matter if we were on the floor or in the bed? Something told me Gaige would think it did. So, I saved my breath and let him order what he needed from the constructor to sleep on the floor while I got ready for bed.

I came out of the bathroom to find Gaige already sound asleep with his shirt, socks, and shoes off. When staying with me, he left the pants on. His sheet only covered him to the waist and his bare chest invited me to caress it or rest my cheek upon it. Something. *Anything*.

I pulled my comforter off the bed, commanded the lights to night-light level, and settled in next to him. I didn't touch him, though, even with my body aching for him almost more than I could stand. Each day seemed harder to resist the pull he had on me. Was it getting more difficult for him, too? I tried to think of other things—moving the hairbrush, spending time with his family, the ship. Nothing worked. He consumed my thoughts. I didn't know if I could resist being with him much longer. Secret or no secret. Me staying here or going home. Lifelong commitment or not. None of it seemed to matter. Could we take that step and figure out the rest later? No. That made no logical sense. Logic wasn't driving my thoughts at the moment, though. I wanted everything else to be decided so we could know: do we take that step or would I be gone from his life? I couldn't help wonder what it would be like if my future ended up being one with his.

*What would it be like, Gaige, to be with you? I want you so badly. I know you feel it, too. Do you want me as much as I want you?*

Gaige mumbled something, his voice lifting softly through the air. But his eyes remained closed.

I pulled myself out of my own thoughts and listened to Gaige, figuring he must be talking out loud to someone in a dream.

"Yes." He rolled onto his side, eyes open now, and ran his hand up the outside of my thigh, lifting my nightgown to my waist. "I want you," he whispered in my ear. Then in one smooth, silent move, Gaige was on top of me, kissing me deeply.

Confused at first by what was happening, I decided I didn't care about the *why*. *Something* had opened a door I was sure we'd go through, despite all the things left unsettled, and I was okay with that. I couldn't fight it any longer. I laced my fingers into his hair and wrapped my legs around him.

Gaige jerked back. "What? No!" He pushed himself off me, eyes wide and face panic-stricken. "Victoria, I'm sorry. I didn't mean to. I didn't realize . . ."

"You didn't *realize*?"

"No. Not consciously, anyway. I'm sorry. Are you all right?"

Not able to find any words, I nodded.

"Okay. Good. I need a minute." Gaige rushed into the bathroom and slammed the door behind him.

What had happened? Had he pulled me into his dreamland where being together would have no consequences?

I could hear him banging things around, obviously upset. I'd never seen him like that. I heard the water for the shower come on—no ion beam for this job. In a few minutes, the water shut off.

I went to the bathroom door and tapped. "Gaige? Are you coming out soon?"

He opened the door, soaking wet and shivering with his pants sticking to his wet body. Soon the temperature control would cancel out his cold shower. Would we be in trouble again then?

"I'm sorry, Victoria. I can't believe what I tried to do."

"Were you dreaming?"

"I don't know. I must have been. Did I say anything?"

I thought back to what happened and when he'd first spoken. "I couldn't make out your words at first. Then you said, 'yes.' "

"Was I responding to something you said?"

By this time, the fog of the incident had cleared and I remembered the rest. "Oh no. I didn't say anything. But I was wondering if you wanted me as much as I wanted you. Could I have . . .?"

Gaige lowered his head and rubbed his brow. He dropped his hand to his side and raised his head. "Yes. Seeing what you've been able to do so far, you probably could have. Not that you forced me, by any means. You just caught me unguarded."

"Gaige, I'm sorry. I didn't realize."

"It's all right. You didn't know. Nobody knows quite what you're capable of. You sleep in the bed. I'm sleeping on the floor. Don't come down there. And don't think about us like that. Can you do that?"

"I can try—no, I *can* do that."

I crawled into the bed and Gaige settled back onto the floor. After what had happened, I tossed and turned most of the night, not able to sleep. Deep into the night, I finally decided enough was enough. Living like that tortured us both.

The secret had to be told, whether he thought I was ready to hear it or not.

# CHAPTER 83 - TAS

Bec stood over the thin disk that lay on the table, practicing her mind skills. The object, with barely any substance at all, quivered and shook, but didn't move beyond that. She'd worked hard for years, but the Kian's evolution hadn't included sharpening their telekinetic abilities. That put her generations behind. She'd build her skills eventually. It was tough to watch her struggle in the meantime, though.

I walked up behind her and put my arms around her waist. "You're doing great."

She let out a defeated sigh. "I'm not sure about great, but at least I'm getting some movement out of them now. That's more than I could do when I first arrived."

"Wait and see. One of these days it will fly right into your hand." I pushed some energy into her. "Try it now."

"Don't do it for me," she said.

"I'm just letting you use some of my energy, that's all. What you do with it is up to you."

Bec inhaled, exhaled, and then held up her hand. After a few seconds the disk lifted into the air and floated slowly to her. She grasped it when it got near enough, then turned to me and kissed me on the cheek. "Thank you."

"You're welcome. You should use my energy when you practice."

She laid the disk down on the table. "I feel like that's cheating."

"Nonsense. We're bonded. What's mine is yours. You should use that to your advantage."

I'd voiced that same statement for years, but she wanted to succeed without any help. Had she used my energy all this time, she'd have probably been able to move things on her own by now. But I respected her tenacity. Eventually, she would do it, all by herself. There was no hurry.

"Sit with me." She took my hand and led me to our seats.

I sat and pulled her onto my lap. Why be apart, even by a foot, if we didn't have to be?

She curled up against me. "Victoria is doing really well."

"Yes, I'm glad about that."

"She's going to have to be told eventually, probably sooner than later. She's adjusting very quickly."

"I know." I dreaded what Victoria's reaction would be. *Would she understand?*

Bec patted my chest. "It will all be okay."

"I hope so."

# CHAPTER 84 - VICTORIA

Sitting with my legs dangling over the side of the bed, I waited for morning to come. Gaige tossed and turned on the floor all night, probably not sleeping much either. I allowed him the chance at least.

The room finally began to lighten. It was time.

"Gaige," I whispered.

"I'm awake." He pushed his covers back and sat up. "Don't do this, Victoria. Not yet."

"We nearly had sex last night. Do you want that to happen with me in the dark?"

He rested his arms on his knees. "It won't happen. I won't let it."

"And what if you can't stop it? Regardless, I want to know and I want to know now."

"You may not be ready to handle it."

"I can't handle the way things are now. It's too much. For both of us. Is it my choice whether or not to be told? Is that my decision?"

Gaige lowered his eyes in silence, and then raised them back to me. "Yes," he said, quietly.

"Then tell me, and do it now."

Gaige put his head in his hands and said nothing for several minutes. I stayed quiet and let him wrestle with what he *had* to do. Finally, he lifted his head and stood up.

"All right. I'll tell you."

"All right," I repeated, agreeing, but truly not sure I was doing the right thing. I'd made my decision, though. Regardless of the outcome, we would not put off the inevitable any longer.

"Link to Bec," Gaige said. "Can you come to Victoria's quarters, please? It's time. Yes, bring it with you." When he finished his conversation with Bec, he sat down on the bed next to me and took my hand. "Everything will be okay." By the uncertain feel of his energy, I wondered if he was trying to convince me or himself.

My hand felt perfect in his. Right. I didn't want this to be the end for me and Gaige. A wave of dread hit me. My stomach burned and tears tried to form. I wouldn't let them. I had to be strong.

"Find your balance, Victoria. If you have to know right now, at least do that. And remember, no matter what, I'll always be here for you. If that's what you want. You don't ever have to worry about that. Now find balance."

I could do this, and anything else. I searched for balance and the dread dwindled to a nervous anticipation.

"Good," Gaige said. "That's good."

A chime rang and the door became transparent, showing Bec on the other side. I put my hand on Gaige's cheek. He nodded. *It's okay, let her in.* But I couldn't. Not yet. I moved in close to Gaige, my lips just touching his. I wouldn't be deprived, not of one more *or one last* kiss. So I took it, that kiss. Gaige didn't object. After a long, wonderful moment, I pulled back and gave the computer permission to allow Bec in. Gaige and I stood to greet her as politely as if she'd been invited to a formal dinner party. But this was far from a party. When she entered, I noticed the photograph in her hand.

"I assume that's for me," I said, nodding toward the picture.

Gaige took the photo from Bec and handed it to me. "Yes, it's for you."

The group picture was taken at some kind of celebration. I recognized Bec and Tas, and Daigon and Sena, though they were all younger. Then, a little boy caught my eye and I knew immediately it was Gaige.

"That's you, isn't it?" I asked Gaige. But before he could answer, I saw her, and I saw her *eyes*. Her beautiful *aqua* eyes. "The eyes. I knew they were blue, but not *this* color blue. I was so young to remember exactly, I guess." My world felt like a dream. Everything disjointed and hazy.

"Sit down, Victoria," Gaige said.

"I don't want to sit down." All I could do was stare at the photo. Trying to remember for myself. I couldn't. It was too long ago. But there she was—my mother—with her *aqua-blue eyes*. My legs went rubbery and I decided sitting might not be a bad idea after all. I took a step backwards, still not taking my eyes off the photo, and sat slowly down on the bed.

Gaige put a hand on my shoulder. "You understand?"

"I understand." I let my hand drop to my lap. I'd seen enough. "My mother's in this picture."

"Yes, she is."

"Anuan."

"Yes."

"My father?"

"Kian."

"She was on Earth for him, then. But she was no Earthling." I continued to roll the fact over in my mind.

"No, she wasn't." Gaige stepped closer, shifting his hand from my shoulder to my neck. He kneaded gently. I could feel his calm essence. He was trying to help this go smoothly.

My mother was Anuan, which meant I was, too. Things began to make sense. "That's why I have all these abilities. *'Humans have the potential.'* Yeah, right. Human Anuans, you meant. Human Earthlings, might have this potential in a thousand years!"

Gaige didn't say anything. Bec didn't say anything. They waited for me to work through the revelation in my own time.

"How did she end up on Earth with my father?"

"Bec?" Gaige said. "You'd remember the details better than I would."

"She was Tas's little sister, and he adored her," Bec said. "She was a Peacewalker, an Anuan who went to Earth to spread calm and peace by their presence. She met your father there and wanted to stay on Earth to marry him. The Council agreed since her request would have caused no detrimental effects to others. She had to promise not to share Anuan technology or influence Earth in any direct way by who she was. She agreed.

"Peacewalkers were only permitted on Earth for a few months at a time while the mission ship was in the area. Since she'd relinquished the program and Anu to stay on Earth permanently, she couldn't always be protected. Tas and the ship were on Anu when he felt her presence fade. He couldn't reach her by any means, so we departed for Earth immediately. By the time we arrived and found out your parents were dead, you were already settled in with your father's brother and his wife.

"Tas wanted you brought back to Anu. After extensive discussions, though, we realized that kind of upheaval would have been too upsetting for a child, especially after recently losing your parents. We knew your aunt and uncle would provide you with a good, stable home. We didn't expect you to feel the emptiness of not knowing your Anuan people when the decision was made.

"Tas has worried about you all this time." Bec pulled a tissue from her pocket and dabbed at a tear on her face. "Our constant surveillance of Earth began because of you, so we could always look after you. We incorporated it into our scientific research of the planet, but it was initiated for you. Though weapons are always a last resort for us, The Council agreed that if anyone ever tried to harm you, weapons could be used to defend you—initiated remotely from Anu if a ship wasn't in the area. Tas has been anxious all these years to give you the choice to come home. To your other home, that is."

My head felt like it was the size of a watermelon and my ears buzzed. Receiving this news on top of having had no sleep made it hard to think everything through. "Why did you leave me there all those years?"

Bec spoke again in her loving tone while Gaige continued to massage my neck and emit calm energy. "The decision was made to allow you time to heal from your loss, to mature so as to better understand the situation, and to make your own decision about where you wanted to be. You are only now an adult by Earth standards. That's the time everyone agreed would be best to approach you. Gaige was preparing to do just that and gradually introduce you to this information. Tas knew Gaige would be the best one to carry out that mission. He knew you'd be in good hands with him. But when Gaige was captured, things became complicated."

My saturated brain was only catching bits and pieces of all the information Bec provided, and I missed some of the details that came while my thoughts churned. "Wait. You said everyone agreed. Who is everyone? Did my parents—my aunt and uncle—know who I was? *What* I was?"

Gaige finally spoke. "They knew. It wouldn't have been fair to them otherwise."

"They know I'm here now, don't they? That's why my father didn't give me any of his usual advice when I spoke to him."

Gaige's hand paused—his calm essence disjointed for a moment—then resumed its kneading of my neck. "Tas has kept them informed."

"Then *everyone* has been lying to me my whole life. I hate to be lied to." My head felt like it might explode, a headache taking quick and full control. "I want to be alone. I need to think."

"You shouldn't be alone," Gaige said.

"Gaige," Bec interrupted. "Let's give her some time."

"She shouldn't be left by herself after all this," Gaige protested.

My skull felt close to splitting open. I couldn't deal with the arguing. I grabbed my head in both hands to hold it together long enough to speak. "Gaige, go!"

"Gaige," Bec said. "Come with me. Please give her time to process."

As the two argued back and forth, Bec tugged the still-protesting Gaige out of my room. When they were gone, I laid back on the bed, scooting up enough to rest my aching head on the pillows. I kept my eyes closed for a while, trying not to think of anything besides getting the pain to subside. After some time, and perhaps a few minutes of dozing, the headache eased.

Next, I had to process what I'd learned. Had I used the skills Gaige kept helping me uncover, I could have figured this out on my own. I *should* have figured it out on my own. But who could have ever imagined they'd be a college student one day and an alien the next. I turned my head to look at the photo of my biological parents on the dresser, the *black and white* photo. Even it had betrayed me.

I went into the bathroom, filled my hands with water, and splashed it on my face. Out of the corner of my eye, I caught sight of my pink Anuan ship suit hanging on a hook next to me. I grabbed a towel and dried my face, then took the suit off the hook and threw it in a heap on the floor. At that moment, I didn't want to be Anuan. I didn't want to be an Earthling, either. I couldn't run around the ship naked, though, so I rifled through my dresser drawers, pulled out some jeans and a sweater, and put them on.

I couldn't think in that dichotomy of a room, but knew exactly where to go. I ran out of my room and down the corridor. Yellow lights up the hall blinked to indicate a gravity change. Gaige must have thought I might leave my area. Even from a distance, he still protected me.

# CHAPTER 85 - GAIGE

Slumped down in a chair and holding a copy of the photo I'd given Victoria, I stared out my window. The stars and galaxies blurred into their black background and I let them. I didn't want focus. Victoria consumed my every cell. If the only place I could have her was in my tortured thoughts, then I'd hold on to them for now and search for balance later.

"Conner requesting entry," the computer said.

"Allow."

I listened to the door open and close. Conner's footsteps grew closer, but I didn't bother to turn around. I didn't have the strength or the desire.

Conner gave me a consoling slap on the shoulder and sat down in the chair next to me. "She'll get over this."

I rolled my head in his direction. "She was pretty mad. She hates to be lied to. Now she finds out her whole life was a lie."

"She needs time to absorb it, that's all."

I straightened myself up in the chair to relieve the crick in my neck. "She's headed to the observation deck. Will you check on her?"

"I can," Conner said. "But you already know how she is. What do you feel from her?"

"Everything—anger, hurt, confusion. She's lost. I don't want her to be alone. She already sent me away once. I'd rather she not have to do it again."

Conner stood. "I'll go to her. In the meantime, you need to take care of yourself. Is everything ready for your mission this evening?"

"I want to talk to you about that." I tossed the photo onto the table next to me. "I have a bad feeling about something. At first, I thought it might have to do with Victoria. But, the closer the mission gets, the more I think the feeling is connected to the mission rather than Victoria. I can't be sure, though. This stuff with Victoria has me muddled. I'm having a hard time getting any clarity about it."

Conner sat back down. "What do you mean? What do you feel?"

"A sort of hesitation or dread, like something bad is about to happen. The captain had a talk with me about the Tamanacke possibly still being around and I know your Dad has concerns about them, too. Maybe they planted a seed of paranoia, and that's all there is to it."

"It's a sore subject for the two of them. Do you think they may be overreacting?"

"Maybe, but still, we need to consider it." The timing of the mission couldn't have been worse. I wanted to focus on Victoria, but I couldn't leave Brian down there to die. I'd send someone else, but he knew me and trusted me. *And* if the Tamanacke were still around, as the mission lead, I had to be the one to take on that risk. I rubbed my temples to ease the headache that had been growing stronger by the minute. "I'm going in cloaked, just in case."

"That's a good idea. It doesn't hurt to take extra precautions. Do you want me to pull a team together to accompany you?"

"No. If they can't see me, they can't be a threat to me, Tamanacke or not."

"Okay, you take care of getting your cloaking suit and I'll check on Victoria."

Conner left me to my misery. I knew he'd look after Victoria in my exile, so, for the mission's sake, I turned back to the universe to look for balance. After several attempts, it managed to elude me. Maybe balance wasn't meant to be. Not at that moment. Maybe that worried edge was exactly what the universe intended me to have.

# CHAPTER 86 - VICTORIA

When I reached the relatively empty observation deck, I walked the distance to the edge of the room and stared straight out the window. I tried to find some balance in the vast universe, but all I could feel at that moment was Gaige. The dedicated "mission lead" was terribly worried. Was I just a job to him? Is that why he thought things might be over with us once I knew the truth and his mission was done? He said he loved me. Anuans were loving beings, though. Could that have been all he meant? Could I have misinterpreted Gaige's feelings because of my mixed up emotions? *Emotions!* Of course. Anuan *Empath.* Being bombarded with all that emotional energy was another thing that made sense now. Could what I felt merely have been an effect of the damn emotional adjustments that took over my life? I didn't know what was real and what wasn't anymore.

"Gaige thought you'd be here."

I looked over my shoulder and saw Conner standing behind me. I turned back to my view of space. "What are you doing here?"

"Gaige is worried about you."

"I'm okay. No. I'm not sure if I am. I'm confused."

"Can I help you with anything?"

"So many things make sense now. Except one—Gaige."

"He just wants you to be okay."

"Because it was his job?" I searched for Conner's reflection in the window. I wanted to see his reaction, but the space-view windows offered no such property, nothing to disrupt the view. I had to occasionally touch one to prove to myself they really were present.

"His job? Oh, you mean because he led your mission?"

"Yes. Was that all his connection was to me? Looking out for me because it was part of his mission?"

Conner stepped up next to me, the two of us now side by side. "Gaige has been watching over you for years. Long before his mission to approach you, or any other kind of official duty."

I glanced at Conner, not quite sure what he was talking about. "Why?"

"He was drawn to you."

"But he didn't even know me."

"Actually, he did. My dad and Gaige's dad were best friends long before they were married or had any children. They and their families have always spent time together. Including you, Victoria."

I turned to face Conner. "But I've been on Earth."

"Not always. Not when you were little. You used to visit the ship with your mom during our missions to the area."

"I did?" I remembered how connected I'd felt to this place from the very beginning of my stay. "Yes. I did. That makes sense." Realizing I'd already been a part of this world once, I felt its loss as if it had just been taken away. But that was only an echo of a time staunched by circumstances. I could have it back now, if I chose to. "Tell me more."

"You were barely a toddler. I suppose young enough not to be confused by it all. I don't remember your visits, being only a baby myself. But Gaige was old enough to remember you. Dad says Gaige used to follow you around to make sure you didn't fall or run into something and hurt yourself. Gaige already felt a connection to you then. Not the same as now, of course. But something. It stayed with him all these years."

"Gaige has always been overprotective, then." I laughed, thinking of a mini-Gaige being as protective of me when I was young as he had been with me lately. The magnitude of what Conner said soaked in and I swallowed the laugh. "All these years, he's waited for this time? For me to be here? To find out exactly what that connection would mean for us as adults?"

"All these years."

"That makes his hesitation all the more confusing. If there was a connection even as children, why would he doubt what we have now? Or what I *think* we have. *Thought* we had."

"He has his reasons to be cautious, and they make sense. You should talk to him about it. And when you talk to him, remember, you have potential you can't even comprehend. Use it. Set your fears and your doubts aside and find the truth about this situation for yourself."

I knew what Conner meant. It was the same quest Gaige had sent me on when I'd first met him. *Find the truth.* My intuition would know. Once I understood Gaige's concerns, I'd sort everything out. I'd go searching for the truth and know for sure.

"Will you tell Gaige he can stop by my room this evening to talk?" I felt Gaige's worry ease a little. "Never mind. He already knows."

"Yes, I suppose he does. I'll give you some time." Conner started walking back to the center of the room where the ibbs was located.

My life no longer looked the same in so many ways. With knowledge of my heritage, I realized Gaige and that place were only parts of the new picture. The other parts all rushed at me and I ran to catch up with Conner. "Conner, wait!"

He stopped and turned back, quicker than I'd expected. He had to put his hands out to keep me from running into him.

"Sorry." I took a step back. "Can you help me with something?"

"Sure. What is it?"

"I'm Anuan and I have family on this ship. You. You are my family. And Tas. I want to meet Tas. Will you take me to meet him?"

A warm smile creased the soft, little crow's feet back into the edges of his eyes. "He would love that."

# CHAPTER 87 - GAIGE

After briefing the team about the Tamanacke suspicions, I arrived at Engineering to pick out a cloaking outfit for the mission that evening. Victoria had taken the news about who she was as well as could be expected and had agreed to talk with me. I hoped taking extra precautions for the mission would put the other potentially precarious situation on a positive path, too, and the uneasy feeling plaguing me would settle.

When I walked into Engineering, Kearon held a black, mesh cloaking suit out in front of her. “Try this one on Gaige. It should fit.”

I pushed my shoes off and looked the suit over, front and back. It seemed about the right size. After smoothing down the legs of my flight suit so they wouldn’t bunch up, I stepped into the outfit. The boots gripped my feet and calves snugly, but left enough room to wiggle my toes. I put my arms into the gloved sleeves and bent my elbows to make sure I had enough length in the arms to maneuver. I did. Kearon helped with the intricate double closures at the front of the suit. When everything was connected securely, the suit fit well. Kearon had picked the perfect size.

“Now the hood,” she said. “We don’t want you to be a floating head.”

I pulled the hood on. The rough metallic mesh scraped across my face.

"Can you see all right?" she asked.

"The room looks darker through the suit, but I can see well enough to get around."

"Great. Let's test it." Before starting, she ran a scanner over the entire suit to make sure the integrity was solid. "Okay, Gaige, I'm going to turn it on now. We'll be monitoring for any stresses to your body. If things get uncomfortable, we'll know and we'll stop the test. You don't have to worry about trying to tell us."

"Got it," I said.

A quick vibration surged through the suit, sending a prickly tingle through my body. The vibration dissipated. The noticeable, but tolerable, tingling remained.

Kearon circled me, checking her readouts, and then shut the cloaking suit down. "We didn't see a trace of you, Gaige. And your medical values stayed within range. How do you feel?"

I pulled the hood from my head, slowly enough not to take skin with it. "I feel fine. The usual tingles, that's it."

"Stop by here this evening and I'll make sure you're sealed up tight before your transition."

I thanked Kearon and left Engineering, looking forward to seeing Victoria before my mission. Arranging for the cloaking suit hadn't lessened my uneasy feeling. With extra precautions taken for the mission, could the feelings be about Victoria? Maybe the conversation with her wasn't going to go as I hoped it would.

# CHAPTER 88 - TAS

"Tas, your pacing is going to wear a hole in the floor," Bec said.

"I know. I can't help it. What if she can't forgive me for leaving her behind?" I took another pass by the door, waiting for Conner and Victoria to arrive.

Bec stepped in my path and placed her hands on the sides of my face. Standing on tiptoes, she drew my head down to her and kissed my forehead. "You didn't leave her behind. It was her home and had been for years. It was all she knew."

"Still, we should have taken her. She'd have adjusted."

"Tas, you're not being reasonable. It would have been an incredible shock on top of everything she'd already been through. Victoria will understand that."

The door turned transparent with Conner and Victoria waiting to enter. Bec took my hand. "It'll be fine," she whispered. "Let them in."

"Allow," I said.

The door slid open. Victoria stood before me with her father's eyes, but her mother's face—like I was looking at a ghost. I stepped back. Bec squeezed my hand and I pulled from her calm energy for emotional balance.

"Come in." I moved aside so they could enter.

Releasing my hand, Bec stepped away to give us room.

Victoria stopped in front of me and stared into my face. She tilted her head one way then the other. "I can see the resemblance."

"As can I."

She smiled and reached for me with outstretched arms. I embraced her and never wanted to let her go. She was *finally* home.

"I'm not upset at you for leaving me on Earth. You don't have to worry about that anymore. I know you all had my best interests at heart."

She released her hold and I let go of my guilt, feeling lighter than I had in years.

"Can you tell me about my mother?" she asked.

"Yes, whatever you want to know."

"Please, come, sit," Bec said, holding her arm out toward our gathering space.

We sat and talked for a long while. Victoria had so many questions and I answered them all. I tried to comfort her by sharing that her mother would never really be gone. She understood. She'd felt her presence, too.

"Do you have any more pictures of my mother?" she asked.

"We have better than that. We have virtual image streams." I ordered up a family stream and the transparent scene filled the room. "This is the stream from which we made the photograph. It was taken during the party we gave your mother before she left for her Peacewalker mission."

The stream showed me and Bec, Daigon and Sena, and Gaige as a boy. In the middle of everyone was my beautiful sister, Tessy. We were all speaking Anuan. I saw the disappointment in Victoria's face when she couldn't understand what her mother was saying. Then my image began to speak in English and Victoria's face lit up.

> *"You'd better practice your English, Tessy. You don't want to stand out."*
>
> *"Yes, big brother," she said, patting my cheek. "Don't worry so much. I'll be fine. And I'll be back home before you know it."*
>
> *"I'll see to that," I said, filling my plate with more food. "But there's no reason to ask for trouble."*
>
> *Little Gaige ran in circles, chasing a friend, then veered back to our group. "Tessy, will you bring me a souvenir from Earth?"*
>
> *She took his small chin in her hand. "How could I say no to that sweet face? Of course I will."*
>
> *Daigon messed Gaige's hair. "You spoil that boy, Tessy."*
>
> *"He deserves it. He's a sweetheart." Tessy gave Gaige a wink.*
>
> *Gaige jumped into her arms. "I'll miss you Tessy."*

Victoria sat, absorbed in the stream with only the slightest smile on her face. But her eyes sparkled with pure joy. "It's like I was right there with her. She was so full of life, so happy. And Gaige. He knew her well?"

“Yes, he did.” I said. “He’d known Tessy all his life. Daigon was right; she spoiled him rotten. She adored him and he adored her.”

“She never came back from that trip, did she?” Tears formed in Victoria’s eyes. She fought to keep them from rolling past her lashes.

Bec handed me a tissue and I passed it to Victoria. “No. That’s the trip in which she met your father. Earth became her home then.”

“Thank you.” Victoria took the tissue and dabbed her eyes. “It’s not your fault, you know. It was her choice.”

“I tried to talk her out of staying. She was strong-willed and very determined. She’d made up her mind and that was that.”

“They were happy together. She had to follow her heart. That’s hard to fight.” Victoria looked down into her lap. “Thank you for all this. I need to go now.”

I knew her mind had drifted to Gaige. She had to resolve where things stood with him now. I showed her how to retrieve the virtual streams so she could watch them any time she wanted. We said our goodbyes with words and hugs. She was definitely her mother’s daughter, and I was thrilled to finally have her with us.

# CHAPTER 89 - VICTORIA

I stopped outside my quarters and drew in a deep breath. With it, I willed the energy of my Anuan people to strengthen me. I felt empowered. Life finally made sense.

When I stepped up to the door, it opened to my old Earth bedroom, which seemed out of place now. There was a time it had provided comfort. I didn't need that anymore. I didn't need to *feel* at home. I *was* home.

I meandered around the room, dragging my fingers along the rough drywall, tracing the smooth finish of the mahogany headboard, squeezing my fists into the thick comforter, and smelling its familiar scent—saying goodbye to it all.

Out the window, my dormant Ohio yard remained locked in winter. Now, I'd keep it frozen in my memory instead—where it belonged. I no longer needed that anchor. As soon as could be arranged, I wanted an Anuan room with an Anuan view of the stars. My future lay there now, somewhere out in the vast wilderness of space. I wanted to give my Earth family a proper goodbye and visit when we returned for missions. I looked forward to that. I'd miss them. But my place was with my other family now and I wanted to step into that Anuan heritage as soon as I could.

As I told my old world goodbye, I noticed the pink lump lying on the floor of my bathroom. I walked in and hung the ship suit neatly back on its hook. It was part of my new world and I was okay with that now.

I stacked my pillows against the headboard and settled myself onto the bed. Sinking back into the pillows, I summoned one of the virtual streams of my mother. She appeared in my room, so beautiful, so alive. I relived those moments with her, and then called up another stream, and another. There were so many, it would take me weeks, maybe months, to get through them all. I especially liked the ones that included Gaige. He and my mother seemed so close. Her death must have been difficult for him, too.

So engrossed in every scene and every word of the streams, I jumped when Gaige arrived. I shut off the images and watched him for a moment through the transparent door, knowing he couldn't see me. He looked so handsome in his flight suit, but I didn't want to leave him waiting another minute. He'd already been waiting long enough—we both had. So, I walked to the door and told it to open.

He stepped into my room and hugged me, letting go slowly. "Are you okay?"

"Yes, I just needed time to think. Come in. Sit down." I stepped aside to let him pass. While he walked by, I looked around my room again. No matter what the outcome of our conversation, I would stay with the Anuans and that room would be gone. Its Earth version, anyway. I did hope Gaige would be part of my new life, though. The way I wanted him to be.

"You're far away." Gaige had stopped and turned back, waiting on me to join him.

"Oh. Yes. I guess I was. But still with you."

"That's good to hear." His weak smile struggled to meet its normal glowing standards. "Is there anything I can do for you?"

I stepped up to him and took hold of his hands. "Yes. But first, I need you to know that I'm not upset with you, or anybody. I understand that you were trying to do what you thought was best for me."

"We were. We always will."

"Now, the thing you can do."

"Anything."

"Tell me why you thought this would make a difference for us. Was I just a mission to you?"

"No!" He shook his head, his dark brows drawn together like I'd hurt him to the core. "Of course, not. You mean everything to me, Victoria."

"Then why, Gaige?"

He led me to the chair, and then knelt down in front of me, placing his hands on my legs. His touch caused my soul to stir and reach out for him. He started to speak, but stared into my eyes instead. We were back in another one of those moments that locked us together in our own world. He began to rub his thumbs along the insides of my thighs. I sucked in a quick gulp of air and held it.

Gaige pulled his hands away. "I'm sorry. I didn't realize . . ." He balled his hands into fists and held them at his sides. "Victoria." His voice had turned serious, deep and frustrated. "You've felt a longing for a life you didn't even know existed. Now you can have it. If that's what you want."

"It is."

He smiled, the features of his face falling into a peaceful relaxation. "I'm glad you've resolved that. Now, as far as *I'm* concerned, you have to search within yourself to be sure the connection we've shared is really for *me*, and not for the planet and the people you felt *within* me—the connection to a heritage you'd been longing for. You need to be sure you didn't attach to me because I was the first Anuan contact you'd had since your mother died."

I eased one of Gaige's hands open, and placed it over my heart. "There used to be a hole here. Now it's gone. This place and these people have filled it and I'm staying. But they haven't filled all of it. To be here without *you* would mean being incomplete. There is no choice between whole and incomplete. The decision has been made for me, right here, where your hand rests. You are more to me than an *Anuan attachment*. You are my other half, Gaige, and nothing will change that."

## CHAPTER 90 - GAIGE

Since we were children, I'd felt *something*. Then, being with her as an adult, the attraction had been unbearable to fight. Now, I no longer had to. She understood what she felt. Knowing all there was to know and how that could have skewed her interpretation of her feelings, she knew. And I knew, too. I always had, really.

"Gaige." Victoria gripped the collar of my flight suit. "You're staring."

My thoughts came back to the present. I still knelt in front of Victoria in her bedroom chair. "I'm in shock."

"Let me help you." She took my hands in hers and placed them back on her thighs. "I believe we were right about here."

"Yes, I think you're right." Stroking her legs, I leaned in close and kissed her. I savored every slow and lingering second without fear of taking advantage of her now.

She let out a soft, relieved moan, and pulled the front of my flight suit open.

"Mission Commander to Gaige." I heard in my ear. "Mission Team is assembled, waiting on you."

"No!" I yelled.

"No?" Victoria pulled back, complete confusion on her face.

"No?" Tas said through the mission channel in my flight suit.

"I'm sorry, Commander. I need a moment. Disconnect from mission channels."

"Commander?" Victoria sank, letting go of me. "Your mission is *now*?"

It would have been easy, though rude and unprofessional, to keep going and let the mission team wait. But I wasn't going to rush bonding with Victoria. It deserved more respect than that. She deserved more respect than that. And Brian might not have time to wait.

I stood, refastening my flight suit. "I'm so sorry, Victoria. I'll be back as soon as I can."

She followed me to thc door. "You're serious?"

"I'll hurry, I promise." I kissed her on the cheek. "Okay?"

She threw her head back. "The timing could be better, but go." She waved her hands to shoo me off. "Go get Brian."

"I *do* love you." I kissed her again and ran out the door, ready to be back where we'd left off.

# CHAPTER 91 - GAIGE

Running down the corridor on my way to Engineering to get my cloaking suit, I linked back into our mission channel. "I'm sorry, Commander. I'll be there soon."

"Nice of you to join us, Gaige."

"Yes, sir." I grimaced, embarrassed I wasn't showing better leadership qualities at the moment. "How does everything look?"

"The solar energy should be low enough not to cause a problem with the ship's cloak within thirty Earth minutes," Tas said. "The captain is standing by to move the ship into position. That should take less than a minute. Slight problem, though. Pags just gave us another update on the general. He's still going at a damn good pace and even in the short time since this afternoon's briefing, he's progressed quite a bit. At the rate he's going now, it'll be close. I told Pags to notify us when he gets within fifteen minutes of the facility."

"Copy, Commander. I'll be there shortly."

After suiting up in my cloaking outfit, I arrived at External Transitions, X-Tran as we called it. Trigget, the transition controller, stood at his transition console with Conner, studying readouts suspended in front of him. Tas stood back, arms crossed, watching the team work. He gave me a nod with a critically arched eyebrow when I entered. If I hadn't been helping his niece through her transition, I'd have gotten one hell of a reprimand for this one. I returned his greeting, glad he hadn't said anything about my tardiness.

I tossed my cloaking hood on a table that lined the wall. "Sorry I'm late. Is everyone else ready?"

"I took roll," Conner said. "The bridge, Engineering, Surveillance, sickbay—all the ground mission support locations and functions are linked in."

"Thanks, Conner." I wedged myself between Conner and Trigget so I could look over the solar values with them. "Are we going to be within an acceptable solar range before the general arrives?"

Tas stepped forward. "The timing's still tight, Gaige. We're staying with the plan to wait until the ship's cloak will hold. If it looks like the general will arrive before that time, we'll have to reassess that plan."

Conner tilted his head, scrutinizing the numbers. "Maybe the mission should be postponed until after the general's gone."

I stepped away from the displays. There was no need to stare at the numbers. It wouldn't make them change any faster. "No. We don't know what the general has planned. He could take Brian underground someplace where we wouldn't be able to transition. Or worse. And Brian can't go much longer without adequate food."

"I agree," Tas said. "If we're going to have a chance of getting him out, we have to do it before the general gets to him."

Trigget still watched his display, waiting for the solar values to reach the cloak's tolerable range, while the rest of us debated.

"But what if you're right, Commander?" Conner said to his father. "What if the Tamanacke really are behind things?"

"All the more reason to get Brian out now," Tas said. "What do you think the Tamanacke will do to him?"

Conner shook his head. "Worse than not feeding him. Maybe you shouldn't go down to get him, Gaige. We could transport Brian up alone, and then deal with the rest once he's on the ship. I think we can all agree he won't want to stay there, so it's not like we'd be violating his wishes. It will just be a matter of him deciding where to go—with us or somewhere else on Earth. At least that way, you won't be putting yourself in danger."

"I agree that he won't want to stay there," I said. "But, if at all possible, I need to give him the courtesy of explaining what's happening before we jolt him out of there."

Pags' voice sounded through the mission channel, interrupting our discussion. "The general has reached the fifteen-minute point."

"Team Lead," Tas said to me. "What's your recommendation?"

I checked the readouts again, which still weren't within range. "How much longer Trigget?"

"Seven Earth minutes," Trigget answered.

I turned to Tas. "Our schedule is getting too risky. I agree with Conner. The best thing to do at this point is to bring Brian out alone and explain things to him once he gets here. I don't like it, but our goal is to get him to safety, not put two people at risk."

"Agreed." Tas nodded.

I turned from Tas to Trigget to make sure he'd heard the new plan. "Trigget, we're going to forgo the planned mission. As soon as we can move the ship in close enough, we'll transition Brian out rather than me going in to get him. Send him straight to sickbay. Once Zada has addressed any medical needs, I'll talk him through his options. He can take whatever time he needs to decide here on the ship."

"Got it, Gaige. You're not going to the surface. I'll transition Brian to sickbay." Trigget's eyes stayed fixed on the numbers.

I reiterated what I'd said to the entire team. "Mission change report. I will not be going to the surface. Brian will be transitioned out alone and sent directly to sickbay. Repeat, mission change, no surface attempt. All mission team members hold positions and standby."

One by one, all the team members echoed back through the open mission channel that they were clear on the order and they were standing by.

"Solar values are within tolerable cloaking range," Trigget said.

After about twenty seconds, the captain confirmed that the ship was cloaked and in position.

"Trigget, initiate transition sync," I told him.

"Initiating," Trigget answered.

"Transition Brian as soon as you get a lock on him," I said. "I'll head down to sickbay to meet him. Conner, you take over here."

"Wait, Gaige." Trigget frantically began changing settings on the transition controls. "Gaige, I can't get a lock on Brian. I can't even locate him. His life signs must have dropped too low for us to pick up. I'm boosting our sensors at his last known location to see if I can detect him there."

"Pags, what's the estimate on the general's arrival?" I asked.

"Five minutes now," Pags answered over the open channel.

"Trigget, have you detected Brian yet?"

"No, Gaige, not yet."

"We have to get him out before the general gets there." I grabbed the clocking hood and turned to Tas. "Permission to re-engage original mission plan."

"Permission granted," Tas said, quickly. "But grab him and get out immediately!"

I pulled the hood over my head. "Mission Team, resume original mission. Trigget, prepare to send me down." I stepped onto the transition pad. "Conner, it's yours."

"Ground Mission Team resume original mission!" Conner yelled. "Repeat, original mission is a go!" Conner quickly scanned the suit to make sure the hood was properly sealed. "You're good, Gaige. Kearon, initiate cloak," Conner told her over the mission channel.

Conner stepped up to the controls next to Trigget. My body tingled and I knew the cloak was working. Trigget held his finger over the transition symbol, ready.

"Cloaking suit is at full shield," Kearon's voice echoed from Engineering. "He's clear to go."

"Initiate transition!" Conner said.

"Transitioning." Trigget touched the transition symbol on the display.

Before X-Tran faded away, my eyes met Conner's and I heard his thoughts loud and clear. *May peace surround you, Gaige.* And I prayed that it would.

# CHAPTER 92 - VICTORIA

My gloved hands slapped against the concrete floor, searching for something in the darkness. I couldn't recall what I searched for. Only that I had to find it before . . . *Before what?* Before *something* happened—something bad.

"Gaige, Pags reports the general has arrived at the building. You don't have more than a couple of minutes."

I heard the message clearly in my ear, but couldn't see Gaige anywhere in the thick blanket of darkness.

"I can't find him. It's too dark. I know he's here. He has to be unconscious." I felt Gaige's voice resonate in my throat. I didn't understand, but didn't have time to figure it out, either. I crawled faster, groping around the floor with my hands. The sound of my breathing echoed throughout the blackness.

Finally finding what I sought—a person—I picked the lifeless body off the floor.

Out of nowhere, light flooded the room and I saw the eyes. The yellow snake eyes.

"NO!" I sat up in bed screaming, clutching at my throat. "I know how the dream ends, but it's not me. It's not me. It's Gaige! And it's not a dream. They're real. The monsters, they're real! Link to Gaige!" I said, throwing off my covers. "Link to Gaige. Link to Conner. Link to Bec."

"Yes, sweetheart," Bec answered.

"Where's Gaige? I can't reach him."

"No, sweetheart, you won't be able to reach him now. He's on the surface and will only be in communications with the Mission Team."

Her words faded into a garbled buzz. Waves of nausea rocked my stomach, one after another in quick succession. Bile burned its way up my throat, but came no further. I wouldn't allow it. There wasn't time to be sick. I had to stop the mission.

Still in the silky nightgown I'd put on to wait for Gaige, I rushed from my quarters. When I left my sector, the Anuan gravity nearly stopped me in my tracks. I pushed my body to cut through the dense, simulated atmosphere. I needed to run like the wind. Instead I trudged along in slow motion, fighting through a wall of molasses-thick air to get to the bridge. I didn't know where else to go. But Daigon, I was sure, could give the order to bring Gaige back.

After only a short distance, I could barely breathe, but kept going. Gasping for air, I fell to the floor. My chest tightened and a sharp pain shot down my right arm. I stretched my other arm out and pulled at the floor, trying to crawl forward. Excruciating cramps clamped down throughout my body and my muscles fought every movement. Still, I forged ahead. Nothing was going to stop me.

Something, no, some*one* touched my arm. "Victoria, it's me, Zada. The computer notified me of distressed medical values in your area. I have an assistant with me. He's going to carry you to sickbay."

Someone lifted me off the ground and began carrying me through the ship. I couldn't tell who through my blurred vision.

"No. Can't stop. Gaige." Wheezing, I tried to push away from whoever held me.

"It's okay, Victoria. Sickbay isn't far. We'll give you something there to make you feel better."

"No! Gaige. Have to. Warn Gaige." I fought to be put down, but wasn't able to break free. I had to make them understand.

"Gaige is on a mission right now," Zada said.

I heard a door slide open and Zada's assistant placed me on a bed.

"Gaige. Have to. Save him. Going to. Die."

"He's *what*?" Zada said.

"In danger. Will die. Help him, *please*," I begged, hoping she could make out the choppy information.

"Report this to the rest of the mission team immediately. The commander has to get Gaige out of there *now*!" Zada said as she waved something in front of my face and everything faded away.

# CHAPTER 93 - GAIGE

A shroud of darkness blanketed Brian's cell. The one dim light bulb that hung in its center didn't put out enough energy to light more than a couple of feet of the area directly below it. I couldn't see Brian, but knew he was there. With no illuminator, or any other accessories available while in the cloaking suit, I'd have to find him without any aid to help cut through the blackness. The diminished vision through the cloaking hood wasn't helping. I whispered Brian's name. He didn't answer. By his weak presence, I suspected he wasn't even conscious. I moved to the dark edges of the cell, spreading my arms close to the ground to feel for him.

After a few minutes of groping around the floor for Brian, Trigget's voice resonated in my ear. "Gaige, Pags reports the general has arrived at the building. You don't have more than a couple of minutes."

"I can't find him, it's too dark. I know he's here. He has to be unconscious." I couldn't leave without him. I moved quickly around the cell, sweeping my arms back and forth in front of me. Finally my hand brushed against something. I squeezed the object—an arm.

"Mission abort!" Tas yelled. "Gaige, we're bringing you out *now!*"

“Wait! I’ve found him.” I followed the arm up to Brian’s head, which lay lopped over to the side. “He *is* unconscious. Lock on two at my position and get us out of here.” I bent down and picked Brian up as the lights flicked on.

“Damn you, Anuans!” I heard from outside the cell.

I spun around with Brian in my arms to see the general—vacillating between himself and a Tamanacke—tear the cell door off its hinges. A clawed hand swung down on me before I could utter a word.

# CHAPTER 94 - TAS

Gaige, holding the Kian, fell to the floor of X-Tran in a heap, blood everywhere.

"Transition them to sickbay, Trigget, *now*!" I yelled.

"Report!" Daigon shouted over the mission channel.

Disconnected from the reality of it, my shaky voice answered as if acting on its own, not a part of me. "It's bad, Daigon. Get to sickbay as fast as you can."

I reached sickbay, with Daigon bursting in only seconds behind me. Gaige lay on a bed with Zada hovering over him. Bright red blood pulsed onto Gaige's cloaking suit from a wide-open gash in his neck. Victoria and the Kian lay on their own beds, still and unaware. Bec, there with Victoria, cried quietly while she tried to link to Sena.

Daigon took hold of Gaige's hand. "Come on, son. You're strong. You can do this. Fight!" He repeated encouragements over and over again with no response from Gaige's blue-gray lips.

Zada worked fast, never taking her eyes off Gaige. "I have the hemorrhaging stopped now, but he's already lost so much blood." Her voice cracked as she spoke. She didn't let her emotions slow her down, though. She held the wound closed with one bloody hand and with the other, waved a medical wand back-and-forth over it. "Miccan, regeneration patches," she called out.

While Zada continued to work to mend Gaige's wound, Miccan opened the front of his cloaking suit and applied two blood regeneration patches to his abdomen. She loosely refastened the closures of the suit when she'd finished.

After several minutes, Zada finally had Gaige's wound completely seamed together. The mark left behind was thick and bright red, but at least it was mended.

Sena ran into the room. Her tear-filled eyes fixed on Gaige immediately. She rushed to him and, hanging over his lifeless body, lay her hands on his chest. Soft whispers escaped her barely moving lips. "No, no, no, no."

Thankfully, she had been spared the initial gore of her son's condition. The sight that remained told the story well enough, though.

Daigon overlaid his hand with one of Sena's on Gaige's chest and put his other arm around her shoulder. The two, mother and father, with one mission, continued to will Gaige to live. Conner had slipped into the room and put an arm around his still-crying mother. I couldn't believe the scene before me. Gaige looked bad, really bad. There was so much blood. The wound was unmistakable. They were back.

"Zada," Miccan whispered. "His numbers are fading."

"No!" Sena cried out.

Throughout the room, voices wrapped themselves together into white noise praying for Gaige's recovery, willing it, affirming it, over and over. I'd watched Gaige grow from an infant into a man, like another son to me. I couldn't grasp what might happen to him now.

"Zada," Miccan said. "It's Victoria. Her numbers are fading, too."

Zada snapped her head around to Victoria, then to me. We locked eyes, knowing.

"Bring her out!" I shouted.

The room quieted and heads turned to me, to Zada, to Victoria, to Gaige, as the pieces came together.

I ran to Victoria's side and took her hand. "Seeing him like this will scare her."

"Yes, it will," Zada said, looking at me, waiting.

"Do it," I nodded.

Zada waived the medical wand over Victoria's face. Victoria opened her eyes. "What happened? My dream. Is Gaige all right?"

I leaned over Victoria to block her view of Gaige until I could explain. "I need to talk to you about something."

She sprang up in the bed, eyes searching. "Where's Gaige?" Her eyes fixed beyond me. She'd found him. "No!" Pushing past me, she ran to him. She took his face in her hands and laid her cheek against his. "No. Don't leave me. Please." With tears streaming down her face, she stroked his hair. Smears of his blood covered her face and hands.

Opposite Victoria, Daigon and Sena remained by Gaige's side. Desperation clung to their faces. The rest looked on, watching and waiting and praying. Silent hope hung in the air.

I took Victoria by the arm and turned her toward me. She fought to turn back, but I forced her in my direction. I had to. "Victoria, listen to me." She still fought me. I had to make her understand. "You can help him."

She stopped resisting. "How?"

"You and he are one. Reach out to him. Help him back. You're the only one who has a chance."

As if in a trance, she turned back to Gaige and placed her hands on his face once more. This time she didn't cry or beg. She closed her eyes and took a deep breath. Daigon and Sena stepped back. Victoria moved her hands down Gaige's face and onto his wounded neck, then glided them onto his chest. She spread her fingers, covering as much of his chest as her relatively small hands could.

Zada, Miccan, and the rest of the sickbay team watched Gaige's numbers with stark faces. I held on to hope as Victoria continued to move her hands over Gaige, forcing her energy into him. Red on black, her bloody handprints covered his suit. Minutes felt like hours. Eventually Gaige's skin turned from blue-gray to a pale white.

A cautious smile crept across Zada's face. "His numbers are rising."

Victoria continued to work. Gradually Gaige's color improved to a light cream. Not his usual tan complexion, but still, a living human shade.

After a few more minutes, Zada gave another update. "His numbers are steady. Not quite normal, but close enough."

Victoria let out an exhausted breath and laid her head on Gaige's chest. She remained that way for only a moment before crawling in next to him. She immediately fell asleep, her energy depleted.

"Let's leave them," Zada said. "Her presence is the best medicine for Gaige right now. He'll continue to improve as long as she's with him. We'll clean them up later. Miccan, transfer Brian to the next room."

I patted Victoria on the arm softly as she slept, thanking her. Then I went to Bec and Conner and hugged them. Members of the medical team moved Brian to the next room. The rest of us filed out of sickbay, with the exception of Daigon and Sena. They stood silently next to Gaige for another minute or two before leaving him with Victoria.

Gaige looked so much better than when we'd first pulled him on board. But only time would tell how successful his recovery would be.

# CHAPTER 95 - VICTORIA

I woke with a gasp. A vision of snake eyes lingered in my mind. Gaige lay next to me covered in dried blood. It caked his neck and the top part of his suit. Handprints spread across the rest of the black mesh outfit. A thick, pink scar stretched from just under his left ear to the top of his right collar bone. Fuzzy scenes came back to me and I remembered what had happened.

Shaking, I held my hand underneath Gaige's nose. His breath warmed my fingers. I didn't want to take my hand away from the validation that Gaige was alive, but I couldn't see him like that.

I figured a sink must be tucked away somewhere in all the hidden compartments. Too impatient to figure out where, I rolled off the bed and went to the constructor. I told it to give me a warm, wet towel, and a dry one, too. After some exchange about how, exactly, I defined *warm*, it provided what I'd asked for.

I squeezed a corner of the wet towel over Gaige's raw wound. Drops of water trickled onto his neck. He made no movement. Barely touching the area around the freshly healed gash, I dabbed the blood from Gaige's neck. I continued to clean him until his neck and face were free of blood and glistened with moisture. After patting him dry with the other towel, I disposed of them both in the constructor.

If not for the scar on Gaige's neck and his soiled clothing, I'd have never known he'd been injured. His skin coloring had almost returned to its normal bronzed shade and his chest rose and fell in an easy rhythm. I knelt down at eye level with his chest and watched, thankful for each breath he took. I'd feel even better once he woke. *Please wake.*

After an hour or so, Gaige moaned and raised his hand to his neck. He didn't open his eyes.

"It's okay. Zada healed it."

His hand relaxed and dropped to his chest. Then he was still again. I pulled a chair up next to him, watched, and waited. After another couple of hours, Gaige stirred and opened his eyes. They fixed, lifeless, on the ceiling.

The way he looked scared me and I jumped up. "Gaige?"

His eyes closed. He was trying to come back to me, but he'd been through so much. I'd helped him before. I had to help him finish this. Crawling back into bed with him, I lay on my right side and wrapped my left arm and leg over his body. Focusing on nothing else, I willed all the energy I could gather into him. Concentrating and concentrating, willing and willing, I kept on until finally he pulled in a labored breath and tried to clear his throat.

"Gaige? Can you hear me?"

"Mm-hm," he said in a raspy voice.

"Can you open your eyes?"

His eyelids flickered, were still, then flickered again and opened. The life was back in them this time. I leaned over so he could see I was there. His eyes grew large. He tried to grab for me, but his arm didn't work quite right. It dropped to the bed after only rising halfway.

"Gaige, what is it?"

He raised his arm again and managed to touch my face this time. "You're . . . hurt!"

"No. I'm not hurt."

His arm dropped. His eyes rolled back and he struggled to breathe.

"Gaige, stay with me." I placed my hands on him and saw what he'd seen. Except for where I'd touched the wet towel, my hands were covered in dried blood, just as my face must have been. I'd paid no attention to myself before, but now I saw plainly what had scared him. "It's not my blood. I'm not hurt. I'm fine. Please come back. I didn't mean to scare you." I pushed more of my energy into him and willed him calm.

Gaige's breathing slowed and his eyes looked straight at me. He reached for my face again and rubbed at the blood on my cheek. "Not . . . yours?"

"Not mine. I'm not hurt."

He slid his hand behind my neck, pulled me against him, and fell back to sleep. Only a few minutes later he tried to clear his throat again.

I eased myself from his loose grip. "Would you like some water?"

"Yes. Please."

I made out his hoarse words and ran to the constructor, bringing back a container of water. He took it. I held his head so he could sit up enough to drink. The bed quickly adjusted, providing the support he needed.

He emptied the container in one long gulp. “Thank you,” he said, his voice clearer.

I took the container from him and set it on the floor. “How do you feel?”

“After my injury?” He paused as if gathering strength. “Or the heart attack you gave me . . .” He took a breath. “. . . with all that blood on your face?” He smiled. Gaige was back.

I crawled in next to him and tucked myself under his arm. “I’m sorry. I didn’t realize I was such a mess until I noticed my hands.”

He lifted one to examine. “That’s a lot of blood. Mine?”

“Yours.”

“You should shower and get some rest.” He paused. “I’ll be okay while you do.”

“I’m not leaving you.”

He sat completely up. “I’m fine.” He placed his feet, still in the boots of his black mesh outfit, onto the floor and started to stand.

I held him back. “You need to stay in bed.”

He swayed and lay back down. “Maybe another few minutes wouldn’t hurt.” Within seconds, he’d drifted off.

Exhausted after expending so much energy helping Gaige, I must have fallen asleep, too. I wasn’t sure for how long, but the next thing I knew, I opened my eyes and Gaige was sitting by the bed in a clean robe, quietly watching me.

“Feeling better?” I asked.

“Much. But I can’t stand to see you like that. You look injured. There’s a shower here where you can get the blood off.” He stood and took one slow step. “Come on. I’ll take you to it.”

I'd felt exactly the same way about seeing him all bloodied. He didn't need to overdo it, though. "Can't you just tell me?" I asked, getting out of bed.

"No. I need to stretch and move around. I've been in that bed long enough." He took my hand and moved a few more steps forward. "See? I'm steady."

His hand felt warm and his healthy color had improved even more. He took one solid step after another with no wobbling, sweating, or anything else that might indicate he struggled.

"Use your other senses," he said.

"What?"

"Your other senses. Don't judge by what you see. You can know with certainty how I'm doing."

I moved past sight and sound and touch. I tapped into him, beyond all those things, as easily as if I'd stepped into a pair of shoes. He *was* well. "Okay, I believe you. You can show me the shower."

He pushed a button on the wall. An outline next to it opened to reveal another room, a bathroom.

"Water?" he asked.

"Yes, water. I'll try the ion thing another time."

With smooth, strong movements, he started demonstrating how to use the shower. I no longer worried about his well-being and my mind filled with other things. His words drifted into the air and never met my ears. My eyes were too busy poring over him for my ears to function.

". . . then select this one." He slid his finger across a symbol on the wall and water blasted down next to us from the ceiling. "That's all there is to it."

I'd missed most of what he'd told me. But how hard could it be?—if you were an Anuan who could read the written language.

"I guess I shouldn't quiz you, huh?" His dimples punctuated his smile this time. "How about you just tell it instead?" He reached his hand into the water and rubbed it across my cheek, rinsing the blood from it. He did the same for my other cheek, then my forehead, my chin, my nose.

I couldn't move. His touch hypnotized me. Paralyzed me.

"I should let you finish." He traced my lips with his index finger then removed his hand from my face. He didn't leave, though. Instead he leaned in. My heart leapt, jumping toward him and the moment I'd been waiting for. He shook his head and took a step back. "You should finish. I want things to be better than this."

*Better?* I didn't care if we were in a cave. But the experience belonged to both of us. If he wanted better, then better it would be. "I'll hurry."

He left me standing next to the flowing water. I stepped under the stream and took the quickest shower on record. When I finished, I towel-dried my hair and smoothed it out the best I could. With no constructor in the bathroom, I wrapped the towel snuggly around my body and left my blood-stained nightgown abandoned on the floor. Checking myself in the mirror, I decided that, under the circumstances, it would have to do. We didn't need to wait any longer for makeup and sexy clothes that wouldn't stay on long anyway. I pinched my checks to add some color and stepped out of the bathroom.

Gaige stood nearby, a fluffy white robe in his outstretched hands. He wrapped it around me and I let the towel drop to the floor.

"I've been cleared to leave," he said. "Are you ready to go back to your quarters?"

"Are you sure? Was Zada here?"

"I linked to her. My medical values were being monitored from another section of sickbay. Thanks to you, Zada, and a couple of blood regeneration patches, my numbers are all back within normal ranges. The worst is over."

I let out a sigh. "Oh, thank goodness."

"So, are you ready?" Gaige held out his hand and I took it.

"We're not really dressed for roaming the halls." With my free hand, I lifted the hem of the robe, soft as a cotton ball between my fingers.

"No one should be in the medical section right now unless it's one of the medical staff. They won't mind."

My room seemed so homey, I'd forgotten it was a converted well room—the Anuan version of a hospital room. "Okay. I'm ready."

But was I? The closer we got to my room, the more my heart raced. Not with excitement. With fear. My raw nerves twitched with anxiety, causing a chill to settle on me. What if I did something wrong? What if he didn't like the way I did *it*? I squeezed Gaige's hand, hoping to draw strength from him.

"It's the same for me, you know?"

"It is?" Gaige's words caught me by surprise. Always so strong and capable, I'd forgotten this would be new to him, too.

"Mm-hm. But, I think we'll figure it out." Despite his words, Gaige looked hesitant when we stopped in front of my door. "Victoria, maybe we should talk about what happened—"

I put my finger over his lips. Not even monsters would make me change my mind. "It doesn't matter. My decision is made." But it occurred to me that something else *did* matter. I couldn't give myself to Gaige looking like a marshmallow. "Wait here."

I left Gaige in the hall so fast he didn't have time to ask why. Shucking my robe in the floor on my dash to the constructor, I ordered a silky, and very skimpy, nightgown. And candles. I slipped the gown over my head and placed the candles around the room, lighting them as I went. After commanding the room to go dark, I watched the orange flames flicker in the blackness. They provided just enough dancing glow for us to find our way around each other. Perfect. I kicked the robe under the bed and let Gaige in.

He'd been resting his back against the wall, but stood away from it as soon as I opened the door. His eyes glided over my scantily clad body and his jaw dropped open. "Whoa."

"Don't talk." I pulled him into the room and kissed him.

From that moment on, neither of us worried about what to do. We explored each other, moving from the small, gentle touches in places so natural to us, to those places less familiar, to the intimacy of togetherness. His body warm against mine, parts of him touching me, in me, that no one *but* me would ever know. Every touch of his hands, every kiss of his lips, every movement of his body resonated through my entire being like I might explode into tiny bits of sensation. Our bodies, locked in rhythm, soon became overtaken by a pleasure beyond imagination.

Our souls merged. Fused.
One body.
One mind.
One being.
Bonded.

# CHAPTER 96 - BRIAN

My circumstances had definitely changed. All I could discern was that I no longer lay curled up on some cold concrete floor. I was somewhere warm, and soft, and comfortable. Not hungry. Not thirsty. And not conscious. Not quite, anyway. Hell, maybe I wasn't even alive. If not, I was okay with that. So far, it seemed to be an improvement.

I strained to pull my eyelids open. After a minute or two, my will finally won out, and they slowly parted. Just a slit, but enough to verify I was no longer locked in a dark cell. I saw only whiteness, a soft whiteness, but still light. Not coming from a single bulb hanging from the middle of the ceiling this time, but emanating directly from the walls, seamless and pure. Maybe I *was* dead and heaven really did exist. *Yeah, right. Like they'd actually let me in.* I laughed to myself, more disgusted than amused. No sound escaped my lips, though. My eyes might have been working, but the rest of me hadn't caught up.

Before I could figure out what had happened, a movement to my left caught my attention. I opened my eyelids wider and saw a little droid hovering above me.

"Hello, Brian. My name is Toji," the thing said.

*Ho-ly shit!* I was *not* in Kansas anymore. Or Ohio. Or Earth, for that matter. Since Gaige had been the only alien I'd bumped into lately, and I seemed to be in some alien place *somewhere*, I figured he had something to do with this. I hoped that meant he and Tori were okay.

"Where am I?" I asked the droid. I figured since he'd introduced himself, maybe he could actually carry on a conversation.

"You are on the Anuan scientific vessel, Mission Earth." Small lights blinked on the disc-shaped droid when he spoke. "You were rescued from an Earth incarceration facility and brought on board the ship to recover."

The lightness in the room brightened and a young rosy-cheeked woman approached my bed, her jet-black curls bouncing against her shoulders. "Hello, Brian. My name is Miccan. Like Toji said, you were brought on board to recover. We're sorry for any inconvenience, but your situation was very dire. We figured you'd want the assistance."

"Inconvenience? I wouldn't call this an inconvenience. I'd have died in that pit. So, thank you and whoever else saved my life. Who actually did get me out of there?" Feeling that the rest of my body might be catching up and actually work now, I wriggled myself up in the bed. It adjusted on its own to help me sit. No remote. Just my movement. I liked this place.

"That would be Gaige. I believe you already know him." She brushed a curl away from her face with the back of her hand then pulled something from the wall. A screen protruded from the surface of the handheld device on the side that had been hidden within the wall. She waved the device through the air above my forehead and torso then looked at the readouts on the screen. "Your numbers look good."

I leaned forward trying to see the details. "May I?"

"Sure." She tilted the readout screen in my direction.

I had no idea what the garble meant. It looked to me like something between ancient Egyptian hieroglyphs and Russian.

"Oh wait." She pushed a symbol at the top of the screen.

The garble turned to English—pulse, temperature, blood pressure, hydration, and numbers for heart, lungs, liver, kidneys, and every other organ a person could think of. I had no idea what all the numbers meant, beyond the basics, only that they *looked good.*

"Fascinating," I said.

"Yes, they tell us everything we need to know to make a proper assessment." She placed the device back into the wall where it merged smoothly. "I'll let Gaige know you're awake so he can come by and discuss your options with you."

"Wait!" I called out as she turned from me.

Spinning around, she jerked the medical device from the wall. "What is it?"

"Oh, sorry. I'm fine. It's just that you said Gaige would be coming to talk with me. Does that mean he's okay?"

"Yes, Gaige is fine." She snapped the device back into the wall. "There was an incident during your rescue, but he's recovering well."

"Incident?"

"You don't need to worry. Gaige is fine. He'll explain everything to you."

"Good, then. And what about Tori? Do you know anything about Tori?"

"Tori?" She tipped her head to one side and searched the ceiling like the answer was up there somewhere. If Tori wasn't with Gaige, what had happened to her?

The hovering droid's lights started blinking. "I believe he is referring to Victoria."

Victoria *was* her full name. I'd seen it on her application package. I didn't realize she ever went by that name, though. "Yes, Victoria. Is she okay?"

Miccan's face lit up as the pieces came together. "Oh, of course! Victoria. Yes, she's doing quite well. She's here, on the ship, with Gaige."

A weight lifted. I was safe. Gaige and Victoria were safe. General Ash and his posse hadn't captured them. Or, if he had, they'd been able to break free. We were all now far from his reach in—*what had the droid called it?*—the scientific vessel, Mission Earth. But what came next, I had no idea.

# CHAPTER 97 - VICTORIA

We slept soundly the rest of the night in my bed. Together. Before we'd fallen asleep, we'd made love again, and again when morning came. I was sure I could never get enough of him.

I lay with my head on Gaige's shoulder, tracing my fingers through the thin layer of dark hair at the center of his chest. "So, you knew me when we were little?"

"And you knew me," he said.

I placed my hand on his cheek. Feeling the vibration of his energy, I knew why he seemed so familiar when I'd first met him in the lab. I might have been too young to remember *him*, but I'd recognized his energy from all those years before. "I guess I did."

I removed my hand from his face and instinctively started to touch the pink line running across his neck, to make it feel better or something. Not wanting to hurt him, I pulled my hand away and laid my arm across his chest. "Your neck looks a little better today. Does it hurt?"

"No." Gaige put his own hand on the scar. "Well, maybe a little. But Zada did a good job. It shouldn't be sore much longer."

The Anuan's medical technology was incredible. Only the day before, Gaige lay near death. Now he was very much alive, in every way, and almost completely healed. Everything I knew of the incident came from my dream, but I wanted the real story. "What happened down there, Gaige?"

With his hand still touching the scar, he said nothing at first. Probably processing how to present it to me, still trying to protect me. "Mission mishap," he finally said.

"Obviously." As soon as the word left my mouth I wished I could take it back. "I'm sorry, Gaige. I didn't mean to be rude. But I'm better now. I don't need protecting. I don't *want* to be protected. I'm here to stay. This is my world and *you* are my world, whatever that involves. So, no more secrets. Okay?"

"You're right." He removed his hand from his neck and patted my arm, the one that still lay draped across his chest. He let his hand rest there. "It was an old enemy, back to haunt us. We thought they were all dead." He looked away from me. "We thought we'd killed them all."

"It's okay, Gaige. Look at me. Tell me why? I know Anuans are peaceful people. You had to have a good reason."

His eyes came back to me. "We are peaceful, but sometimes the ability to choose peace is outside of our control. They were trying to take over our planet. We had to defend ourselves."

"Why were they trying to take over Anu?"

"It all happened when I was a baby, so I don't remember it firsthand. But I'll tell you what I know."

"Okay." Holding onto the covers, I sat up in the bed and faced Gaige so I could listen better to his story.

With a sad smile, Gaige watched me reposition myself before continuing to tell me what had happened. "They'd destroyed their own planet warring amongst themselves with technology they didn't respect. We took in refugees—all their women and children. The men were still off fighting each other, even after destroying their planet. They didn't learn. Some never do." Gaige stared off in the distance, like he was imagining that place and time. "We helped the refugees. They weren't responsible for the chaos, just helpless, homeless victims. But they weren't used to our planet. Many died from diseases they had no immunities to. Our medicines weren't always enough to help them. The warriors—the men—accused us of deliberately killing their families, and didn't want our help anymore. They wanted revenge: our planet and our lives. We couldn't let that happen."

"No, you couldn't." I lay back down next to Gaige, heartsick the Anuans had gone through that. In equal measure, I was mortified that these beings were still around and had almost killed Gaige. "Will they come after the Anuans again?"

"I don't know." He pulled me tighter against him. "I'm sorry, Victoria. I should have tried harder to talk to you about this. You know, before we—"

I put a finger over his lips, just as I'd done when he made the attempt to tell me before. "No. I told you it didn't matter. Together is what matters. For better or worse. That's what we say on Earth."

"This is definitely a worse." He ran his fingers across the pink line on his neck. "Definitely a worse."

I realized then, talking about this enemy after what he'd just been through, had to be keeping the trauma of his attack fresh. "Gaige, I'm sorry. Let's talk about something else." My mind reached for a topic, any topic. With him lying next to me, naked under the covers, the choice was clear. "Us. Let's talk about us."

"Yes. I can't think of a better subject." He gave me a long kiss, but then got out of bed and pulled on his clothes. "I'll be back."

"Where are you going?"

"Get ready. I have a surprise for you."

And with that, he was gone.

# CHAPTER 98 - VICTORIA

Gaige arrived back at my door wearing a navy blue Earth suit and matching tie. In his hand, he held a flowing white dress.

"You look nice, Gaige. And the dress, it's beautiful. But what's all this for?"

He handed the dress to me. "We have an event to attend."

I took the dress, admiring the delicate lace. "What event? Gaige, what are you talking about?"

"It's our celebration."

I remembered him saying Anuans didn't have marriage ceremonies, but celebrated their unions. We *had* just taken that final step. "The celebration of our union?"

"Yes, exactly." He kissed me on the top of my head. "Hurry, put on your dress. Everything will be ready soon."

"Hold on." I spread the dress out neatly on the bed and turned back to him. "I know you told me about this event, but let me get this straight. We're going to celebrate, with other people, the fact that we've just had sex?"

"It's more than that, Victoria. You're thinking like a Kian."

"I *am* a Kian."

Gaige cradled my chin in his hand. "I didn't mean that in a negative way." He kissed the tip of my nose. "But you're also Anuan and this is an important event. Mom and Dad are getting everything ready, and are excited to welcome you into our family."

"You told your Mom and Dad we had *sex*?"

"In this world we're married now. Intimacy is just one part of that. Don't you think us committing our lives to each other is something to celebrate?"

I started pacing, not sure how to sync the two worlds. Our commitment was worth celebrating. Spending our lives together was worth celebrating. Having sex was even worth celebrating—but with each other, not the world. I continued to pace back and forth between my bed and the wall, wanting to be okay with the Anuan custom. I was, after all, Anuan—half, anyway. I wanted to be comfortable with everything that meant. But *wanting* to be comfortable with something was far from *being* comfortable with it.

"Victoria, you're going to make yourself dizzy."

"Just give me a second." I grasped desperately for the courage to celebrate our most intimate moments with his parents and everyone else on the ship.

Gaige waited patiently. The shimmer in his eyes extinguished a little more with each second that passed. "If you're not comfortable, and you obviously aren't, we don't have to do this. Let's skip it. We know we're together. That's what matters."

He stood in front of me with such disappointment in his eyes, ready to sacrifice something really important to him *for me*. Knowing what a selfless, loving, protective, strong, compassionate person he was, how could I not want to scream to the world that this man was a part of my life, in every way? The two worlds reconciled. "No. Don't cancel. I'm not uncomfortable with it. Not anymore. I just had to wrap my head around it. Thank you for waiting." I adjusted his tie and kissed his lips. "Besides, you look pretty hot in that suit. I should probably show you off."

A smile spread across his face. "I love you."

"I love you, too. My first Anuan event will be one celebrating us. I can't think of anything more perfect." I caught a glimpse of the silver jewelry box on my dresser. "Or maybe I can."

"What?" he asked.

My parents' rings pulled me to their little velvet-lined home as strongly as if they'd reached out with hands and grabbed me. Gaige followed me to my replicated dresser and, still behind me, slid his arms around my waist.

"In this Anuan world we're committed now. Married. I know it's silly, and we don't need a symbol of our commitment. But . . ."

He leaned close and whispered in my ear. "There is no *but*. Whatever you want, it's already yours." He reached a hand toward the jewelry box and opened its lid.

I lifted the rings from their resting place and read the inscription in the smaller one. "May peace and love surround us, always." Sliding the rings off their chain and laying them in the palm of my right hand, I turned to face Gaige. "Anu's motto?"

"You could say that, yes."

"Anu's motto on these gold bands, which are an Earth symbol of love and commitment. A blend of Anu and Earth. The perfect combination for my parents."

"And for us." Gaige removed the smaller ring from my palm and took my other hand—the left one—in his. "Victoria, I take you to be my wife, forever and ever." He slid the band onto my ring finger.

It fit perfectly. I wiggled my fingers, watching the ring settle into place. *Gaige's wife.* That fit perfectly, too.

Now it was my turn at our little slice of Earth tradition. I looked at my father's ring, then at Gaige's Anuan-sized hand. "It's not going to fit."

"We can fix that." Gaige picked up the ring and went to the constructor. He put the ring snuggly on the tip of his left ring finger and tapped the wall next to the constructor drawer. When it popped open, Gaige placed his hand inside. "Size ring to current finger." After a moment he pulled his hand out. The ring now hung loose at the end of his finger. He let it drop into my hand. "Go ahead. It'll be fine now."

I picked the ring up. "Gaige, I take you to be my husband, *for better or worse*, forever and ever."

"Nice touch," he said. "Me, too."

I pushed the ring onto his finger, past both knuckles. Like mine, it fit perfectly. "Now for the best part." I smiled. "You may now kiss—"

And he did.

"That *was* the best part." He gave me a full-dimpled smile. "I love you," he said.

And I loved him, too. Enough to celebrate our most intimate milestone with his parents and everyone else who would be at the celebration of our union. And to stand by his side, for better or worse, even if worse meant facing monsters who could tear a person apart in the blink of an eye.

# CHAPTER 99 - LOME

After taking time overnight to calm myself, I marched into the conference room with Cruck following closely behind. The Anuans had to know we were on Earth. So there had been no reason to drive back when we could transition and give up nothing that hadn't already been given. Thanks to my anger, I'd flashed our presence like these Earthling's neon signs to whatever cloaked Anuan carried that floating scientist. Only estimating where to aim, I'd felt the resistance as claws dug through flesh. The Tamanacke swath I'd carved into the would-be rescuer's neck—or someplace close—would be unmistakable. Dead or not, that Anuan would talk. His wound would tell them, even if he couldn't, that we'd survived their massacre.

"Be seated!" I yelled.

With Cruck taking the seat to my right, my soldiers quickly disbursed themselves around the conference table to await my words.

Back in my own form with my head held high, I stepped to the head of the table. I would not admit defeat. This was not over. "Stop gawking. Yes, we're back early. The Anuans will know we're here now. They came for the scientist and the timing was, well . . . bad. But no matter, it's time for us to get to the business of avenging our people, anyway."

"Why would they come for the scientist?" Tull asked.

"For his knowledge?" Dath offered.

Tull waved off Dath's suggestion. "Phsssh, the Anuans already possess everything any Earth being would know."

"Who knows why they do what they do," I snapped. "Who would have thought they'd come back for the girl after all these years. But they did. They think differently than we do. We will probably never know why they came back for either of the two."

"Maybe they wanted to make a pet of the scientist," Tull joked. The rest snorted in amusement. "Thcy take pleasure in stupid things like that."

I slammed my fist down on the table. "Because of this *pet*, I've lost the girl and the Anuans know we're here!"

Remembering their places, the room fell silent and heads bowed.

"We must firm up plans. Our armies are strong enough now. My sister and nephew were lost at the hands of Tas and his family. I will give that pain back to them in equal measure, or as close as I can. An eye for an eye, as these Earthlings would say. I have not given up on the girl being a part of that. So, prepare yourselves, warriors. It is time for our revenge."

Thank you for reading The Anuan Legacy. If you enjoyed this book, please consider leaving a review on Amazon, Goodreads, or other review sites.

§

For more information about me or my books,
please visit
www.traciisonschafer.com

Thank you!

Made in the USA
San Bernardino, CA
25 May 2018